I0744233

TRUE DEATH

VAMPIRES & VICES NO. 4

NINA WALKER

ADDISON & GRAY PRESS

Copyright © 2023 by Nina Walker

All rights reserved.

No part of this book may be reproduced in any form or by any electronic or mechanical means, including information storage and retrieval systems, without written permission from the author, except for the use of brief quotations in a book review.

Editing by Ailene Kubricky

Character Illustration by Kalynne Art

Cover by Clarissa at JOY Author Design Studio

Ebook ISBN: 978-1-950093-36-6

Paperback ISBN: 978-1-950093-39-7

For The Booktok Girlies

CHAPTER 1

ADRIAN

When you live as long as vampires do, time almost becomes irrelevant. *Almost,* because our existence is chained to an endless countdown. Sunrise is our constant reckoning, a reminder that we were made for the darker halves of this world. Trying to change that is like trying to change the speed of light. Impossible.

"Two weeks," Mangus grumbles. "How are we supposed to round them up in only two weeks?" My vampiric brother and I are hiding out in a decrepit basement somewhere in rural Ireland, waiting for the sun to set so that we can run.

Mangus isn't my real brother, but we have the same maker and he's the only other prince I've ever considered a true friend. Now that I don't know how much longer I'll have him, I'm finally allowing myself to accept him as the brother I never had. He's not doing well since Kat's death. The man doesn't want to be here anymore. I understand that because I felt the same way for ages after I killed Eleni. I wanted to crawl into the grave with her, to find her in the afterlife and beg her forgiveness, and then to burn in hell for what I'd done.

But mostly, I wanted to kill Brisa for what she'd let happen to us.

And that's the other thing about being undead--we learn to be patient. Even when we don't want to be, it's forced upon us. Days. Months. Years. Centuries. Eventually the patience runs out, and when it does, someone always ends up dead.

"Two weeks is not a lot of time, but it's almost too much." I hate to point out the obvious, but we're in trouble if Isadora's spell doesn't work, and there are plenty of vamps who would love for the spell to fail. We can't forget that the council wasn't voted in unanimously.

"It's not going to be easy to contact the right people without leaking the location to the wrong ones," he agrees. "Or to tip them off as to why we're meeting in the first place."

That's the other thing I'm worried about.

Isadora said that we need to meet with the rest of the vampiric council under the full moon to complete her spell. That only gives us two weeks. The royal blood bond has already been transferred to the council, but the magic containing it is still unstable. If we fail to heed that fae witch's instructions, the bond could be stolen or destroyed completely.

That can't happen.

If anyone stole it--namely Brisa--I'm as good as dead. And God forbid it's destroyed because then the only thing we will be able to rely on for some semblance of rule is the Vampire Enforcement Coalition, and there's no way the VEC is strong enough to keep so many vampires under control. An inevitable bloodbath would follow, and with it, far too much death. The humans have more weapons and people than ever before. They'll regroup and fight back, and the resulting war will be catastrophic for both of our kinds.

"What are we going to do about Sebastian?" Mangus asks.

I lean back against the stone wall and drag my boot along the dirt floor, casting up the stench of mildew. "Ah, the question of the day." I curl my lip. Hugo used to be the thorn in my side, and now that Seb has shown his hand, he's no better than his dead twin. "We don't tell Sebastian about the meeting until a couple of days before. That way, if he's still helping Brisa, they won't have a lot of time to prepare an attack."

Mangus goes quiet, and I know what he's thinking. He doesn't want to tell Sebastian at all. But we have to, the entire council needs to be there. That, and even though we hate our brother, he was still voted into this position. He has a right to it, and to undermine that now would be to undermine the council as a whole.

"We should wait to tell the others until a few days before. This is on a need to know basis." Mangus is lying on his back on the dusty floor. He's so still, he'd look dead if his mouth wasn't moving. I know he's still angry about what happened in Dublin. The coven was supposed to be our ally, but it turned on us for Brisa's sake. We don't know who to trust, but we never did. It gets old.

I begin to pace like a damn dog. I'm so full of anxious energy that I can't stop moving. Even my hands are flexing and unflexing, a habit from my human life that I thought I'd long since broken.

Nine council members. The three remaining princes, and the other six council members, have all been elected with a seventy percent majority. The first official vampire council is here and primed for success, but Brisa will try to stop us. That's exactly why we must get this spell solidified. The bond has to be untouchable. There can be no question about who's in power. Not from Brisa herself and not even from the lowest level fledgling belonging to the smallest coven.

"Brisa will never back down," Mangus says, as if reading my mind.

"Brisa doesn't have any power anymore, and in two weeks she never will again," I spit.

I hate Brisa. Always have. Always will. Seeing her fall from grace has been the greatest joy of my afterlife.

But even as I think that, I question if it's true. Aren't I forgetting something?

Mangus sits up, raking a hand through his tangled bronzy hair and nods, a satisfied grin tugging at his lips. He hates our maker just as much as I do. She's the reason both of our wives are dead. It's not something I would ever wish we had in common, but we do and we always will. So the question remains, what are we going to do about it?

"Where do you want to do this ritual anyway?" Mangus asks.

The witch didn't specify where it needed to be done, just when and how, so wherever we go, I want people I can trust nearby. I need to get back to my own territory.

"New Orleans," I say with finality. My coven needs me, and I need them. I can't imagine doing the ritual anywhere else. "We'll meet on the roof of The Alabaster Heart."

"That works for me. I haven't been there in years."

And I've been gone for over three months, which is far too long. As the coven leader it's unacceptable, but I didn't have much choice.

Mangus nods and hands me his cell phone. "Make the call."

I turn it over in my hand, amazed it still has juice after the last thirty-six hours we just had. I dial into my coven and my new number two, William, picks up on the first ring. He's no Kelli and he's not bonded to me, but his master is long gone and he's loyal to our coven. He'll do what I ask of him, no questions asked.

"It's me," I say. "I'm flying home tonight. Is everything okay there?"

"Everything is fine," William answers tentatively. His voice is different than it normally is. He's usually so cool and collected, but right now he sounds worried. "Something strange happened last night. I can't quite explain it."

"Try anyway," I reply carefully.

"That woman we were supposed to be protecting? Virginia? Well, she's gone. She and I were in the lobby talking and it was as if some unseen force picked her up and took her right out of the casino. I've never seen anything like it before."

I blink, my mind trying to grab onto something slippery. "What woman?"

"Virginia Black––something."

Blackwood.

My mouth goes dry.

Why do I know that name?

I turn to Mangus. "What are we forgetting?"

He blinks up at me and shrugs.

"Does the name Virginia Blackwood ring any bells?"

He squints. "No, should it?"

It should––I know it should, but I can't remember why. Worry floods my system, and I return to the phone. "Thanks, William, we'll look into it more when I get back. Until then, prepare the coven for my return."

I hang up and hand the phone back to Mangus. He calls the helicopter for our pickup, and I keep pacing. I can't stop thinking about that name, *Blackwood*, but it's also as if the more I think about it, the more I lose track as to why it even mattered in the first place. More prickling unease washes over me. Something isn't right.

"How did we get here?" I turn to Mangus, suddenly feeling very disoriented at our surroundings: the dank basement, the old stone walls, even the fact that we're in Ireland in the first place. None of it feels right to me.

Mangus glowers up at me like I've lost my mind, and maybe I have. How is it that I'm feeling this so strongly and he's not? "We came to Ireland to secure the blood bond by making a deal with the fae witch, Isadora."

Yes, I remember that. "What was our side of the deal?"

He frowns and thinks for a long moment. "That's strange. I can't remember."

"Something with blood?" I question, raising my eyebrows. It's always blood with vampires.

He nods once. "Yeah, that sounds right."

"Who's blood?" A girl. There was a girl.

"I don't know," his voice trails off, but less in confusion and more in apathy.

No. No, this is definitely wrong. I should know the answer to this question. I was there. So why can't I remember? What did that witch do to us? "And what happened after we left?"

Memory sparks behind his eyes, and he jumps to his feet, anger seeming to overtake him. "We were seeking refuge with the Dublin coven, but they were housing

Brisa and they turned us over to her. We didn't know she was still alive. We fought. Then we . . ."

"Then we?" Only bits and pieces of memory will come to me, along with the sick feeling of panic. I was forced away from someone. All the vampires were blown off the rooftop of the Dublin coven's headquarters. It was as if the unseen hand of God had reached down and plucked us up all at once, flinging us away from that girl.

What girl?

And why? Why did that happen?

"Angel," I blurt out, the word coming at me fast. "What does Angel mean in all this?"

"Nephilim?"

"Maybe?"

"No idea, brother. I can't remember the details either." He shrugs, his eyebrows drawing together in frustration, and I know exactly how he feels.

Because I can't recall the details either, nor can I recall anything about the girl who we were being forced away from. It feels important that I remember her, that I remember what happened on that rooftop, but by the time the helicopter arrives, I've not only forgotten all about her . . . I've forgotten why I should care.

CHAPTER 2

"Is this the right one?" Camilla demands as we pull up to yet another graveyard. She rolls down the window for me to take in the scene.

We've been traveling the countryside all day looking for The Gateway and haven't found it yet. More cars have joined up with us; the group is bigger than I thought. And everyone is acting like I'm purposely messing with them, as if I'm somehow to blame for the abundance of graveyards in Ireland.

When Camilla went into my head, she wanted a detailed map of the location, but that's not what she found. My mind only held onto what I thought was important at the time, and didn't include the exact details of getting there, just what it looked and felt like. She saw what I saw, but I had only followed Mangus. He's the one with the map, not me.

And I was hoping that without him, we'd never find The Gateway.

But as I catalog the newest graveyard, I'm filled with dread. This is it; I recognize it immediately. I can't undo the last day of my life, I can't make this not happen. We're here now, and the fae realm on the other side of that portal is the absolute last place I want to be.

"Not it. Sorry." The lie rolls off my tongue, and the other passengers exchange frustrated glances. Camilla grabs me, her bony hands circling my wrists in an iron grip.

"Do not lie."

"Ouch, you're hurting me," I sputter, not that she cares.

"Hush." She pushes her gift past my barriers and into my unwilling mind.

Her intrusion is a sickening violation, so I close my eyes and fight back, willing her out. Already, I can feel her sifting through yesterday's events, peeling back the layered memories one by one. She may think she has control over this, but I'm done playing these games. She's supposed to be my family, my own grandmother, but none of the De Lucas care about my well-being. I'm a tool to be used, and if I don't participate willingly, then they'll force their gifts on me. And if they can kill my father for defying them—if Camilla can order the hit on her own son—then there's no doubt they'd do the same to me.

My stomach hardens as the aged matriarch peers

into my private moment with Adrian in the farmhouse basement and the hungry kisses we shared.

"Out!" I hiss, wishing her from my mind. I imagine my memories to be a photobook, and I firmly slam it shut. She drops my wrists, and I open my watery eyes to find her glare hot and enraged.

"How did you do that?" she demands.

An undercurrent of worry accompanies her question, and a wicked smile curls up my lips. "Maybe I'm stronger than you think."

And I am strong. Brisa bit me again last night, so now with more venom than I've ever had before, it stands to reason I will have even stronger capabilities. The nephilim know all about the venom's abilities and have killed vampires to get it, but do they have Brisa's? Adrian's? Hugo's?

No--they don't.

My blood is ripe with royal venom. It's the oldest and strongest in the world, and it's made me powerful enough to make even Camilla De Luca feel threatened.

Fortunately, as long as I don't exchange actual blood with a vampire, then I don't have to worry about becoming one of them. I'm thankful to whatever God that could be out there that it didn't happen last night, as was Brisa's intention. I never ever want to go through fighting off the vampiric transition again. I'm so lucky to have survived it the first time; I'm not sure I could survive it again. Just the thought of it makes my skin crawl.

"Yes, you are strong," Camilla says slowly. "But so am I. And I still saw enough." She turns to the others, a calculated smile playing at her overly-lined lips. Everything about her is too much, too intense, too fanatical, too controlling. Since she's old, it's almost like she's bound and determined to get her way before she dies, growing more dangerous with each day. "We're here," she announces.

I let out a groan. There's no denying this is the correct graveyard.

"I'll stay in the car," I try.

They don't bother to reply to that.

The other vehicles join us, and a wave of excitement courses through the group as we all climb out of the cars. The entire De Luca family is here now. Enzo and Nicco tuck me between their hulking forms, becoming my prison guards or bodyguards, I'm still not sure which. Others go to the trunks and retrieve medieval-looking weapons. Swords and daggers and little balls with spikes, all shining from recent polish despite the lack of afternoon sun.

"Iron," Nicco says wickedly. "It's deadly to the fae."

I fight back tears as I take the weapons in––this isn't going to end well. War never does.

I nod to my friends Felix and Seth. They are also outfitting themselves with the weapons, but they don't have angelic gifts. They shouldn't be putting themselves in this kind of danger. "Okay, but the humans don't have to come, do they? They don't know anything about the fae, and they're not equipped for this."

They both stare at me with their eyes glazed over, and I know Tate has been in their minds again. How many times until it's too many? Until he breaks them entirely?

"The humans will do as I say," Tate replies. "And I say they come and fight with us."

For as much as I hate Camilla, I think I hate Leslie Tate more.

He's not even blood-related, he married into the family, and yet he's bound and determined to be Camilla's iron fist, as if that will ensure his wife, Bianca, and his children, Bella and Greyson, are the favorites. But at what cost? Is manipulating human minds really worth it? I scowl at him with my nastiest glare, wishing that looks really could kill. That would certainly be more useful than the unreliable light I have hidden somewhere within me.

"How are you so sure that God will forgive you for hurting humans?" I challenge Tate. "You think God wants you to protect them, and yet you're willing to put them in harm's way? It's hypocritical."

He doesn't even deign to give me an answer, but his children sure do. They both stalk up to me, vitriol in their hateful expression. "Keep your mouth shut about things you don't know," Bella threatens. But she doesn't scare me, not even a little bit.

"Or what?" I prod.

"You don't want to know." Greyson offers a cruel grimace. "But trust me, your friends here will be the first to find out."

Felix and Seth step back from me, and I force myself to shut up despite my white-hot anger. Greyson just got added to the top of my shit-list.

The sky has dimmed to an ominous swath of thick gray clouds, and the sun will be setting soon. We should be worried about that considering the vampires will be out, but we're not, thanks to me. Thanks to my messed up agreement with Isadora. I still can't believe I made sure that the vampires have to leave me and my friends and family alone. I should've been more specific because now the entire De Luca family has an advantage and are under the protection of that spell. Do I consider them my family? No. Does the spell know that? Also, no.

"Now what?" I say, wondering how I can stall because Faerie is the last place I want to be. We only visited one tiny corner of it, and I was held down by vines. I don't want to find out what else the realm has to offer.

"What do you think?" Nicco asks under his breath, and I'm almost surprised he's even addressing me at all. When I was in the car with him and the others, he kept his mouth shut and barely even looked at me.

"I think we're all about to die if we go in there." He doesn't reply to that, so I speak louder. "And we don't have a lot of time before the vampires will be out again, hunting us down." It's a long shot, but maybe someone in this group will fall for it.

Tate shoots me an incredulous smile. "We're not worried about the vampires anymore."

"Thanks for that," Enzo adds.

"Thank the *fae* magic," I grumble, making sure to accentuate the fae part because hello, if they kill off the fae then it stands to reason the magic protecting this family from the vampires will be gone too. "No more fae magic, no more vampire protection."

"Fae are immortal beings, and so their magic is immortal too. Even if they are all killed, the protection from that spell will last forever."

"You really believe that?" I snort.

"Blood is blood," he says. "You cannot change your bloodlines, so yes, I really believe that the De Luca line is protected."

My stomach hardens––I really hope he's wrong.

"But *we* don't share blood, Leslie. You're only my uncle through marriage."

He laughs. "And through marriage, I am your family. I am still protected. In fact, I'm pretty sure all nephilim are protected, not just this family, but time will tell."

"Enough," Camilla announces, surveying the group. Save for Seth and Felix, all of these people are related to me in one way or another. I wish I could change it, but that's impossible. Tate is right, they're all protected. "We don't have time for bickering. We need to move."

As we set out on foot, I study the familiar graveyard,

noting that something about it has changed. It doesn't look any different, but it feels different. It's the same Irish graveyard that I journeyed to just last night with Mangus and Adrian, but it feels brand new. Has something changed so quickly, or is my mind playing tricks?

I shake my head. No, it's not my mind playing the trick, it's the fae. They are known for their tricks, and right now they have every right to play them considering the evil intentions of my companions.

"I can feel the wards," Bella points out, sounding sinister and gleeful at once. It's completely unsettling.

Camilla smiles. "Me too, even now I have the urge to turn back."

"Good idea," I try. "Let's go back."

Enzo glowers down at me. "Do you need me to get the duct tape, cousin?"

I roll my eyes. "Don't call me cousin. I don't claim you."

Nicco just laughs.

Tate shoots the three of us a sharp-toothed grin, and my stomach lurches. These people are excited to gain access to the fae realm because they're zealots who believe they were put on the earth to kill everyone besides the nephilim and the humans. They've already obliterated so many innocent creatures, and gaining access to this realm will help them continue their mission. A mission they believe comes from God, but I know couldn't possibly come from a higher power. I don't care that Chloe showed me the avenging angel in her records; I still don't trust it. Because how could a god want to kill his own innocent creations?

"This is wrong," I plead, bypassing Tate and Camilla, and looking instead to everyone else in the family. Uncle Dario shoots me a pathetic look while Aunt Lainey completely ignores me. I turn to Felix and Seth, wishing I could reach out and stop them myself. "You don't have to do this."

"I mean it about the duct tape," Enzo snaps. "You don't know what you're talking about, and I can't stand hearing your crap for another second."

"She's already proven her loyalty isn't to her own kind," Camilla says. "Please, everyone, you would be wise to ignore her."

"Don't you dare talk to me about loyalty! Tell me, were you there when my father died? Did you kill your own son, or did you send one of his brothers to do it for you?"

"Enough!" Camilla strides right up and slaps me across the face. Pain erupts on my cheek, and I stumble back. My face is all tingles, and hers is all rage. "Don't you dare speak again. You are to be quiet, or I will make you be quiet."

I keep my lips sealed after that, not because she deserves any kind of reprieve from her wrongdoings, but because I'm in a weak position and I really don't want that threat of duct tape to become a reality. But I do make a vow right then and there--as soon as I get the chance, I'm fighting back against the De Luca's. I'm going to stop their madness. And then I'm going to avenge my father's death.

"It's this way." Tate leads everyone forward, weaving between the headstones without a care to the actual graves themselves. It's disrespectful, but these people are only focused on one thing, and respect certainly ain't it.

"What are we allowed to do when we get in there?" Enzo questions. He wants blood, I can tell.

"We're going to scope it out, make sure the portal works, then come back with a nephilim and human army, killing anything living in Faerie." Tate makes it sound like it's going to be easy, like it's inevitable, and like it's not vile.

They're sick.

And they're complete fools. The fae will fight back, and they have strong elemental magic, not to mention they also deal in blood magic. When it comes to supernaturals, it's not an even playing field. We're not even in the same league.

"We won't fail," Tate reassures the group. "We've been prophesied to be successful. Have faith."

"What a load of crock," I mutter under my breath.

For the first time since we got out of the cars, Chloe catches my eye. She's not like the others––her face is ashen, and her demeanor is uncertain. Maybe she doesn't want to do this either, and that gives me a small flicker of hope.

Sure, I saw the history being stored away in her head when she took me back in time to show me the records, but does one memory of an angel telling our people to kill supernaturals make me want to actually go out and do it? Hell no. The nephilim are part angel, and so they believed this angel without question, trusting that he was a messenger from God. But what if they were wrong? Or if they were right, then what if God was wrong? Because this is evil.

I don't voice the things I'm thinking out of self-preservation, but also because I've been thinking about something Dario said to me at the Christmas party. He'd asked me if I knew about the different factions of nephilim, and then he said that the neph fight amongst themselves almost as much as they fight supernatural races. That information didn't make me trust him, but it did make me start to think more about my history.

There must be good nephilim out there, people who think the way I think. Maybe those people can help me gain control over my gift without having to feed on human emotions to do it. Chloe sure made it seem like there was another way. And after being forced to feed on a human's emotions at Christmas, I never ever want to do it again unless I know for certain it won't hurt them.

As we approach our destination, the graveyard grows thick with fog. An eerie sense of foreboding surrounds me, seeping into my skin and tightening my lungs. My heart races. My fingers flex.

The urge to run is all-consuming.

"There it is." Camilla points, and my heart drops

because she's found the tree with every season clinging to its branches.

It's still as ethereal and otherworldly as it was before with its massive trunk and gnarled outstretched branches, and just seeing it makes me feel ill. Because I know that nothing is ever going to be the same after what we're about to do. And it's all because of me, all because I led them here, because I couldn't protect my mind from Camilla, because I made a mistake and magically distanced myself from the vampires who were protecting me.

"When we touch the trunk, we'll be sent through the portal. Kill anything you see." Camilla smiles at me. "You're the answer to our prayers, Evangeline."

My stomach twists. "You're delusional if you think you're going to make it back out of Faerie alive. You can't just go in there and kill without retaliation."

Enzo unsheathes his sword with a metallic whoosh, as if to rebut my warning.

"All together," Camilla instructs, and the group links hands.

Nicco grips one of my hands in his free one, and Enzo takes the other. "You're not getting out of this," Enzo says. The twins are so strong from their angelic gift that I can't break away from them, even with the vampire venom.

I shake my head violently. I can't keep silent. "But I don't want to go. I don't want to hurt anyone. This is wrong."

"Now," Camilla commands, and against my will, the twins press my hands to the rough bark.

Nothing happens.

Camilla growls, turning her vitriol in my direction. "Why isn't it working?"

I smile prepared to gloat, thinking that maybe the magic has changed and the portal is closed, when I'm yanked through time and space.

The world ignites into shimmers of silver and gold.

CHAPTER 3

"*D*id it work?" A gruff male voice sweeps through my mind, tugging me back to consciousness.

I'm surrounded by rich scents of earthen moss, a wood-burning fireplace, and warm cedar. I could stay cocooned here forever, safely sleeping my life away on this wonderful bed. Too bad that's not how life works.

"I think so," a softer female voice returns, and a prickle of familiarity courses through me. I know her voice from somewhere, somewhere that doesn't make me feel so safe anymore.

"You think so or you know so?" the man returns harshly.

"I know so, Your Highness." Her words come out rushed, a bit fearful and a bit annoyed.

My mind catches on the way she addresses him, noting that this man must be some kind of royalty. I can't remember if "Your Highness" is used for kings or princes, but my head throbs so violently that I can hardly hold onto the question for long. My eyelids are a million pounds as I fight against the impossible weight to blink them open.

Gazing around, I find myself lying on a soft bed in a dim room. It's not like any room back home. The walls are made from river rock, and the roof looks like thatched straw. Lining the walls are knobby wooden shelves with countless glass jars, each filled with a different substance. There are butterfly wings, plants, stones, powders, and all kinds of dead insects. I spot one that looks like it's filled with inky crusted blood, and I wince.

Isadora.

This is her home––the place Mangus told us never to enter.

"I see you're awake," Isadora says calmly, kneeling down in front of me. She brushes her calloused palm over my forehead and holds it there. "You're no longer feverish. That's good."

"So she'll live?" That man's voice speaks again, and I nearly jump out of my skin. I'd forgotten he was here.

I turn toward his voice and forget to breathe. I'd always heard fae were otherworldly, that they were beautiful, that they could make people do unimaginable things. And obviously Isadora looks like she belongs to the forest with her emerald skin, bright amber eyes, and white-blonde hair. But this man is the most fae-looking creature ever. Not even my imagination could have created him and come close to getting it right.

He appears to be in his late twenties, but I suspect he's much older than that considering fae are immortal beings. His hair is inky black, seeming to absorb light completely. It's tied back behind long pointed ears, each with several jewels pierced along the shells. His skin has a soft pale blue hue to it, and his eyes are like liquid silver around two black all-seeing pupils. He's tall and broad-shouldered, dressed in a black tunic and breeches, complete with a black cloak. He's gripping the hilt of a wicked-looking sword, and I hope to never see the sharp end of that thing.

It's like he stepped off the set of a movie, and he's glowering at me as if he wants to kill me simply for existing.

I raise my hands and utter the words, "I mean no harm," just as he unsheathes that damned sword and presses the tip to my throat. I freeze, fear icing through my veins.

"Do not speak, nephilim," he commands.

He says nephilim like it's a sin.

This is it. This is how I'm going to die. I always figured it would be at the hands of a vampire. Never in a million years did I imagine a fae would be the one to do the deed, let alone in another realm, and certainly not like this.

"Stop it, Prince Casimir," Isadora hisses, confirming my earlier suspicions that he's royalty. "The girl is telling the truth. She wouldn't have been able to make it through The Gateway if her intentions were ill toward any of the fae, and you know it."

Casimir continues to glare, but after a tense moment, returns his sword to its sheath with a metallic clang and steps back. "Make no mistake, demon," he threatens, staring me down. "I will kill you at the first sign of obstinance."

"Fine, but just so we're clear, I'm not a demon. I'm actually part angel." I rub at my neck and sit up. My body feels as if it's been asleep for years, and my head is already starting to ache again.

"That's debatable," Casimir spits, and I have to fight not to roll my eyes. He's still the one with the sword.

"Where is everyone else?" My voice croaks, hoarse from disuse.

"You're the only nephilim who made it through." Isadora sounds pleased, like she expected this to happen and now she has bragging rights.

"How long was I out?"

"Three days."

My stomach drops. Three days is enough time for my wicked grandmother to assemble her army. She'll come back. She'll keep trying. There's no way they're going to give up so easily. I close my eyes for a second, wanting to get a sense of what to do about it, when an idea comes to me. "But three days here isn't as long in the human world, right?" I ask, hopeful.

Casimir's laugh is bitter. "Been reading fairy tales, have you?"

I shrug at the prince. "You've been cut off from humans for so long that most humans don't know you actually exist. So how are we supposed to know what's true and what's not about the fae?"

"Ah, but you are *not* human." The venom dripping from his voice is so toxic that I have to look away.

I turn to Isadora instead. She scares me too, especially because I know what she can do with her earthen magic, not to mention blood magic, but at this moment, she's giving me answers and helping me. I'm certain she doesn't want me dead, but I can't say the same for Casimir. She's sitting on the edge of the bed now, watching me as if she's looking for something dark to uncover, some buried secret that she must unearth. "My family will come back for you. They're not going to give up."

"As if we'll let them touch us," Casimir barks. "We can kill any threat easily. We're the *fae,* and nephilim are no match for us."

He says that, but I know for a fact that nephilim killed so many of the fae that they retreated to their realm ages ago, sealing off every single portal except for one, which they managed to keep hidden for years. It's only recently been discovered, and if they seal off The Gateway before I get out of here, I'll never make it home.

Isadora's smile quirks as if she's thinking the exact

same thing that I am. She looks to the haughty prince and then back to me. "I'm good at my job, and my job is to protect The Gateway. Rest assured, your family members didn't get through, and they won't get through. We have no plans to seal it off completely. The wards will hold."

I swallow my relief, not because I actually consider those people my family and care about their well-being, but because I don't want innocent blood on my hands. And because I'd really like to make it home. "Okay, but that doesn't explain why I'm here and the others are not."

"Your blood links you to *all* nephilim," she supplies. "Blood given willingly can be used in our spells, so I used yours to strengthen the wards here. Now anyone with ill-intent toward the fae who are also linked to a nephilim bloodline cannot use The Gateway to cross into Faerie."

Her answer sinks in slowly at first, and then all at once it floods me with the truth.

"You're brilliant!" I lunge for her before I can think, wrapping her in a tight hug. With the strengthened wards, I no longer have to worry about a war between my people and the fae. Isadora has done a wonderful thing here. When I gave her a thimble of my blood in exchange for helping Mangus and Adrian, I imagined all the ways she could use my blood against me. Never did I imagine she'd use it for good and not evil.

"Would you like me to remove her?" Casimir deadpans to Isadora, the sound of his broadsword being unsheathed yet again.

"Are all the fae men like this?" I ask her, and she chuckles, the sound reminding me of aspen tree leaves blowing on a warm summer's day.

Maybe she's not so bad. Maybe I even like her.

"Yes," she confirms, "especially the princes."

How many fae princes are there? From what I do understand of Faerie, there are multiple courts, and the kings here have oodles of immortal children. Casimir is probably one of a dozen or more. But he's still threatening, still standing there with his sword ready to lob my head off.

"I'm fine, Casimir. Not all of us hate humans," Isadora tuts. Her hug feels so good that I nearly melt right into her. If someone would've told me I'd be hugging this woman when I first met her, I wouldn't have believed it. She terrified me, holding me down with vines, asking for my blood, spelling me . . . and now we're hugging.

"As I've said before," Casimir cuts in, "Eva is *not* a human. And all fae should hate all the nephilim. Do you not forget what they did to our people? To your own parents all those years ago?"

Her body stiffens, and I take that as my cue to release her. I sit back on my haunches and frown up at Casimir. "I don't claim the neph as my people, just so we're clear. I only recently learned I'm one of them, and I don't buy into the whole righteous-genocide stuff. Besides that,

I've recently learned that only some of the nephilim factions want to hunt you guys. We're not all bad, you know."

He tilts his head at me, eyes blazing in disbelief.

"If she was lying, she wouldn't have been able to come through the portal." Isadora backs me up, and once again I want to hug the witchy woman. She pats my back and gives me a wry grin. "Intention is a bigger part of that spell than you realize."

Casimir cuts her off. "Be that as it may, orders are orders." He steps forward, his silver eyes pinning me down as he addresses Isadora. "Now that the aftereffects of your spell have worn off and she's awake and well enough to travel, the neph is coming with me."

My mouth pops open. "Where?"

Because I don't want to go anywhere but home.

I miss my bed, the Moreno family, my old job at Pops, and even my roommates who I barely got the chance to know. It's been months since I've been home, and I have a good life in New Orleans that I intend to return to, a life that has nothing to do with this place.

But then there's Adrian––we had just gotten together when we were separated, and I need to figure out how to undo that part of Isadora's spell. I still hate most of the vampires, but I don't hate him––I might actually love him. Her spell needs to be amended enough so I can actually be with the man I want to be with, the man I want to choose if fate would stop messing things up for us. Yeah, it's a little insane that I want to try to date a vampire, but the heart wants what the heart wants, and my heart yearns for Adrian.

Isadora is the only one who can help me get back to him.

I turn to her. "I need your help with the spell--"

Casimir interjects, "You're a prisoner of my father's. You are to be brought to him at once."

"Who's your father?" I'm stalling. Of course I already know. If Casimir is a prince, that would make his father . . .

"The High King of the Unseelie court."

My mind races. "Yeah, I don't know enough about Faerie to know what Unseelie even means," I blurt out.

"The dark fae," Isadora answers, squeezing my hand once. "Remember what I said about intention," she adds with a cryptic whisper.

Casimir chuckles wickedly, and then all at once he's surrounded by thick billowing shadows. They materialize into my worst nightmares, physically lifting me from the bed and carrying me away.

CHAPTER 4

Casimir strides from Isadora's hut, the shadows dragging me close behind. I expect to be thrown into a carriage or onto a horse, but there's nothing out here except for the sparkling gold and silver forest. I briefly register how pretty it looks during the day compared to when I was here during the night, admiring the way the sun reflects off everything, turning it to glitter, and how a flock of birds match the silver trees, their wings bright as mirrors.

I've never seen birds like that. They swoop in my direction, zooming straight toward us. Something unseen cracks as loud as a bolt of lightning, but I don't see where it came from. I squeal when Casimir grabs my hand and tightens his grip, those terrifying shadows surrounding us growing even thicker, and the birds dive in, circling us like we're their next meal.

I try to scream again, but I can't. It's as if the oxygen

has been ripped from my throat. And then all at once, the light returns and the air with it. I cough, my eyes watering, and the clouds in my vision clearing as I take in my new surroundings.

We're no longer in a forest. The scenic trees and great blue sky have been replaced by the wide courtyard of a literal stone castle. The birds are still there. They take off into the sky, disappearing over the massive castle walls.

"How did you do that?" I rasp. "I thought teleportation was science fiction."

"Do not ask me about my magic again," Casimir responds harshly, then his shadows drop me on my ass right there on the cobblestone floors. Pain shoots up my backside, and I groan.

"Really? Thanks for the warm welcome."

Ugh . . . why don't I know more about these people? Ayla would have an inkling of what to do around someone like Casimir considering she's obsessed with the fairy romance books everyone raves about on social media. I, on the other hand, never got into the fantasy romance thing and know nothing about this new world. Then again, that's all fiction anyway, the strange imaginings of authors tucked away in their home offices. This is the real deal, and I'm completely out of my element.

At least Mangus's voice comes to mind, reminding me not to eat or drink anything. And also not to enter Isadora's hut. The second one happened while I was unconscious, so I can't be blamed for it, but the first one

I can still work on. As if on cue, my stomach releases a painful growl. I hope I'm not here for long because I really don't want to starve.

I know me, I like food too much. I'll give in before I get too hungry.

"Follow me," Casimir instructs, stomping off in the direction of a large oak door. We're alone in this courtyard, but I have a feeling that wherever we're going, we're not going to be alone for much longer. My stomach begins to claw at itself for reasons beyond hunger, but I'm not stupid enough to hang back.

I scramble to my feet and take off after Casimir. He's so tall that he has at least a foot on me. His stride is long, and he definitely doesn't have the patience to wait for me to keep up with him. I practically have to run to match his speed as I cut across the courtyard and slip through the oak door moments before it shuts. I find myself in an arched hallway but don't have a lot of time to take it in because I'm too busy chasing after the prince. I quickly follow him into what is obviously a throne room.

It's not the first time I've been in one of these, but it's definitely the most terrifying. Brisa's throne doesn't hold a candle to the throne made of actual *bones* laid out before me.

Really, does it have to be bones?

Unseelie means dark, so I shouldn't be surprised. But it's not the bones that are the most terrifying thing about this place—it's the people. The room is filled with human-like creatures of all shapes, sizes, and colors. Some even have wings. Intermixed with the creatures are loads of beautiful fae elves. Many here have pointed ears, and every single person is dressed like they not only belong in this medieval castle, but like they belong to its court. There's not a stitch of modern human clothing here, and I stick out like a sore thumb in my days-old jeans and t-shirt.

They hiss and glare, already targeting me as their enemy, malice burning behind their strange eyes. My gaze locks with the king sitting upon the bone throne, and my breath catches. The king sits alone, no queen at his side––power emanating from him as if he were his own sun.

He's an older version of Casimir with thick black hair hanging around his shoulders and sharp features. Unlike his son, he doesn't have pale blue skin, but skin of blue-black midnight. And his eyes are so light, they're almost white. They shine like moonstone, not even looking real. If we were in my world, I'd assume he was wearing contacts.

Questions begin to fill my mind as we stare at each other. How many children does he have? How much power? How long has he been king? Was he born royal or did he have to kill for the title? And most important-ly––what does he want with me?

As if reading my mind, his eyes flash, and it almost feels as if he can see beyond the physical, like he can see me at my basest layer. My fears. My hopes. What makes me different and what makes me the same. He *knows* me.

A shiver jolts through my body.

If this man wants me dead, I'm dead. If he wants to keep me as his prisoner for eternity, I'll rot in the realm and never be able to leave. Because whatever he wants, he gets.

It doesn't matter how quick I am. How cunning. How powerful.

He's so much more.

Do I bow to him? Do I speak?

Casimir shoves me forward before I get a chance to decide. "Father, as requested, I've brought you Isadora's nephilim girl."

More hissing from the spectators, their hatred of me becoming this palpable thing that could easily kill me if the king allows it. I decide right then and there that I value my life more than pride, and I offer the king a deep bow.

He begins to speak, his voice holding depths unheard of in my world. "I'm King Orlyc, the High-King of the Unseelie Court of Faerie and you are . . ." This is my time to say something, but my mouth is as dry as dirt. "Not what I expected," he finishes with disappointment. "But I guess you'll have to do."

I'm not sure what to do with the insult, and I'm almost too scared to ask, but I have to speak. "I'm Eva Blackwood. And I'm wondering . . . why am I here?" I stand tall and force my voice to come out much stronger than I feel inside. If there was one thing I learned from Brisa's court of nightmares, it was to never show weakness. Of course we all know I'm weak compared to them, but if I show it, they'll take advantage, and they definitely won't respect me. And I'll need some semblance of respect to survive this place.

"You'll see soon enough." His response is cryptic, which feels very fae to me. I remind myself not to think of these people as humans. They're not going to act how humans act. They won't value the same things or do what I expect a human would do. If I want to survive their games, I have to play to their level. I have to be more cunning. And maybe even more wicked.

"Now about your magic," he continues. "Tell me, what can you do?" I hesitate, unsure how to answer or if I should. "I know that all nephilim have gifts, so what's yours?"

He stands from his throne of bones and stalks toward me. He's slightly shorter than his son, but still towers over me. I'm not used to looking up so much to talk to a man, and I don't like it. "Do I need to pry answers from that mouth of yours?"

I narrow my eyes and shake my head. "It's not that I don't want to answer you, it's that I'm not entirely sure how to. I just found out what I am two months ago, and I've barely scratched the surface of my gift."

He holds up a hand encrusted in golden rings, several with inlaid gems glimmering like hard candies. A few stick out and look sharp enough to cut, and I take note to avoid the back of that hand. "Excuses, excuses."

I shake my head carefully. "I'm not lying, Your Majesty. I mean no harm to you or your people, I swear on my life."

He raises an eyebrow. "Ah, but don't you know not to swear on anything in Faerie?"

To that, I have nothing to say. Did I just unwittingly bind myself to something?

"I know you're safe to us," he says slowly, narrowing his eyes as he steps closer. I catch the scent of something sweet and cosmic, as if cotton candy were made of stars instead of sugar. My mind grows fuzzy. Intoxicated. He hardly notices as he continues to speak. "You wouldn't have been able to come through The Gateway if your intentions were impure toward my kind, but the fact remains you are still the child of nephilim, and therefore the spawn of our great enemy."

"I wasn't raised by them," I argue, blinking several times to shake myself from that intoxicated feeling. It isn't easy, but I somehow manage. "I don't claim them, and I don't agree with them. You have my word that I won't defend their prejudices."

He holds my gaze for a long moment. "And for that I should spare your life?"

"Yes." It's the only thing I can say, but it hardly feels good enough.

"So far, you are innocent, but that could change."

"Okay, but as far as I understand it, my blood is now

tied to your wards protecting The Gateway. Don't you need me alive? If you kill me, won't you kill the added protection that you need there now that the portal has been discovered?"

I'm stalling.

I know I'm stalling, but at least my headache is gone, and I no longer feel intoxicated. I feel terrified. I feel foolish. Lost. Alone. Out of my element. But I have my mind and my thoughts. I can find a way to get out of here, even if it takes a bargain.

"Our spell will be forged by the upcoming full moon, and then nothing can break it, not even your death. In ten more days we will no longer have any need of you."

I have no idea what any of that means, but it doesn't bode well for me.

Casimir stirs, and I almost forgot he was standing beside me. "She's stalling the inevitable, Father. You may as well lock her up and let me do the honors when the time comes."

I inch farther from Casimir, but his shadows reach out and drag me back so fast that I don't even see it happen.

This is it.

Even if I try––and I will try––I won't be able to fight all of them off. There are just too many fae here, and every single one of them looks like they're out for blood. I know very little about these creatures except that they're immortals, that they're strong, and that they're ruthless. They have grudges that reach all the way back to ancestors I'll never know a thing about but whom they'll never forget. Their memories are just as immortal as they are. They still hate my kind for starting a war and pushing them out of the human world, not to mention all their friends and family that were killed in the process. My death is their revenge.

But maybe they'll play with me first, and if I'm smart enough, I'll find a way to play them right back.

King Orlyc tilts his head and looks me up and down. "Do you know what power my throne gives me?"

I blink rapidly. Of course I don't know, but considering it's made of bones, it can't be anything good.

"I can manipulate any and all magical gifts, can see what's beneath the surface of a person, can even change your very DNA," he says cryptically. "So if you won't reveal your gift to me, I'll take the answer by force."

Quick as a whip, he reaches out and places his hand on my forehead, practically palming my skull like a basketball. Before I can pull back, icy magic zips through my entire body, rooting me in place. I can't move. I'm completely at his mercy.

I can't even speak.

That's when the light erupts from my hands, bright white and violent.

But it doesn't hurt them. They're either immune to it or I don't know what I'm doing. Or both. Either way, it doesn't matter because the crowd erupts in mocking laughter. Shame burns me to the core. What do they care about? I haven't impressed them. I've become the entertainment.

"That's it?" Someone cackles from a group of gorgeous elvin women standing nearest to the throne. "What's she to do with that?"

"Be nice," Casimir teases back, but he's laughing right along with the crowd.

"I'm not ashamed," I lie, spitting at the prince. And then I speak my truth. "I don't want to hurt people, but I could. With this light I could, and I have."

Casimir sneers, and the king raises his hand to quiet the crowd, before turning back to me. "You mean vampires?"

I swallow and nod, not saying anything else. My mind races to Adrian, and my heart does a little squeeze. I feel like everytime we have a chance to make something work it's taken away from us. I don't even know where he is or if he's okay. And now that I'm here in Faerie, I don't know when I'll see him again. If ever.

"Very interesting," the king speaks, and the laughter dies down. "I wonder what we could get for trading you to them. There are vampires who would probably do anything to get their hands on you."

Brisa comes to mind . . .

"No, they can't get their hands on me," I point out. "Thanks to Isadora's spell, the one that you need right now, they've been forced to leave me alone."

His eyes sparkle, and he barks out a laugh. "Alright, you can stay."

What did he just say? I'm taken aback and have to fight not to get upset that he doesn't see how much I want to leave. "I don't want to stay here. I want to go home to New Orleans."

His gaze turns hard, the ice in his white eyes nearly burning me. "You will leave when I say you can leave."

"Am I your prisoner then?" The words are bold, maybe even too bold.

He smiles wickedly, lifting his arms out wide. "You're my guest." A guest who is forced to be here? No, that's a prisoner, and I won't be anyone's prisoner. "Besides, I have a feeling you won't be here longer than ten whole days."

He winks at his son, and I'm clearly missing something here. Something important. Something about the forging of the spell happening in ten days.

Even though ten feels like ten days too long, at least I have a date I can count on. I'm so tired of being at other people's command, stuck under their roofs, made to pretend to go along with things I don't agree with. First it was the bloodsuckers, then the nephilim, and now the fae. It needs to stop, but it's only ten more days . . .

"Don't be so ungrateful, nephilim," Casimir says. "Don't you know we have the most fun in Faerie? You should be so lucky to enjoy our company."

More peals of laughter.

"My son is correct. This is a great privilege. Your kind has never been invited into my home before, and if you're very lucky, you will get to meet my consorts, maybe even my other children. One may take a liking to you."

Dread fills my body, pooling in my belly and turning it sour. I don't want anyone to "take a liking" to me so I can become some kind of nephilim plaything. How much trouble do these fae get up to? I'm afraid I'm about to find out they're even more wild and dangerous than the vampires ever were, and the vampires wanted to drink me dry. Worst of all, in this court, I don't have Adrian's protection. I'm completely on my own.

The king nods toward the corner of the room where a string quartet is waiting. I don't recognize most of the instruments, but when they begin to play, weaving together their earthy tune in a perfect melody, I find I no longer care. I just want to keep listening, for their gorgeous music to last forever.

Before I can protest, Prince Casimir draws me into his arms and begins to lead us in a waltz, dragging my feet along with him whenever I miss a step. He laughs when I ask him to slow down, and he's so much stronger than I that I can't force him to. Even with my vampire venom, he keeps me locked in an extreme grip, shadows nipping at our heels.

A flash catches my eye, and one of those silver birds lands on his shoulder. The little monster's eyes sparkle like precious rubies. It stares at me like it can see into my soul. Maybe it can.

"What is that thing?" I ask, grimacing at it. It squawks right in my face.

"I told you not to ask about my magic."

So they're *his* birds . . .

I roll my eyes. "I wasn't born yesterday. I can already tell it's some kind of magic bird, but I didn't realize it was yours until you gave that away. So what do they do? Spy for you? And how many do you have?"

I've never liked birds. Always thought they were kinda gross, pooping all over, eating worms, throwing up into their youngs' mouths. Not to mention their sharp beaks and beady little eyes and avian flus and who knows how many parasites.

"You reek of vampire venom," Casimir hisses into my ear, moving in closer and changing the subject completely. "I hate the smell of vampire venom almost as much as I hate the stench of nephilim. But lucky for you, my sister Cressida adores vampire venom. She was in love with a bloodsucker once, though, that was many years ago, and that vamp is long dead. Poor thing got drunk on faerie wine and accidently walked into the sunlight."

He laughs and passes me to the woman called Cressida. Tall and beautiful, she also forces me to dance. A few minutes later Cressida passes me to a different woman, and then she throws me into the arms of a different man. I'm tossed through the ballroom for what feels like hours, from prince to princess and courtesans alike. It reminds me of when the vampires made me dance, but it's also different. There's magic here, which makes it so much worse--because I like it.

I can't help myself.

There's something to the otherworldly music. The strange magic weaves through the air like secret whispers. And that wonderful smell has returned, all sugary and ethereal and cruel. It makes my thoughts go soft and hazy.

Soon, I find myself enjoying the endless dancing. I laugh so hard I cry. I can't remember the last time I did something like that. At one point, the king has me in his clutches again, his arms holding me up as we twirl around the room. He says something I don't catch, and once again, the light is emitting from my hands. White. Bright. Ageless. Boundless.

"That's good," he whispers in my ear. "Keep practicing."

I do.

"That's good," he breathes in the other ear. "What else can you do?"

And then I'm glowing with the golden light. It's so warm and wonderful. It feels like coming home to myself. It's pure. Sweet.

And then he's passing me off to someone else. Someone with gossamer wings this time. I can't tell if it's a man or a woman. "They're so beautiful," I say, reaching out to touch them, but my hand is slapped away.

"Never touch our wings without permission," they are telling me.

I should feel ashamed, but I don't. I can't feel anything but happiness.

And then someone else is saying something about my soul. Asking if it's strong enough to handle the vampires, to forge with the bonds. Is it strong enough for immortality? For magic? I don't know what to think about that—*I can't think.*

I don't know what's happening, don't *care* what's happening. My mind comes back to me and goes out again like breathing, easy in and easy out. Like the ocean waves crashing on the shore. And the party continues. The dancing lasts forever. The food is delicious. The wine is heaven.

What did Mangus say? *Whatever you do, don't eat or drink anything in Faerie.*

I stare down at the goblet of crimson fairy wine in my hands, tasting the sweet nectar on my lips, and wonder how much I've already had to drink tonight.

CHAPTER 5

ADRIAN

*E*veryone is here. All nine of us council members are now standing in a circle on the roof of The Alabaster Heart, the sky dark and the full moon almost in position for the spell to be forged. The time has finally come, but now that it's here, I don't trust it. Something feels off. Even though everyone knows that attempting to usurp the council is an automatic true death, there's still a very real possibility someone is going to try.

"It's always circles with witches," Mangus grumbles, looking around at the lot of us. We represent the three remaining princes and six continents where vampires reside--four women and five men.

Each of us is old.

Everyone is powerful.

All of us are deadly.

"Circles mean infinite possibilities." Sebastian smirks from his position across the group.

I watch him intently because as far as I'm concerned he earned the true death when he allied with Brisa and tried to attack us two weeks ago. But Mangus and I already decided that it would be Seb's word against ours, and Sebastian's got way too much sway with the others here for us to deal with that right now. What the rest of them don't know is that our dear brother is back in Brisa's good graces, and I plan to hold that information over his head. If the other council members knew she was still alive, they would see her threat to our power and want her as dead as I do.

And I plan to do just that after the spell is forged tonight.

"I wasn't talking to you," Mangus snaps at Sebastian, and the other council members exchange annoyed glances.

Since the moment Seb showed up here an hour ago to complete the ritual, he and Mangus have been at each other's throats. It's growing tiresome. I can't say I blame Mangus because I hate Sebastian too, but at least Brisa is nowhere to be seen, so that part of the plan is working. She will want to take the blood bonds for herself, but she's still weak and won't be able to fight all of us. We're the strongest vampires in the world.

She would know.

"I think you and I are in agreement about fae witches." I turn to Mangus, who's standing directly at my side. "Avoid them at all costs after this?"

Because something is wrong and has felt wrong for two weeks. I still can't put my finger on it, but I know Isadora meddled with my memories.

Mangus curls his lip, his voice going low. "I never cared for magic."

"Unless you really need a witch, and then you do whatever it takes to find one, isn't that right, boys?" Seb cuts in, his eyes narrowing in on us, and a few of the other council members nod their agreement.

He's not wrong, but that doesn't mean I have to like agreeing with him. The fae witches are the strongest and most stable who deal in spellcraft, naturally deriving their magic from the earth herself. However, this spell wasn't only derived from the elements, but also from the moon, and it's about to be forged in our blood. Considering we're vampires, it makes sense that she would have us use blood, but it still makes me uneasy. I can't remember the last time I felt this nervous. And I can't stand the tickle at the back of my mind telling me there's something else I'm forgetting, something that I should be even more nervous about. But that's the problem, I can't just force a memory when I don't know where to start.

Shaking the infuriating feeling away, I retrieve the steel knife from its sheath under my shirt. The blade shines in the moonlight, slate gray and razor sharp. This is the part that Mangus and I didn't tell the others about, and they gaze upon the blade with mistrust.

"What is that for?" Nadia asks. She's the newly elected councilwoman from Russia. I've always liked her, and I don't blame her for questioning things. Her eyes thin into mistrustful slits as she stares at me. "You said no weapons, Adrianos. Explain yourself."

"Relax, Nadia. We're all weapons," I reply casually, holding up the knife. "Your fangs are sharper than this blade, and it's not silver, it's only steel."

Except for the gusty wind that's rattling the trees below, for the rumble of the Mississippi river a few blocks away, and for the few humans still out in the streets at this early hour, everything is eerily quiet. Nobody speaks, and Nadia finally nods her head and relaxes her shoulders.

I point the blade into my fleshy palm and cut deep, the cool blood dripping down my fingertips. "We are here because the royal blood bonds have been transferred to our council by a fae witch. She has called us here tonight to forge her spell in our blood," I explain, knowing that this news is probably hard to believe for most of them. "We must be quick. The wounds will heal themselves within five minutes, but the moon will be at its peak within three." I cut the other hand, then pass the blade to Mangus. He doesn't hesitate, cutting with calm precision and then passing the knife to the next person who quickly does the same.

"Fae blood magic?" Sebastian questions when the

knife gets to him. He holds it for a moment, hesitating to make the cut.

"We're vampires, so of course she chose blood," I say harshly, but only because it's Seb and I'm tired of him. He can step out of the council for all I care.

"And we're just supposed to take your word for it?"

A few of the others go stiff, and Mangus smirks. I'm sure he'd love nothing more than to exclude Sebastian from our circle, but he was elected to be here, same as we were.

"As far as we know, blood magic dates back to our origins. What are vampires if not magicked to live our eternal lives at the mercy of blood?"

Live by the blood . . . and die by the sun.

"This is the only way to ensure we'll be bound together," Mangus adds with a bitter hiss. It's no secret that the last person Mangus wants to be bound to is Sebastian, especially after what happened to Katerina. "It's the only way our council bond over the covens will be as strong as the royal blood bond once was. Keeping our covens in line is the only way to ensure that our empire doesn't fall."

Sebastian scowls, but he makes the cuts.

I wish I knew what Seb was thinking. He wants power, so does he really still want Brisa now that she's lost everything? Now that he knows the truth, that our mother was planning to kill her princes and that she was behind the murders all along, have his feelings toward her changed at all? She wanted to make a new generation of royals that didn't include him--it's not often that someone like Sebastian forgives such a betrayal.

The knife returns to me, all the cuts have been made, and eight pairs of expectant eyes scrutinize me. I return the knife to its sheath and continue. "Now we clasp hands, sharing our blood, until the moon passes directly overhead. The magic is already in play, but this will forge it, making it untouchable. After tonight, the blood bond can never be lost."

That's the thing about magic. It's unstable. This final part of Isadora's spell is supposed to rectify that, to make it so nobody can ever come after the blood bonds again. But just as we clasp hands, the rooftop door flies open, and a young vampire races out. Recognition hits me like a freight train.

It's Kenton--but how do I know Kenton?

"I'm here to join the council," the young man announces boldly, his voice echoing into the night. "I am also Brisa's child, so I have just as much right to the council as the other three remaining princes."

"Don't let go!" I demand of the others. "Kenton, you need to leave."

"But it's true, isn't it? Kenton is a prince too." Sebastian smirks when the other council members murmur their disbelief. "This young vampire is Brisa's newest child. I saw the transformation happen with my own eyes."

Of course he did, always Brisa's loyal puppet.

Mangus swears under his breath. He must be

thinking exactly what I'm thinking. With Kenton on the council, the numbers won't be odd anymore. Even numbers will create imbalances, and it will give Seb sway to have someone like Kenton in his pocket when it comes to voting power. Not to mention, it will give Brisa sway for whatever she's planning, because there's no way she's going to hide in the shadows for the rest of eternity.

"You can't be a prince. Brisa is dead," Santino argues. He's the councilman elected to represent the South American covens, and a man whom I know little about. I still haven't been able to peg him as reasonable or a zealot. I only know that he comes from Brazil and that his maker died many years ago.

"And yet, he is a prince." Sebastian laughs. "Come, Kenton. Join us."

Employing my telekinesis, I lift the knife from its sheath, spin the blade toward Kenton, and aim it straight for his throat. In all of a second, it's tipped right against his dark skin. One more inch and it'll be lodged into his jugular. "I'll rip your head clear off before you step foot in this sacred circle."

Kenton turns on me then, and those familiar eyes of his spark something within my soul. Something deep.

A memory.

And then another. And another.

The knife falls to the pavement with a clatter. I am frozen. Undone.

Kenton quickly snatches the knife, slicing open his

palms, but I don't even care--all I can think of is these memories as they fill my mind.

Memories of her.

And all I can see is her face, all I can feel is her hand in mine, all I can hear is her voice teasing me. Challenging me. Hating me. Loving me.

Eva.

Eva is all that matters. Eva is how I know Kenton, because he belongs to her. He's not Brisa's, he's Evangeline's. And she's mine.

She's mine.

The memories fall into place, completing the puzzle of Isadora's treachery. Separately, each memory doesn't reveal the whole picture, but putting them together now, I can see it all so clearly. I remember everything that happened, how Eva and I got to this moment, but most of all, I remember how I lost her.

And how I forgot her.

Kenton steps into the circle, clasping hands with Sebastian on his left and Nadia on his right. Any minute the moon will slide into position and this spell will be immortalized, and I'll never be able to step foot near Eva again.

Because that was her end of the deal. The vampires had to leave her friends and family alone. We had to leave *her* alone.

And so we will forget her entirely.

I drop my hands.

"What are you doing?" Mangus hisses.

"Leave him," Sebastian says, his lip curling in a smug smile. "If he doesn't want to be a part of the council then he shouldn't be."

"I never said that," I mumble, my mind racing for a way to make this work.

Sebastian looks pointedly to my hands, unclasped from the group, because my dropped hands certainly say something different.

I don't know what to do.

I don't know how to save the human and vampire races if I don't go through with forging the spell. If there's no vampire council, then the covens will have carte blanche to do whatever they want. War will surely be the result. War and death.

I've lived through too many wars already, and this is one I don't want to experience, but if I do go through with the spell, I'll lose Evangeline forever. I've had countless lovers over the centuries, and I've fathered vampiric children that I deeply cared for, but there's only been one other woman that I actually loved with true romantic affection. I lost her in the most horrific way imaginable, and I can't stand to lose Eva too. Not like this. Not now, not before we've even had a chance to really be together, to see what we could become.

"When did you turn?" I address Kenton, trying to buy a little time before the group cuts me off and proceeds without me.

His face stills, and Sebastian straightens.

"What does that matter?" Kenton asks.

My mind races back to what I thought was Brisa's demise but had actually turned out to be the royal blood bond being transferred to Eva. I narrow my eyes on Kenton, and the kid turns fidgety. He's out of place with us, and he knows it. "Brisa lost the royal bond, so if you didn't become a vampire while Brisa was still queen, then you're not actually a prince."

"What are you talking about?" Santino demands. The other council members are growing restless, but I am the only one who has unclasped their hands from the circle.

"Now is not the time," Mangus is seething, his chest rising and falling as he stares up at the moon. He's right. I need to move this along quickly, but I definitely don't want Kenton to be part of the council if he's Brisa's pawn and Sebastian's friend.

"Brisa is still alive," I announce, hedging my bets.

Mangus freezes, Seb smirks, and the silence from the rest of the council grows palpable. Nobody knows what to believe or who to trust, but Brisa being alive is not a good thing for our council. She never wanted such an organization to exist. She's a threat to our success. She's got enemies all over the planet, but she has allies too.

"Explain yourself," Antara, the council representative from India, asks with cool disdain.

"Brisa lost the royal blood bond, but she never died. She's still alive, Sebastian can tell you all about it."

Everyone turns on Seb, but he keeps his mouth shut. He turns his hateful gaze on me, and I'm certain that he'd love nothing more than to kill me right now. He would if he could, but I'm an equal match and he knows it.

"Is this true? Is she alive?" Santino asks Sebastian, and Sebastian nods once.

I continue my point, "Brisa didn't turn Kenton until after she'd already lost her royal blood bond, so that means he's not a prince. He's just a young vampire, nothing else."

Nadia tosses Kenton's hand away like it's made of rotting meat.

The moon is approaching its perfect position, shining its full light right down on us, and I feel like I'm standing on the edge of a cliff, one that's on either side of me. No matter what step I take, no matter which direction I go, I'm doomed to fall.

"Now," Mangus roars, looking up to the moon. "We do it now or else we face Brisa's wrath."

And somehow, that's enough for the rest of them. They all clasp hands again, except for Kenton, who's stumbling back toward the exit. That's fine, he should go, he doesn't belong in the council.

But I do.

If I don't enter into the council at this moment, I'll be without power, and whether I want this spell to happen or not, it's happening. There's no turning back. I can either be a part of the council without Eva or I can not be a part of the council and still be without her. There is no easy choice because there is no solution I can live with.

I'm sorry, Eva.

I hate myself for doing it, for not being able to find a better way, and for losing Eva in the process, but I've run out of time. So I take their hands, mixing our blood, and bury my pain down deep with all the other ghosts.

The moon slides into its exact position.

The magic is undeniable. It zaps through us like an electric current, racing from one body to the next and to the next and to the next. The wind picks up, swirling around us like we're the center of the universe. Shadows descend. Thick and otherworldly.

Everything goes dark.

I hold on even tighter, and the world becomes bright with lightning and the sound of cracking thunder. A flock of silver birds flies through my periphery. There one second and gone the next.

I hold on even tighter still.

And then all at once, the magic ceases to exist. The night returns to exactly how it was only a minute before. The moon shines as it always does. The wind blows at the same strength. Even the sweet electric smell of magic has dissipated.

It's all as it was, save for one very important detail.

In the center of our sacred circle, with her brown eyes gaping up at me, lies the body of a young woman.

And not just any woman.

My woman.

CHAPTER 6

I blink up into the night and questions come at me so quickly I can barely grab hold of them. Where am I? How did I get here? How long was I in the fae realm? Am I still in it? They swirl through my head until I catch sight of Adrian towering above me like an avenging angel.

My thoughts disappear.

His golden hair spiderwebs across his forehead in the wind, and his black trenchcoat flutters about his boots. Hot tears fill my vision, and my heart swells with relief—I never thought I'd see him again. But here he is, beautiful and terrible and very much real.

I glance down at myself, my fingers splaying over a strange velvet green dress. I've never seen this dress before, and I have no recollection of putting it on. Then I peer up at the circle of vampires standing around me, and my insides flip. I may be stronger than I've ever been, but there are nine of them. They could end my life in a millisecond.

I look back to Adrian and then to the viking, Mangus, at his side. At least I can trust two to have my back.

Can I, though? Adrian and Mangus tricked me into surrendering the royal blood bond. I unknowingly had it for almost two months. It could've changed everything, *and they lied to take it back.*

Blinking up at the silvery full moon, I feel ensnared by its pearlescent light. Something about it looks different tonight, as if it's holding in a secret.

As if I'm that secret.

Fear chases the confusion straight from my lungs in a painful gasp. I'm hardly myself right now. And Adrian . . . Adrian's looking at me like I'm a ghost.

"What happened to me?" I ask. My voice is raw and raspy, as if I've been screaming at the top of my lungs, but my mind is too foggy to remember how it got that way. What did the fae do to me?

Adrian doesn't answer my question.

"Nephilim." Sebastian's single word announcement comes out like an accusation. "Now I remember you. How did you make me forget?" He steps closer.

Fae magic . . . but he remembers me now. I don't understand what changed.

"I've been looking for you," he breathes, his fangs beginning to extend.

"Sebastian," Adrian warns. "Don't."

But it's too late. I already know it's too late. They've got me right where they want me. If Brisa is nearby, she'll be turning me into her little blood princess. Either that or she'll kill me. And if she's not nearby, surely Sebastian will do it for her.

Sebastian directs his next statement to the others in the circle, bypassing Adrian completely. "This is the girl I was telling you about, the one who we thought had killed Brisa, the nephilim with the gift of light."

Several vampires step closer, unbridled hunger shining in their dead eyes. A woman reaches her hand out, her smile turning wicked.

"Don't," I command, and she stops--they all stop. Maybe there's something left from Isadora afterall? But I still don't know the extent of it, and I'm not willing to test it and lose Adrian again.

"Eva, do you remember what happened in Ireland?" Adrian asks carefully. Fear is etched into his features, it's not a look I've often seen on the man.

I rake through the memories of Ireland, but all I can think is he wants me to remember my deal with Isadroa. I can make it so vampires have to leave me and my friends and family alone. If it's still in play, it would be so easy to demand it now, to send them all away. But what had Isadora said to remember? Something about intention . . . I don't remember a whole lot of what happened after that.

So if I really want the vampires gone, they'll be gone. And if I don't, then they won't be. But right now, I'm just so happy to see Adrian. I'm not going to dare mess this up for us.

"Can I?" he asks.

I nod, and slowly, he kneels at my side.

"Do you remember?" he asks again. All I want to do is crawl into his lap. To get away from these other people. For it to be just him and I here and nobody else. But I don't dare speak anything of the sort because Adrian is one of them, and I can never forget it.

"I remember most of it," I answer.

"What's this about?" a man demands, but Adrian ignores the question. Instead, he asks me if he can touch me, and when I nod, he scoops me into his arms and turns to the others, many of whom are still staring at me like I'm their meal ticket.

"She's mine," Adrian growls at the others. "Do you understand that? Mine."

"She's not just yours, Adrian," Sebastian argues. "Looks like the fae brought her for all of us to enjoy."

Part of me wants to stay tucked in Adrian's arms, but I've never been the damsel in distress, and I'll be damned if I start now. I shimmy myself out of his grip, but still stay close. His hands rest on my hips, and I don't remove them. He's behind me now, backing me up, no longer in front of me like I need saving, but behind me like he knows I can handle myself. With the familiar skyline surrounding us, I can see now that we're on top of the casino. Being back in New Orleans is a comfort, at least. I've missed this city so much, but I don't have time to process how it makes me feel to be back.

"You landed in our circle." Sebastian continues scowling at me. "You belong to all of us now."

"I belong to no one," I say boldly.

"The vampire council is all here. Shall we put it to a vote?" He motions to the others in the circle.

I turn to Adrian. His expression has grown murderous. "I said, she's *mine*. There is nothing to vote on."

"The vampiric council is set? The blood bonds have been transferred? Is that what was happening tonight?" I ask him. Suddenly I remember the circle of vampires that I woke up in--the blood on their palms, the full moon shining above them, and the electrical charge of fae magic sizzling through the air.

When Isadora had cast the spell the first time she'd been giving them instructions, but I hadn't listened. This meeting must have been part of that.

"Yes, it's done," Adrian confirms.

"So what does that mean for me?" I search his eyes, hoping for good news but expecting the worst.

"That remains to be seen, Angel." His reply is crisp. Succinct. Careful.

"We don't know yet," Mangus drawls with a pat on my shoulder.

Sebastian adds, "We don't, but we will."

"Enough," Adrian growls. "Touch her and die."

"You can't kill me now," Sebastian cackles. "The magic of our bond won't allow it, remember? No members of our council can kill the others. Those were your rules, and now we get to play with them."

"I'll kill you myself," I challenge, and the others laugh.

"That would be fun to watch." Mangus winks playfully, but I know him, and he'd probably love to watch me kill some of these people.

I find their "no council members can kill each other" edict pointless. These men and women are powerful enough that they could plot around that magic, using their covens and progeny to do their dirty work for them. Adrian leads the coven here, but he doesn't have any progeny, so he's already at a disadvantage. And as far as I remember, Mangus has nobody. I can't speak for the others, but I'm certain that Sebastian has powerful resources up his sleeve.

"The spell is complete, and that's what matters," Adrian addresses the others, all of whom have inched closer to me throughout this conversation.

It seems that when I gave Adrian permission to come closer, I gave all the other vampires license to do the same. A prickle of unease goosebumps over my skin. What are they going to do to me? I'm still not even sure why or how I ended up here, except that the fae are the ones responsible for it. But if I have to, I'll command them away again. It's my last option, but at least there is one.

"We are a council now," Adrian continues. "There is much work to be done."

Mangus claps sardonically. Everything about that

man drips sarcasm and resentment, and right now it's aimed at the other council members. There was a time when it used to be aimed at me. I'm glad we've moved past that. "Go team," he deadpans. "Now can we go have a meal please? We can talk all about our plans for world domination at our first council meeting tomorrow night."

A few of the others nod, but most are still watching me with distrust.

And a few stare with hunger. They don't even try to hide it.

"The girl stays close," a woman instructs, and the others nod. I expect Adrian to tell them all to stick it where the sun don't shine, but he agrees.

"That's not going to be a problem. Eva's staying with me."

Um--what now?

I want to tell him off, but I also have to remember what happened in Ireland. If I say the wrong thing, we'll be separated again. I don't want that to keep happening. So I pin him with a knowing glare instead, one that says he and I need to talk. And with that, he grabs my hand and pulls me after him, through the rooftop door, down the little hallway, and into the elevator.

It's only once the elevator doors close, once we're blissfully alone, that he wraps me into a tight hug. My body melts like butter under his touch, and my breathing slows.

The nephilim and the vampire. Who would've thought?

"You are not to leave my sight ever again," he growls into my hair.

I inch back to peer up at him. "Yeah, I don't think my staying here is a reasonable request. Did you see those people? They want me, and not in the way you want me."

"I don't care." His eyes are wild as they search me over. "I can't lose you again. I won't let you out of my sight."

There's a fear within him that I've never experienced before. In fact, I didn't even know it was possible for a creature like him to have so much fear. He's the scary one in every situation he walks into.

"You won't lose me again," I assure him, but even as I say it, I know it's an empty promise. I can't guarantee anything. Neither can he.

The elevator doors slide open and we're in the beautiful art deco lobby of the hotel, the sounds from the casino are not far off. I'm not sure where we're going next, but I'd love to see my mother. It's been too long, and my heart can't take another minute. I know we have our differences, that I've played more of the parental role in the last few years, but she's irreplaceable. And sometimes a girl just needs her mother.

"Where's my mom?" I ask. "Please take me to her."

He doesn't say a word, but his eyes flash meaningfully.

The penthouse elevator whisks us up, and then we're in the hotel hallway. One of these two suites belonged to Hugo and the other is all Adrian's. Could my mother be staying in the second penthouse? Adrian said he was protecting her for me, and it makes sense that she'd be hiding out there.

The familiarity of this hallway is unsettling. Something about being up here this time feels so different than all the other times before. So much has happened between us. For one, I don't hate Adrian anymore. I love him. I've accepted it to be true; despite all the odds, I love him. And I need to tell him that.

After I check-in with my mother.

"Where is she?" I ask as we approach the two front doors. He opens his, ignoring the other, and unease spreads through my system. "Is she staying in your place?" Maybe she's in my old bedroom?

We step into his suite, the door closing behind us. He wraps me into another hug before falling to his knees. As if in prayer, my body becomes his altar as he holds my waist and presses his face to my stomach. He clasps my hands and peers up at me. The scent of night still clings to his windswept hair. And his eyes . . . his eyes are filled with torment. "Please, forgive me," he whispers.

CHAPTER 7

"Where is she?" I breathe.

He doesn't respond right away. I try to shake him off me, but he won't budge. I'm stronger than I've ever been before, though, and I know I could push him away if I really wanted to, but all my energy is depleted. It's like I can't even move. "Where is she?" I repeat again. Tears burn my eyes as my mind is pelted with visions of worst case scenarios.

He's still staring up at me when he tells me the truth. "I don't know. I forgot about her."

Those words break me from my trance, and I yank away from his hold, stalking into the living room and whirling around to face him. "You forgot about her?"

"It's not what you think. I lost her," he says. "I lost you, too."

My eyes narrow, the tears thickening. "Explain."

"Do you remember what you asked for as part of that spell?"

How could I forget? "I can't repeat it," I say. "Because even though I'm mad as hell at you right now, I don't want to go through losing you again, and I'm pretty sure if I say it, it'll happen all over again."

He nods once. "It looks like you have some control over that part."

I nod. When Isadora told me about intention, she was referring to exactly this thing. I can't control the vampires, but if I tell them to leave me alone, they will. "It seems that's the case. And that's how you lost my mother?"

And me.

He said he lost me too.

His eyes search me up and down, like he can't believe I'm here or even real. He stands. Steps closer. I step back. He stops, staring at me. Tormented. My fears double.

"I forgot that you existed," he confirms.

Those words are hard to believe at first. I have to sit with them for a few seconds to fully let them in. Never in a million years could I forget Adrian, but he forgot me?

He forgot me.

It hurts, more than anything else. My heart has already been through so much. And now I have to live with this fear that I will mess up and he'll forget all about me. Even though my logical side understands this happened because of Isadora's spell and my own bargain with her, the illogical part of me, the messy and human part of me, is overcome with complete and utter devastation.

"And I forgot your mother," he goes on. "She was ejected from the coven that night. I only just remembered her––remembered you––a few minutes ago."

A tear breaks free, hot rejection splashing down my cheek.

I know I shouldn't blame him.

And I don't.

. . . but I do.

Again, it's my stupid illogical heart. I don't care if I'm nephilim now, I'll always consider myself a human too. I was raised by humans, and at my base I relate to them the most. And this feeling is all human.

"And you're certain that you remember me now?" I chew my bottom lip, the nerves starting to get to me now. "Do you remember us?"

He answers by pulling me into his arms and crushing his lips to mine. I'm frozen at first, still hurt, still disbelieving, still angry at him and angry at myself, but then his lips do what they've always done to me. They open me up to a level of vulnerability I've only experienced with him. Even though they're cool, they warm me from the inside out. Even though they're hard, they're just the softness I need. Only his unforgiving lips can strip away all my defenses and tear down my walls.

I kiss him back with equal hunger, my fears disappearing. I'm not thinking about the fae or the vampires. I'm not wondering about where the nephilim are or what they're doing. And even the worries for my mother are put to the side, just for this moment.

Just for him.

For us.

He deepens the kiss and lifts me into his arms. My legs wrap around his torso and I press my body into his. This reunion feels like a homecoming and a confession. It feels like everything I've ever wanted.

His spicy male scent is intoxicating as he walks us into his bedroom and lays me down on the bed, looking down on me like I'm a present he can't believe he gets to unwrap. And when he joins me, my mind clears in the most peaceful way, and then that same mind is gone entirely as our bodies take over.

I've only done this once before. Last time he showed me what to do and how to trust myself. This time, I'm bold enough to take the lead for as long as he'll let me. And for a while he does, but eventually his possessive-ness takes over and he can't let me have control for another second. And somehow, that's even better.

"You know how to make me feel things I didn't know were possible," I confess, and he chuckles darkly.

"Good girl. Tell me all about it."

We continue like that, him praising me, urging me to speak more freely about what I want, to tell him every-thing I'm feeling. And so I do as we spend the next hours reacquainting ourselves and making up for lost time.

And even when I start to glow, my body emitting my warm golden light from the inside out, we don't stop.

"You're gorgeous," Adrian whispers into my ear.

After spending the entire day in bed with him, only sometimes sleeping, I'm dressed for the coven meeting tonight. The vampires dress up for these things in luxury designer clothing, and though I'm no vampire and never plan to be, I still want to fit in just enough to be comfortable. I don't want to be the thorn among roses tonight.

"Thanks." I place a soft kiss on his lips, and he groans regretfully.

"As much as I want to take you back to bed, we have to go to this."

"I'm not looking forward to it, are you sure I have to go?"

The last place I want to be is in the basement hotel ballroom with all the bloodsuckers. Even if my opinion has changed about certain vampires, I still distrust most of them. Adrian is the coven leader, so he won't let anything happen to me. And Brisa holds no power, so she can't demand things. But I can't get the images out of my mind of the first time I sat in for one of those meetings, of the woman that had been killed, and how Adrian had been forced to take part in it.

"I'm not ready to let you out of my sight," Adrian repeats the same thing he's been saying since he brought up the coven meeting and I said I wanted to stay back in the room. Eventually he's going to have to let me out of his sight, but I know he's not ready. And honestly, I might not be either.

"Fine." A smile crosses my face. "But can I bring a stake?"

"Very funny," he deadpans, and I snort.

He knows by now that I carry a stake as often as I can. It's rather unfortunate that I haven't been able to get my hands on one today. I hate knowing I don't have a weapon right now. Even if I don't plan to use it, it still acts as a security blanket for me, and it has saved my ass on more than one occasion.

But things are different now. First of all, Adrian would never let any of those vampires touch me. And secondly, I've been bitten enough times that the venom in my blood has made me nearly as strong as the vampires themselves. I'm not powerless, and I'm not weak.

And I have angelic light—though I still haven't gotten a complete handle on it.

Except . . . the golden light was easy for me to control while Adrian and I were together earlier. I let it come to me, and when I wanted it to go away, it did. I still don't know what it does or what it means, but I'm no longer afraid of it, and neither is Adrian.

It's the white light that he should be afraid of, and that doesn't come from love. That's my weapon, and it's just as powerful as a stake anyway.

"Have you heard any news about my mom, yet?" I ask, changing the subject.

He shakes his head. "Give it some time. We'll find her. I promise."

I nod, and try to put her from my mind, though it's not easy. I'm so worried, but she's a grown woman, and I know she can take care of herself. That is––if the De Lucas don't find her first.

He drops a kiss to my forehead. "Are you ready to go?"

I nod and clasping hands, we head down to the coven meeting together.

"What's that smile for?" he teases.

"I'm happy," I admit with a shrug. And it's true, even though I feel guilty that my mom could be in danger somewhere, I'm still happy right now. I'm finally seeing myself for exactly what I've always thought was there–– a strong woman. I can take care of myself. I know what I want. I have a strong sense of right and wrong. And I'm not going to back down from a worthy fight.

"I'm happy too," he says, pulling me against the elevator wall and kissing me with reckless abandon.

"I've never liked elevators before, but I think I might love this one," I tease between our kisses, and he laughs wickedly.

"Note to self, get trapped in an elevator with Eva."

But that doesn't happen, and all too soon we're out of this one and waiting for the one that goes exclusively downstairs to the coven headquarters.

When we step inside, we're not alone. "Prince Adrianos," a group of four equally gorgeous vampires address Adrian, bowing their heads low in unison.

He nods a hello, engaging them in conversation while simultaneously running the pad of his thumb up and down the side of my hand.

It's not lost on the others—they shoot quick glances at our clasped hands.

And it's not lost on me either.

This is more than an announcement—it's a claim.

I'm his and he's mine.

They know it, Adrian knows it, but most importantly, I know it.

I squeeze his hand tighter. Three times. *I. Love. You.*

He squeezes back. *I. Love. You. Too.*

The elevator doors open, and we stroll into the foyer and then the coven ballroom—soon, everyone else will know we're together.

My heart speeds as the many vampires turn to look at us. They can hear my heartbeat, and from the looks of it, they weren't expecting me to be here tonight. There are more vampires here than ever before, reminding me of Brisa's court. But looking around, I don't see a single human fledgling or servant.

Not tonight.

Maybe I am a thorn among roses afterall. But who said being a thorn was such a bad thing anyway? Someone's got to be the prickly one.

"The council is here, and they brought many of their

own coven members for added security," Adrian reassures me, but he doesn't say more, probably because of all the listening ears.

I press my shoulders back and stride into the room with him, proud to be at his side. I know I'm safe, protected by more than just Adrian's feelings for me. I'm protected by an angelic gift. And by fae magic.

Fae magic that threw me into the center of their council's sacred circle.

I still don't know why, but I'm starting to have an inkling of what their reasoning was for doing that. Tonight is the perfect opportunity to confirm my suspicions.

A slow smile forms on my face.

"Be good," Adrian says in a low tone, raising an eyebrow at my smile.

"I was your good girl upstairs, Adrian, but down here, I get to be as bad as I want."

CHAPTER 8

The blood is always the worst part at these things. The vampires like to keep it flowing, stocking the bar with loads of blood bags that they can pour into their wine glasses. The distinct coppery smell is undeniable to any human, let alone to a nephilim like me with an incredible sense of smell thanks to both venom and my angelic bloodline. As we mingle, I keep having to hold my breath.

"And who is she to you anyway?" One of the vampires I recognize from the rooftop last night approaches us. She's a stunning Indian woman with black wavy hair, a petite frame, and dark winged eyes—but her voice is dripping in cruelty.

She hates me.

Probably because she knows I'm nephilim, but maybe for more reasons than just that. Showing up in the middle of their sacred ceremony probably didn't earn me any brownie points. But she doesn't know me either, and maybe that's a good thing. She doesn't know what I'm capable of and what I'll do to make sure the people I love are safe. Especially my mother, whom Adrain has people looking for at this very moment.

"Antara, good to see you again. This is Eva," Adrian introduces me. "And she's my girlfriend."

Several of the nearby vampires––all clearly eavesdropping while pretending to have conversations––go quiet. My cheeks warm.

"Have you ever had a girlfriend before?" Mangus approaches, a wicked glint in his eyes.

"No, not since I was a human," Adrian answers, not an ounce of embarrassment or regret in his tone. It's the opposite. He's proud we're together.

So I'm his girlfriend? And his first one? I mean, obviously the man has taken lovers, he certainly knows how to perform in the bedroom, but this? This is vulnerable and real in a way that I wasn't expecting tonight. Anyone who wants to touch me will have to go through him, I already knew that. But now they all know it too.

He's the oldest prince, and the second oldest vampire alive. And most of these people don't know Brisa is still kicking it somewhere, so they consider him the oldest.

He's a founding member of the first ever vampiric council.

He's the coven leader here in New Orleans, but his power and influence reach much farther than just this city, in fact he has authority over the entire continent.

And he's all mine.

And as wonderful as that feels, it also puts a target on my back. I'm not stupid, but I'm also not stupid enough to let go of his hand right now.

"Cute," Antara replies curtly, her tone implying that she thinks our relationship is anything but cute. Do I even blame her? I remember what my cousin Chloe, the nephilim record keeper, showed me back in Italy. My kind and the vampires have been at war for centuries. Hundreds have died on both sides. Maybe even thousands.

And now here I am, Adrian's girlfriend, crashing a coven meeting. Holding his hand. Under his protection. We're like Romeo and Juliet, and we all know how that story ended.

"It's nice to meet you," I pretend, and she pretends too. They all do. The only ones I can trust here are Adrian and maybe Mangus. Suddenly, I miss Kelli. We weren't friends, but I still think we could've been, and I know she would've had Adrian's back no matter what. It would've been nice to have another ally. These vampires have so many children at their beck and call, and Adrian has none. I get his reasoning because if I were a vampire, I wouldn't want to turn anyone either, but the political ramifications might be deadly for us both.

Finally, the conversation dwindles and it's time to get to council business.

Everyone takes their chairs, and the nine council members stand at the front of the room. Cameras have been set up to broadcast this meeting to covens all over the world, and I wonder how many are watching right now. Just thinking about it makes me nervous. Adrian sits me down in the first row, only a few paces from where he's standing with the others.

"When you said you didn't want to let me out of your sight, you really meant it, huh?" I raise an eyebrow.

He drops a kiss to my forehead. "I really meant it."

Sebastian speaks first, and I have to fight to keep my face void of the disgust I feel for that man.

"It is done," he announces, throwing his hands up in celebration, and everyone cheers. He's so sanctimonious and self-satisfied, as if he wasn't trying to take the blood bond back for Brisa just two weeks ago. I still can't believe I was in Faerie for two weeks, but Adrian confirmed it to me earlier. I only remember bits and pieces of the first night, and when we talked about it today, there wasn't a whole lot I could tell him.

Which is killing me because there's got to be something I'm missing. Something important. And it's just beyond my reach . . .

Sebastian bows to the applause coming from both the crowd and the livestream. The other council members do as well, and Adrian's bow is so short lived I have to fight back a snort. He hates this crap. He's not here for applause, he's here to make sure his people are okay.

And all I can think is that somewhere out there, Brisa

is probably watching along with the rest of the vampires.

Watching and plotting.

"Your council has been selected through a democratic process, and the blood bonds have been forged by the moon," Sebastian continues.

The crowd grows even more enthusiastic, and I clap along, though it nearly kills me to be clapping for anything to do with vampires. My prejudices run deep . . . something I might need to work on now that I'm dating one of them.

Logically, I get why the vampiric council is a good thing for humans, that they'll be able to govern and keep suckers in check this way, but emotionally, I can't help but hate the power these creatures hold. No, they're not *all* bad, but so many of them are still monsters and would enslave us if they could. I see the way I'm being watched in here, some of these people would happily rip me to shreds and feast on my blood if given the opportunity.

And of all the suckers here, I think Sebastian would love that opportunity the most. Who else on that council would do the same? If enough of them vote, they could change everything. They could decree that vampires can go out this very night and start killing.

"Our first order of business is to put the current laws to a vote." He turns to the other members. "Are there any that you would like to challenge?"

I don't know what I am expecting exactly, but it's not

the silence that follows. None of the council members want to challenge the status quo? I find that extremely hard to believe, but maybe I underestimated them.

"Now is the time," he presses. "The next council meeting won't be until quarter two."

Again, silence.

"Nobody wants to show their true colors, huh?" Mangus laughs bitterly, looking them each in the eye. "Very well. We set the rules, the VEC enforces the rules, and the blood bonds will keep those rules from being easily broken to begin with. How very special."

"Things will go on as they have," Adrian agrees, patting Mangus on the back. "It's not so bad, brother. There's always next time." He says it with a teasing wink.

Not so bad, huh?

The vampires will get to keep their fingers in human vices, exchanging blood for everything from gambling to alcohol to drugs and prostitution. I hate it, but I understand their logic. This is the best way they have found to get as much of the sustenance they need without biting humans directly and making them stronger with venom.

Couldn't you just just *pay* for that blood instead?

As everyone turns to look at me, I realize that I blurted that question out loud.

CHAPTER 9

"*A*drian, muzzle your pet," Antara spits. She and several other council members look like they're seconds away from ripping my head off.

"Eva has a point. We have plenty of money. We could easily pay for blood." I blink at Adrian's words. They're the last thing I ever expected.

"Are you putting it to a vote?" Sebastian cackles. "Please do, brother. I would love to see your first proposal fail miserably."

"What do you think, Eva?" Adrian shoots me a smirk. "Should I propose this idea of yours?"

Everyone else is staring at me.

Shocked?

Disgusted?

Rageful?

All of the above . . .

Adrian turns back to the others with a long sigh.

"No, I'm not putting this up for a vote. I was simply pointing out that it's not the worst idea. In fact, paying for blood instead of trading for it has been discussed before, as some of you might recall."

"Right!" I can't help but butt in. "Humans *love* money, and if you got all your blood that way instead of how you're doing it now, you wouldn't have to promote human addiction at all." I'm sitting up taller in my seat, my voice turning passionate. "Do any of you know what it feels like to have the person you love the very most in the world love their vices more than you? Because I do, and it sucks. It doesn't paint y'all in the best light, no offense."

"You dare speak to us in this manner?" one of the councilmen snarls. "You don't even belong here!"

"That's enough," Adrian snaps, though, I'm not one hundred percent sure whom he is telling to shut up. Probably me.

I sink back into my padded seat, pretending to be chastised by the council and Adrian, when really I want nothing more than to continue making my point. But I know better, anything I have to say about blood donation is going to fall on deaf ears here. It has to--because they could pay for blood, but why would they? What they have going has provided them with more blood than they could ever dream of, and they're not willing to risk losing that.

At least they don't go around killing for it anymore. And for the millionth time in my life, I praise the sun for making sure these suckers can't roam around during the day like they can at night. At least the daylight is still a safe space for humans.

Well, it's safe from vamps, but it's certainly not safe from all the other supernaturals out there.

My face continues to burn, and I sit on my hands, trying not to feel so helpless for the next few minutes as the council finishes up their meeting. I seriously feel like everyone in this damn ballroom and all the viewers the world over are staring daggers at me and planning my bloody demise. I should've kept my mouth shut, but that's not really me, now is it?

"If that's all, we can adjourn this meeting," Adrian concludes.

The gorgeous Indian woman, Antara, juts her chin. "Actually, I have a little something I would like to propose to the council."

"You have our ears, Antara," Sebastian replies smoothly, and there's something conspiratorial in his tone that rubs me the wrong way. He was expecting Antara's interruption this whole time.

I swallow a hard lump in my throat and sit up straighter, catching Adrian's ever-watchful gaze. He's even more alert than I am, and I wonder if he expected this to happen or if Antara waited for the perfect timing to spring this little request on us.

Her little request turns out to be not so little.

"Nephilim Girl," she points to me, "Stand up, please."

"Her name is Eva," Adrian barks. He's already told

her this, she knows my name, but that's not the point. The point is that she's purposely calling me by what I am because everyone here is enemies with the nephilim.

And I'm guilty by association.

"I thought it was Evangeline?" She bats her eyelashes, and my body goes cold.

This is all a game to her, and I don't know what rules she's playing by, if any.

"She prefers Eva," Adrian corrects, and my heart does a momentary happy dance. It's silly, but I love that he calls me the pet name Angel or the name I prefer and not by the legal name I don't relate to. The name I *never* related to.

But to everyone here, I'm Eva. I know how to be Eva. Eva doesn't back down from a challenge, and she sure as shit isn't going to let these vampires scare her.

"That's right," I say, standing from my seat and walking forward to Antara. "It's Eva, not Evangeline, and not Nephilim Girl."

Antara grins slyly. "Ah, but you are a nephilim, aren't you?"

I shrug. "So? I didn't know I was one until very recently, and I don't align myself with those who seek to kill off innocent supernaturals, nor am I willing to feed on human emotions."

Although that last bit makes me wonder why I was able to control the golden light so easily last night. It's never been that easy before. What really happened in Faerie?

"So you think you're special?" She raises an eyebrow, and several in the crowd laugh.

Adrian is fuming, and I know he's taking notes on exactly who is laughing at my expense. Knowing him, they'll pay later, and knowing me, I'll help him.

"I know I'm special," I respond sharply. "And I think you do too. Why else would you single me out? So tell me, what do you want?"

"You're the first nephilim light-bearer in well over a century," she snaps. "Don't try to deny it."

"I never did," I snap back, "but as I said before, I'm not willing to feed on humans, so my gift is weak, and that's fine by me. You don't need to fear my light."

But she does.

They all do.

I can sense it the way one can sense when a storm is brewing. Something happened to my gift in Faerie, something for my benefit. I can't remember what they did with me for those two weeks, but whatever it was, I'm suddenly able to control my gift in a way I never could before.

That can't be a coincidence.

I can feel it right there below my skin. It's mine for the taking. As if clouds are gathering, the pressure is becoming more dense within me, and it's only a matter of time before the skies open and my gift comes pouring out. I'm the storm standing here right now, and I don't fear it anymore. Let it pour down on all of us because I'm strong enough to handle it.

Antara keeps her eyes pinned on me, as do all the others, when she makes her statement. "I propose that Evangeline Blackwood becomes our prisoner until such time that we can harness her light to help us walk freely in the sun once again."

I blink at her, stunned and horrified that we're doing this right now.

The crowd is silent, but only for the briefest of moments, and then cheers erupt.

Antara turns to her other council members. "Who is with me?"

"You do this and you'll lose her forever," Adrian roars. "You know what happened in Ireland. Are you really so foolish?"

Except for me to push them away would be to break my own heart.

"Let's vote!" Antara calls.

Half of the council raises their hands, the dissenters being Adrian, Mangus, and two others whom I make note to thank later. But the four who are on my side are outnumbered by the others. It's five to four--and I'm the one who will face the consequences.

"No," Adrian sneers, pulling me into his arms for protection. "She belongs to nobody."

"Oh, because you've claimed her?" Sebastian challenges, stepping forward and turning his lip up at us. "Because you think she already belongs to you? Isn't that what you told us last night, *brother*?"

"It's not like that," he argues. "I'm not using her for her light. She's my girlfriend."

Seb cackles. "Save it. Since when have you had a girlfriend? Since never. We all know you really just want her light for yourself. Let me guess, you've already experienced some of it, haven't you?"

They're twisting everything, they're twisting us. But in the back of my mind, I can't help but wonder if they could be right. Is it possible that Adrian is using me? That he found out what I could do and that's what changed his mind about me?

"I belong to myself and nobody else," I bark, peeling myself from Adrian's arms. I stand tall all on my own and glare at the council. Antara and Sebastian my main targets.

"Sorry, it doesn't work that way." Antara flashes her fangs as she laughs. "We've already voted, and you're ours now."

This is it. This is my chance to test why I was thrown into that sacred circle last night. And I have to, don't I? I'm all out of options, and not even Adrian can protect me now. I'm going to have to protect myself.

I'm going to have to become the storm.

Raising my hands, I point one at Antara and one at Sebastian, careful to keep my back to the crowd so I'm only facing the other council members.

"Have you stopped to ask yourselves why I was placed into your sacred circle last night? Haven't you wondered who did it?" I question, mustering up as much courage as I can for this. It's not a lot, but it's enough.

"We already know it has something to do with the fae," Sebastian glares, "They gave you to us as a gift. Maybe they want to repair our poor relationship." He doesn't believe a word he just said, I can hear it in his voice. But I can also hear that he doesn't care so long as he gets what he wants. "Now put your hands down."

"No," I say between gritted teeth. My hands begin to warm.

"What do you think you're doing? Are you asking to die? I said, put your hands down!" Sebastian's eyes are ablaze, but my hands are only getting hotter.

I ignore his threat because I am not afraid.

If they kill me, they kill me. I won't just let them take me as their prisoner––their experiment––and I won't let them force me apart from Adrian either. "The fae had me in Faerie for the past two weeks. That was two weeks to weave their magic into me. And what do you think they did with me during that time?"

Mangus and Adrian are at my side now. I've got back up, but I don't need it because I'm not putting down my hands. I'm not stopping this.

"I'll tell you," I continue, bluffing a little bit here because I don't actually know what they did, but I've got a pretty good guess based on how I feel right now. "They forced my angelic gift to surface and then taught me how best to use it."

"So you were lying about your gift being weak?" Sebastian challenges.

"You, of all people, should know how to spot a liar."

My hands are growing hotter now. This is it.

"You wouldn't dare," Antara shrieks. For the first time tonight, her voice wavers, and her eyes dart to the sides. She's planning her escape. "You're just proving my point. You need to be tamed and controlled, and we're the ones tasked to do it."

Just like I ignored Sebastian, I ignore Antara. I speak to the council as a whole, loud enough for everyone to hear whether they're in the room or streaming from a coven far away. "Let it be known that the fae threw me into your sacred circle at precisely the right moment when the moon was forging the spell. I would wager that they have big plans for me, plans that made me part of your council."

"Impossible!"

"It was the fae who forged the blood bonds, and it was the fae who placed me in your circle at the perfect moment. You say it's impossible, but I say it's more than possible, it's obvious that I'm part of your council now."

"You're not one of us," Sebastian growls. "Is that what you want? Do you want me to turn you tonight? Do not tempt me."

"I'm not a vampire, and I never will be, but I have an idea as to how I can test my theory." I tilt my head toward Adrian. "Adrian, the vampiric council members are protected from killing each other, is that right?"

"That's right," he confirms in a low voice. He's prepared to jump into action at any second, his entire body tense with anticipation. But he's letting me have this because he trusts me, because we're finally on the same team.

I pin my eyes on Sebastian and Antara, though I wish I could glare at each and every one of those vampires who just voted to lock me up and turn me into an experiment. "The way I see it, I have two options. Either I kill you, and your vampire council doesn't have enough votes to sustain hurting me. Or I don't kill you, thereby proving that I am now a part of your council, in which case I'll tie up your vote."

"That's ludicrous," Sebastian says. "You dare to threaten us?"

He's about to attack. I can feel it, but I can feel my own gift more.

My smile splits the sky. "Either way, I win."

With that, I take a chance. My gift explodes from my palms, white and ungodly bright light--a reckoning unlike anything the vampires have ever seen.

CHAPTER 10

$\mathcal{H}$aving a gambling addict for a mother comes with a lot of wisdom that I didn't ask for, but there are a few things that have stuck with me. They're like peanut butter on the roof of my mouth, not always easy to swallow and impossible to ignore. And right now, it's my mother's voice telling me to bet on myself, reminding me that I can't win if I don't play the game. It's her voice that is giving me the strength to fight back.

Sebastian and Antara don't move fast enough to shield themselves from the stream of blinding light because nothing, not even a vampire, is faster than the speed of light. It shoots at them like a laser, and one of two things is about to happen. They're either going to burn alive and all hell is going to break loose, or nothing is going to happen at all. And if that's the case, which I'm hoping it is, then I'll have figured out that the fae really did bind me into the vampiric council.

People scream while Adrian and Mangus move in closer to my sides, offering their protection. The light is as bright as a bolt of lightning, but it's not a flash. It's a steady stream exploding from my palms and going right into the two vampires. It lasts for a solid ten seconds before I let it drop, blinking rapidly as my vision adjusts to the lack of light.

The screaming fades as everyone takes in the scene. Sebastian and Antara are cowering on the floor, but they're not dead. They're not even injured.

"Angel, it looks like you're going to have to explain yourself," Adrian says loudly, but there's a sweetness to his tone that's bordering on amused. He's obviously fighting back a laugh. A laugh that Mangus lets out without a care in the world.

Sebastian is the first one back to his feet, immediately coming at me, but Mangus cuts him off. Antara isn't far behind, but Adrian doesn't give a shit about hurting a woman apparently because he lifts her up and throws her against the wall. She's tough, so she gets to her feet quickly, but she doesn't attack a second time.

I sigh, prepared to explain myself to everyone in the room. Let them hate me, but let them fear me too. It's the only way I'm going to survive. "I don't know why the fae wanted me in your council and I didn't know it was coming, but I swear to you this is the truth of our situation." Mangus continues laughing maniacally while everyone else stays silent, half of them staring at him like he's lost his mind.

"Make no mistake that the light from my palms can kill vampires," I threaten. "But it couldn't kill Sebastian and Antara because the magic forged in our council bond is even stronger than my angelic gift. The council magic forbids me from killing anyone else on the council, same as it forbids them from killing me. And that right there is all the proof you need that I am now a part of this vampiric council."

I don't mention that I could also tell them to leave me alone and they'd have to, that they might even forget me entirely, simply because I don't want to risk losing Adrian. But if it comes down to it, if they try to take my life or my gift, then I'll take that risk. I wouldn't have another choice.

"It can't be true," one of the council women gasps in a thick Russian accent. She didn't vote for me, so I don't really care what she has to say. "This nephilim is not a vampire. She cannot belong with us."

"She just proved to you it is true, Nadia," Mangus sighs. "Don't underestimate fae magic. Or haven't you learned that lesson yet? Remind me, how old are you? A hundred years? Sometimes I forget how young most vampires are these days."

That comment earns him a death glare from just about everyone in the room. They're all pretty young compared to the princes, and I think it has something to do with the earlier nephilim wars and the sheer number of vamps who were killed.

The council stands divided as they take in my news. With me as part of the group now, we're an even split. There are ten of us to vote on matters. Ten of us to vote on my future.

"You can't have me," I announce boldly. I make sure to look each of them dead on so they can see how serious I'm being about this. "With nine votes there was a split, but with ten there's a tie. And I vote for my freedom." I turn to Mangus, Adrian, and the two vampires who also voted for my side. "Thank you for helping me keep my freedom. I won't forget this kindness."

Mangus and Adrian nod. The others don't look so sure, but they eventually nod as well.

"So it's settled," Adrian is quick to say. "We'll meet again at the next council meeting scheduled to take place at Santino's coven headquarters in Rio De Janeiro in three months' time."

"This isn't over," Sebastian says darkly.

And then he turns and leaves, his entourage following him out the door. I recognize his new child, Fiona, who was a fledgling not that long ago. And I remember how she tried to help turn me back in Italy. At the time I'd considered her my savior, but I was under the influence of vampirism and not in my right mind. Now I can only see her as the demon working overtime for the devil that is Sebastian. She gives me a little wave on her way out, her eyes mocking.

"Sebastian always did have to have the last word," Mangus grunts.

I sigh and press my forehead into Adrian's chest. I'm so ready to get out of here. I feel depleted but also so full at the same time. Even though I can't remember it, I'm now certain that the fae king Orlyc forced my gift to surface and, in the two weeks I was with the fae, they taught me how to use it without needing human emotion to feed it.

But how? I thought nephilim had to feed on humans.

Part of me would love to thank him, part of me wants to demand answers, and the biggest part never wants to step foot in his realm again.

"Games are afoot, eh?" Mangus nudges me. "Fae don't just help nephilim for no reason. They hate nephilim even more than we do, no offense."

"I know . . ." I bite the inside of my cheek and try not to freak out. "It's clear they want something from me, but the question is, what?"

Adrian keeps me tucked under his arm as we leave the ballroom. It's not until we're alone in his penthouse that he relaxes a fraction, but he's still roiling with anger. He looks like he wants to kill someone. Probably five someones.

"I'll kill them before they ever lay a hand on you, Angel," he growls the second the door closes us in the penthouse, proving my point.

"You can't kill them. The magic won't let you," I point out.

96

"Then I'll make someone else do it."

I sigh, taking his hands in mine and kissing his knuckles one by one. He goes still as he watches me. "Obviously, I want them dead, too. They're dangerous to me. And if it's between me or them, well, I choose me. But we can't just start a council war over what happened tonight, at least not right now."

He shakes his head and a golden lock falls across his troubled eyes. "Nobody said anything about torture, though. I'll start with Sebastian. Peel his fingernails off one by one."

I snort. "You can't do that. He has his entourage here to protect him."

"And I have my coven. They'll back me up." He's seething. I don't know if I've ever seen him so angry. "I know he was the one who convinced the other council members to try and get to your gift. I'm sure he asked Antara to propose the idea just to piss me off. He's so much like his twin, Hugo. Always playing games with everyone, always making deals and scheming."

At least Hugo is dead, but Sebastian isn't going anywhere any time soon, especially with the protections now in place. But we're not going anywhere either. After losing Adrian on that rooftop in Ireland, then getting him back and spending the night with him, I couldn't care less about Sebastian right now.

Because I know exactly how I feel in my heart, and I can't wait another second to tell him. I take his hand in mine and squeeze gently--three times for I love you. But I haven't said it out loud yet. "Hey, look at me."

His breathing is heavy. He only does that when he's upset. The man doesn't even need to breathe at all, but when his emotions get away from him, he starts to breathe like that, just a human man. His emotions are right here for me to see, they're plain on his face, and yet his mind is far away. With my other hand, I trace my fingertips along his neck, up his jawline, to cup his cheek.

"Adrian, look at me." He does, and there's so much worry and pain behind the glacial blue that it nearly breaks me.

"I love you," I whisper the three words that I've never said to a man before.

His eyes narrow as they search mine. They're so electric blue right now that they would be frightening if I didn't love him so much. He doesn't have kind or soft eyes, and nothing about him is approachable, but that doesn't matter because right now he's looking at me like I'm the only woman in the world.

I am mad with love.

"I would kill them all for you, Eva," he confesses. "Do you know what kind of monster you have fallen in love with?"

It's not what I expected him to say. It hurts. Not because he didn't tell me he loves me back, but because he thinks so low of himself.

"You're not a monster."

"But I am," he growls, dropping my hand and gripping the back of my neck instead, pulling me in closer. "I've killed so many people. I killed my own wife. My unborn child. And I know that I don't deserve your love, but I'm a selfish man, and I'm going to accept it anyway because it's the best thing that has ever happened to me in this morbid existence."

I can't help it. I giggle. "God, you're dramatic. Did anyone ever tell you that?"

His smile quirks, the intense energy loosening, and those wicked eyes transform with happiness. It might be the first time I've ever truly seen him allow happiness in. "I love you too, Angel," he says firmly. "I love you, and I swear to you, I will kill anyone who dares to harm you."

"Again with the theatrics," I tease.

But I love it. I love every second of this moment, theatrics and all. "I don't know if anyone's ever loved me back as much as I've loved them," I confess, suddenly more vulnerable than I've ever been. Being naked with him is not nearly as vulnerable as telling him these deep dark insecurities. It makes me feel weak even though I know it's actually making me stronger. "I'm not even sure my own family could love me fully. I didn't get a chance to know my father, and my mother and grandmother were probably afraid of me to an extent. But this? And you? You're what I've been searching for, Adrian." I press his hand to my heart. "Feel it beating?"

He nods, dropping his forehead to mine with a soft groan.

"It's all for you. I'm yours. My heart is yours."

Finally, I've found someone who will love me enough to put me first and fight for me. I saw it tonight during the council meeting, and it's given me the strength to do this.

He presses a kiss to my lips once. Twice. But then he pulls back. "There's something I have to tell you."

I don't like those words. Those words scare me. But I nod, forcing myself to be strong. "Okay."

He leads me to his sofa, and my mind races with the possibilities of what he's going to say. Does he not want this like I do? Is there something he's been hiding? Is he going to try to let me down easily? Whatever it is, he thinks it's bad enough that I need to be sitting for this conversation.

"I have responsibilities to my coven and to my people," he says.

"I know, and I wouldn't ask you to give those up." But is that really true? If it came down to it--them or me--what would I want? I'm not entirely sure I have the answer to that right now, because I just want us to stand a chance.

"When Isadora's spell was being forged last night, I was faced with an impossible choice." He stares at me expectantly, like I should get this, but I don't understand what he's trying to say.

"Just tell me, Adrian. Whatever you have to say isn't going to scare me off."

He scratches his jaw, a pained expression overtaking

his face. "I love you, but at that moment, I knew that if I didn't join the council, I wouldn't be able to protect my coven, let alone protect the humans from the worst of my kind. It killed me to do it, but I decided to move forward with the council bond." He swallows hard, and his words start to make sense to me. My face burns hot. I hold my breath. "I chose them over remembering you because I couldn't live with myself if I allowed the council to forge without me or not at all. And I'm so sorry."

He drops his head, and I expect to feel betrayed or disappointed.

But I don't.

"I'm proud of you," I say, surprising both of us. "You made the right choice. I would've done the same thing."

His head pops back up. "What?"

"You heard me. I wouldn't have wanted you to choose me over the billions of humans on this planet that need protecting, and I wouldn't have wanted your coven to be in danger either. You understand what's important, and that's why I love you."

"But *you* are important," he growls, pulling me into his lap. His hands roam under my skirt to grip my thighs. "You deserve more than I'll ever be able to give you. You deserve a full life, and you can never have that with a vampire."

"Stop. Don't say that."

"But it's true."

I kiss him hungrily, losing myself in his embrace and

in this safe space we've created tonight. I don't want to lose him. Not like this. It feels like we're building ourselves up and breaking ourselves down at the same moment. I don't know how to stop it before we crumble.

Pulling away, I stare into his eyes. "Listen to me carefully. I get to say what I deserve in my life. And what I want is for us to be together." I take his hand and place it over my heart again. "This is yours. Don't forget it." My heart pounds against my chest, and I know that he can feel and hear it. Finally he nods, relief plain on his face. Mine is probably mirroring back the same thing. "As long as that damn thing is in my chest, it belongs to you."

"My heart belongs to you too, but what need do you have with a heart that's been dead for centuries?" He means it, he really does look down on himself. He's always been so calm and collected, so confident and cold. To see him like this kills me.

"If it's yours, then I want it."

He smiles.

And when he smiles, the golden soft glow emits from my skin, lighting the darkness between us. I run my fingers over his face, his arms, his body. Everywhere. He does the same.

I know what he's thinking. That I should have a normal life, one with a human or even a nephilim man at my side, one with children and motherhood and everything that a human life has to offer someone like me.

A life without vampires.

And before I fell in love with him, I would've agreed. I never wanted a vampire, but I also never thought I would feel the way I do right now. I'm in love, and anything else would be second best. Adrian is the only one I want. I'll gladly give the rest of it away, give it all up, because having him is better.

Just as he's peeling off my dress, pounding booms on the door. Adrian groans into my mouth, and I do the same to him, my hands gripping his white shirt.

"Go away," he calls out.

"Your Highness," a male voice calls back, muffled by the door but still audible enough to send alarm bells through my system. "Please, we need you to hurry. There's been an incident in the casino. You're going to want to see this."

CHAPTER 11

"Stay here," Adrian commands, putting me gently on the couch like I'm made of glass. He stands and goes for the door.

"Don't you know me better than that?" I scoff, jumping up and adjusting my dress. "I'm coming with you."

His mouth lifts on one side. "You're right. What am I going to do with you?"

I waggle my eyebrows. "I can think of a few things."

"And we will do all those things later." He takes my hand and leads me to the door. "Come along. Let's get this over with."

A vampire stands waiting in the hallway. I immediately recognize the pit boss from the first night I met Adrian. I don't like this man. "William, this is Eva. Eva, this is William. He's my right-hand man on the casino floor."

"We've met," I say smoothly, pinning William down with a nasty glare.

He sighs heavily and turns back toward the elevator. "You really need to answer your phone, Adrian. I shouldn't have to come all the way up here to drag you away from your new toy."

Adrian moves lightning quick, pinning the man against the elevator doors. "Speak one sour word against Eva again and I will rip your intestines out and feed them back to you, is that clear?"

William blinks rapidly and nods.

"Now apologize."

"I'm sorry, Eva," he gets out just as the elevator doors open. He steps back into the box, and we follow.

Adrian is busy straightening out his suit and tie as he finishes with William. "You know, sometimes I think I'm too soft on the coven. Do you forget who I am? What I can do? Do I need to remind you?" He says it all casual and smooth, as if this is a conversation about the weather. It's terrifying and hot as hell.

"You're right. I'll do better," William replies. "You know I am loyal to only you."

Adrian stares at him for a long time before sighing. "Your maker is long gone. I took you in because I saw potential in you. And I still do."

"You're right," William offers. "Forgive me."

"You're forgiven." Adrian pats him on the shoulder. It's so strange seeing them together because William appears to have a decade on Adrian, but Adrian is actually much, much older. "I apologize for the outburst, William. I'm very protective of Eva, but I can do better, too."

Okay, that was also very hot.

He pulls me into his arms, kisses me on the top of my head, then continues his conversation with his number two. "Now, tell me what we're dealing with."

William swallows hard, his lips going thin. "The night was going just fine until a new vampire arrived. He attacked a group playing roulette on the casino floor. He drained one of our regulars before we could pry him off the guy."

"Who did he drain?"

"Raymond. He's one of our elderly player's club members. Comes in every day except Sundays because he says Sundays are for God."

Adrian's holding me tighter now, his muscles straining. I can feel the anger rolling off him and wouldn't want to be that baby vampire right now. Whoever it is, they're dead. For real this time. And they should be because that's messed up. Killing an old guy for no reason? I'm sick just thinking about it.

"Did you call the VEC?" Adrian asks.

"Not yet. I knew you would want to deal with the issue first."

Not to mention, Adrian is one of the primary members of the VEC. He nods and rolls back his shoulders, his neck popping in the process. "Thank you,

William. You did good. Did any of the other council members see it? Or their guests?"

William shakes his head. "No, they all think they're too good for the casino."

Adrian chuckles darkly. "They're not too good to drink the blood it provides."

My stomach churns at that not only because he's got a point, but also because the thought of the blood casino still makes me want to vomit.

My feelings are all jumbled up about this. Yes, I'm upset that a vampire killed someone, and yes, I think it should be reported. But I also know the VEC is in the pockets of the vamps anyway. And I trust Adrian. Back when I first met him, he killed a man in front of me as an intimidation tactic, but I later learned the guy was a gangster who deserved it. Adrian may call himself a monster, but he's the kind that takes care of the other monsters.

We head through the casino floor, to the roulette table where this apparently happened. But from the looks of it, you'd never know. The blood has been mopped up and there's a group of humans standing around gambling. They were probably compelled to forget what they saw. I catch sight of a woman with a small splatter of blood on her white dress and have to look away.

It's triggering. Makes my skin crawl. I'd still rather be anywhere else than this place. Up in the hotel I can almost forget this is here, but then I have to walk through the casino, and I'm affronted by the overstimulation. The dinging of the slot machines, the desperate patrons hoping for another hit, the stench of stale cigarette smoke, and especially the people with blood bags slowly dripping while they play. That's the worst part, and it's for show. They could just have people donate in the nurses station, but the vamps like the novelty of it all.

Even though The Alabaster Heart is a luxury hotel and casino, even though a lot of people in this city think it's a nice place, I still hate it.

The memories will haunt me forever.

I can almost see my mother there at that Texas Hold'em table. Her sparkly red purse slung over the back of the chair while she plays her games and loses herself. There's a woman there right now that looks so much like her with that curly auburn hair hanging down around her slim waist.

Wait . . . I squint, and my heart drops to the floor.

No. It can't be.

But it is.

The woman *is* my mother.

I stop dead in my tracks and just stare. Time crawls, and my vision narrows. My hands begin to shake. My mind races far too fast for my emotions to match. What is she doing here? I'm happy to see she's alive, but this is the last place I ever wanted to see her again. She's supposed to have been cured from her addiction. Adrian

compelled her to give up gambling. But there she is––
gambling once again.

I don't understand.

Adrian is saying something to me and then to
William, but I don't pay attention. I can't. His words are
like sand streaming through my fingers.

Without thinking, I run to her. "Mom!"

Her back stills, and then I call her by her name. She
turns to me, standing, taking me in her arms, an IV line
tugging at her hand.

"No," I say. "No." I can't believe it. I won't.

But I have to because the proof is right there. She's
donating blood in exchange for chips, just like she used
to do. Her blood is a red line in a tube of plastic leading
to a plump bag, but it might as well be a knife to my
heart. She was never supposed to donate to the vampires
again, and especially not in this manner. Suddenly, all I
want is to command the vampires to get away from her,
to demand the deal I made with Isadora be enforced.

But at what cost?

It won't save her from her addiction, and I'd lose
Adrian.

So I don't say a word about it, I don't, but I'm
speechless to say anything else.

"Oh, honey," her voice wobbles, "It's so good to see
you. I've been worried."

"What's going on?" I finally whisper, my voice breaking. "I thought you never wanted to gamble again?"

Her eyes well with tears, mirroring my own, and then she shrugs. "That feeling faded and the old one came back. I'm so sorry, Eva. I missed you so much, and then I was hiding out here, and being close to the casino wasn't easy, but I swear I never gambled." She swallows hard. "And then a few weeks ago I was in the lobby and something terrible happened. It was too fast for me to even see who did it, but the vampires threw me out on the streets. Adrian wasn't here to help me. Nobody wanted to help me. I had nowhere else to turn."

"What does that even mean?" I don't understand why that explains her coming back here to gamble. None of this makes sense––but I also don't want it to make sense because then I would have to accept that it's real, that she relapsed.

The man next to her swivels in his chair, a smug grin coming over his familiar pockmarked face, and things become ten times worse.

Armondo.

He's the mafia boss with the sinister grin and the deep scar in his left eyebrow, the one who nearly killed her in September. He gives me and Adrian the smuggest grin that I want to claw off his face. I outplayed him once before with Adrian's help, but he's back for more.

"Nice to see you again, Evangeline. And you too, Adrianos." His eyes flash to Adrian, and I know this has more to do with him than with me. Powerful men are like that sometimes, they underestimate the women, only ever looking to the men as worthy adversaries. "Eva, your lovely mother needed a place to stay while she got back on her feet. What kind of man would I have been to refuse a beautiful woman in need?"

"I know exactly what kind of man you are," I hiss between gritted teeth. I grab her arm. "But thank you, she is safe with me now."

He snakes his slimy hand around her waist and actually pulls her into his large lap, then he peels my hand off of her arm and kisses her neck as if he's done it a thousand times before. "Your mother and I came to an arrangement. She lives with me now."

He grins up at me with a mocking wink, and she shoots me a warning look. I don't know what to do. I truly don't.

Adrian steps closer. "Armondo, what are you playing at?"

Armondo laughs. "I thought I was playing Texas Hold'em. Is there another game I should be betting on right now? Maybe something with better odds?"

He winks.

He's taunting us.

And silence stretches between the group because we all know there's definitely another game going on here. A game of egos and power and the women who get caught in the middle. The dealer finishes distributing the current hand and the gamblers on either side of Armondo and my mother prepare their bets.

"Mom, you don't have to stay with him. Come with

us. Right now, come with us, and we'll pay him back however we have to."

"She's mine." Armondo squeezes her closer to his body, but I force myself to ignore it and will my mother to stand instead. "And if you'll excuse us, we have a hand to play."

She doesn't move, just stares at me with big sorrowful eyes. "I assure you, Eva. We're okay. We're enjoying ourselves. You don't need to worry about us. I'm happy with Armondo."

It's a lie. I know it's a lie.

How are we back here? After everything we've been through, is this really what she wants? Because not only is she in the clutches of this mobster again, but she's out in the open where the nephilim can track her and hurt her, and she's gambling. She's giving in to the thing that hurt her the most, the thing that she loves but that doesn't love her back.

It's all my fault--if I hadn't made that stupid deal with Isadora none of this would have happened. Mom would've stayed hidden by Adrian's coven. Protected and cared for until we could've found a way for her to live her life without the fear of the De Luca family. Once things were safe, we could've gotten her away from here forever.

"We'll see you around," Mom says gently, and then she turns her back on me, placing her bet. And even though I can tell she's sad, I can also tell she likes this, that this is also her choice. Armondo isn't making her do this, he's just enabling her.

And me?

I'm lost at sea, swallowed up by crashing waves of emotion. I'm falling through space with nowhere to land. I'm crawling through the barren desert, reaching out toward an oasis that isn't real, that was never real.

It. Was. Never. Real.

My mother was never really cured of her addiction. She was in a forced remission, but she was never cured, and now I'm going to lose her to it. In the pit of my stomach, I know it to be true. All my worst fears are happening, and I can't stop them.

"Eva." Adrian cups my elbow and guides me from the casino floor. I shuffle along aimlessly, not caring that people are staring at us, that vampires are glaring at me, or that my emotions are exposed for the whole world to see.

He pulls me into a dark side room and flips on a fluorescent light. I wince because it's too bright and too sterile in here. It's only when he wraps me in a tight hug that the floodgates burst open and I sob into his chest. "Shh," he whispers into my hair, and then he mumbles something in another language.

I don't know how long I stay like that. Minutes? Hours? But eventually, I peel away from his embrace and look up into his eyes. I find pity staring right back, and I hate it. I don't want his pity. What I want is action.

"Please," my voice hitches. "Compel her again. Make her stop. Make her better."

He shakes his head regretfully.

"Why not?" My hands fist, and I press them to his chest. "You say you love me, then prove it."

He grabs my fisted hands and holds them still, kissing the knuckles one by one. Eventually, I deflate.

"I will compel her if that's what you really want, but I have to warn you, compulsion can be dangerous if used over again on something as strong as this. She just proved her addiction is stronger than my first compulsion. If I do it again, I could scramble her mind. You could lose her forever."

CHAPTER 12

"How can an addiction be stronger than a centuries old vampire? You're the strongest vampire in the world. If anyone can help her, it's you."

At least my tears have dried up, but it still feels so unfair. I never thought I'd have to cry about this again. I didn't even get a chance to spend time with her while she was better.

"I will try. If that's what you want, I will try, but I can't promise that it won't hurt her."

My mind reels with the implications of his warnings. "And what happens if it does? What do we do then?"

"I can't undo a traumatic brain injury," he explains regretfully. "If her mind was strong enough to fight my compulsion, then I'll have to use even stronger compulsion to get her to stop gambling again."

"So you shouldn't do it . . ."

"Right now, we should be most concerned about Armondo. Would you like me to kill him?"

I snort and wipe away my remaining tears, but Adrian doesn't laugh. "Oh, you're being serious."

"Just say the word."

It's incredibly tempting. "What happens if we kill him?"

"First we have to get your mother away from him, but we kill him and wait for retaliation. That's if they know it's us. We've had a bad relationship with them for years. It won't be pretty, but I'll do it for you."

"Is there another way to get her away from him? Can we negotiate?"

He smiles. "If there's one thing I've learned in my time, it's that negotiating with guys like Armondo doesn't work."

Am I really going to put a hit on Armondo? Is this what it has come to?

It won't solve her gambling addiction, but getting her away from him will help. That slimeball brought her here to goad us, which means that word must have gotten out about Adrian and me being together and back in New Orleans.

Who else knows? My mind flits to the De Luca's. I just know they're lying in wait somewhere, wanting me to answer questions about what happened at The Gateway. But right now, Armondo is my biggest concern. He feels manageable. A bug I can squash. My awful relatives do not. They're more like an infestation.

"Whatever it takes to get my mom back, I want to do it."

Adrian gives me a quick nod and another hug and then leads me to a private bathroom to get cleaned up. I go in alone and glare at myself in the mirror, rubbing off the black mascara tracks that have stained my cheeks. My brown eyes are bright from crying, almost golden, but they're rimmed in red. Proof of my vulnerability. I really hate crying, especially in front of other people. Falling apart in Adrian's arms like that wasn't ideal, but somehow I'm not mortified by it. He's my person now.

I haven't had a person since Ayla broke off our friendship. I miss Ayla, and I'll always love her, but she hurt me. Yes, I made mistakes too. I never should've kept things from her, and I should've listened to her more when she shared her feelings about me dating her brother. I want her friendship back, but only if we're both fair to each other. It's been months, and I just hope that whatever she's doing, she's healthy and no longer hiding in her bedroom. If anyone deserves to live a wonderful life, it's that girl.

Adrian knocks on the door. "Are you ready?"

I shake my thoughts clear and head out to meet him. The detour with my mom wasn't expected, she could've been the one killed in that attack, and we still have to deal with the issue at hand. A new vampire killing a human means true death. That's the rules, and honestly, I'm all for it. If a vampire can't control their urges and kills an innocent, resisting strong blood bonds, then they're too dangerous.

Hell, I'll kill the vampire myself. That might make me feel a little better.

"Will it be a true death?"

"Yes, he's being held right now."

"Can I have the honors?"

"Would that make you feel better, Angel?" he asks. I expect him to tease, but he doesn't. He knows I hate vampires. Not all of them anymore, obviously, but vampires in general, and especially ones who break the rules and kill innocent humans.

Would it make me feel better? That's a good question. And an easy answer. "Absolutely."

A small smile flickers across his otherwise unreadable face. He's already so beautiful when he doesn't smile, that when he does it's like Christmas. "Then yes, you can kill him, but first we need to have a discussion with the vampire, and I need to talk to his maker. There's a proper way that we deal with these situations."

"Proper? Like when Hugo's vampire attacked me in the lobby, so you ripped his head off? Something proper like that?"

"Something like that, yes."

Our banter is making me feel better, and I couldn't be more grateful. I need to get my mind off everything. My life is a mess, and so many of the people I love are also caught up in messes that I can't clean up for them. I wish I could. It would be so much easier that way, but that's not how it works. I can't make my mom better, and I can't just force Ayla to be my friend again. I can't go back in time and stop myself from making mistakes.

I take Adrian's hand as we go back out to the casino floor. The sucker is being held on the opposite end of the casino from the hotel, so we have to walk the whole property. I can't help but notice how Adrian steers me well away from the Texas Hold'em tables. And I can't help but look in that direction anyway.

She's still there, but her blood bag has been removed. At least there's that.

It turns out that the casino has a row of jail cells hidden behind a massive locked door near the cashiers. It's incredibly secure, almost like a second bank vault, and we go from the lavish interior design of the casino to gray everything. That feels like a metaphor for my life lately, but I'm too exhausted to dissect it.

William is waiting for us. "He's in the last cell." He points us down the wide hallway. "He's the only one here."

There are several normal looking cells that must be for humans, a few with what I think are made of iron, and then there are several silver cell doors at the very back. Just seeing the silver takes me back to what it was like seeing Adrian locked up at the Casa. I inwardly shiver, wishing those memories could be erased forever. For both our sakes.

We walk up to the cell door made of solid silver. It has a small window with silver bars at eye level. Adrian peers through first. His shoulders tense, and he goes completely still.

"What?" I ask, already figuring whoever is in there can't be good news.

He turns to me, and his usually stoic face is filled with regret. My heart clenches.

"Let me see." I try to push him aside, but he doesn't budge.

"Maybe it's best if you didn't."

"You and I both know that's not going to happen."

He sighs and inches away, so I look through the little window.

"Kenton." My voice cracks on his name.

My friend is sitting on a bare mattress, and when he turns to look at me, his vampire-bloodshot eyes widen.

"Eva," he croaks. "I'm so glad you're here. You've got to help me."

"What did you do, Kenton?" I ask carefully, trying to remind myself that he's not the same Kenton that he used to be. This isn't the sweet Kenton who cracked jokes and rode around with me in Adrian's Porsche singing at the top of our lungs. This isn't the Kenton who handed me my first stake and stood up for me. This is the Kenton that was attacked in Versailles, that I witnessed die. The Kenton who wasn't actually dead because he was turned by Brisa. He's the man that helped ambush me in Ireland, telling me all about how great being a vampire is, and how much he loves drinking blood.

This is the Kenton who murdered an innocent elderly man earlier tonight.

This is Brisa's Kenton.

Mine is gone.

"Can you come in here so I can talk to you?" he pleads.

My mouth turns to ash. I don't know what to say . . .

"No," Adrian snaps.

I rest my hand on the door handle, trying to remember the friend I used to have. Could he still be in there somewhere? Maybe there's still a chance for him.

"It's okay," I say slowly, my eyes never leaving Kenton. "He won't hurt me."

At least, I hope he won't. I don't really know him anymore.

Adrian growls, "You don't know what he's capable of, Angel. He's not the friend you used to know. He's a soulless killer now."

Kenton starts to cry. I've never seen him cry, he was always the happiest person I knew. And something about the way his shoulders bob up and down and the pain in his voice breaks me.

I turn on Adrian. "You were a killer when you first transitioned. It doesn't make it right, but he has the same maker as you, so shouldn't you of all people have some compassion for what he's going through?"

Adrian rakes a hand through his hair, shaking it out as he thinks of what to say. Finally, he speaks, careful with each word. "You're only saying that because you care about him. If he was any other vampire, you'd have killed him by now."

"You're going to kill me?" Kenton jumps up, flashing forward to the door, only inches from us on the other side of the bars. "For what? For feeding?"

"For killing," Adrian growls. "We have rules for a reason."

And while I know that's the truth, I also know that my Kenton could still exist underneath all the death and destruction. For all we know, Brisa told him to kill in order to gain Adrian's attention.

I turn on Kenton. "Did Brisa make you kill that human?"

Kenton's dark eyes shift away and he steps back. "No, I wanted to feed, and I didn't want to stop."

I can't tell if he's lying, but my gut says he is.

"Brisa is trying to use you, and probably others, to get to the council," Adrian states. "Don't deny it."

Kenton shrugs. "So what? She failed. And now I'm here."

"And now you're here . . . which is a problem. Eva may wish to save you from true death, but I can't let you live. You belong to Brisa, and you operate outside the council's bond. It's only a matter of time before you kill again. You're a liability."

Kenton hangs his head. "You're right. Kill me. I never wanted this to happen, and I never would've asked for it. Just do me a favor and make it quick."

Adrian watches Kenton with interest, his eyes

narrowing, and I don't know what I expect, but it's not what comes next. "No," Adrian states.

"No?" Kenton laughs bitterly. "Why not? Seconds ago you were listing the reasons I should die."

Adrian turns to William. "Keep this area well guarded. Nobody comes in here or leaves without my permission first."

William nods.

"You're just going to keep him locked up?" I cry.

"For now, yes."

"Is that your master plan?" Kenton growls, his tone becoming murderous. "Just drag it out, maybe starve me while you're at it? Or do you want me to sit here and think about how I've become the very thing I hated?"

Adrian doesn't reply. Instead, he takes my hand and tugs me after him. I look back at Kenton, but he's already gone from the cell door window. Kenton's right, I wouldn't want to live that way either, especially knowing I'd killed someone. But despite all that, I can't seem to part with the idea that he could become a good man again. Not the same one, not with the yummy goodness of his human self, but still someone worth saving despite the flaws.

As soon as we're out the door, Adrian turns on me. Taking my face in his cool hands, our gazes lock. "Brisa did this to your friend. Don't be angry at me. Don't be upset with Kenton. It's Brisa we need to stop."

I nod as tears blur my vision. I'm so tired of crying

tonight, but at least I've washed off all the mascara during my last cry. "I hate her."

"Me too," he says with conviction. "And I promise you, Angel, I'm going to kill her."

He thumbs away my tears, and suddenly I'm red hot with anger. Screw crying, I want to punch something, preferably Brisa's face. I wish I could do that right now, but she's in hiding and could be anywhere. "So what's the plan?"

"Your friend just became our plan."

CHAPTER 13

 $\mathcal{B}$ y the time we make it back upstairs to the penthouse, I'm so tired that I fall into Adrian's bed without doing more than removing my shoes. I'm vaguely aware of him tucking the covers in around me and kissing my forehead, whispering something lovingly in that language I don't understand but am pretty sure belonged to the ancient Greeks. I don't spend much time worrying about it because sleep is the break I desperately need. I just want to shut my mind off for the next six to eight hours.

And that's exactly what would happen if I didn't dream.

But I do, and the one that comes for me tonight is lucid and exhausting.

I'm in an old playground that I used to frequent as a child. I'm also keenly aware that this is a dream. I'm alone, and everything is slightly off somehow. The colors are muted into creamy pastels instead of the bright primary colors I remember. The slide should be red, but it looks like a tube of tacky pink lipstick. The grass isn't green, it's gray.

"Wake up," I tell myself, but nothing happens.

I stroll over to the swingset and plop down in the plastic seat, slowly rocking myself back and forth, the tips of my bare feet rubbing against the gravel. I'm wearing the dress I fell asleep in, and find that particularly odd. Kicking up a spray of the gravel, I will myself to wake up again, or at least to move on into a dreamless sleep.

A flash of silver flutters past my periphery, and a metallic dove lands on the swing next to me. My stomach fills with dread--I've seen a bird like that before.

"You can come out now, Casimir," I call, my voice echoing into nowhere.

I stand and turn around in a quick circle. He's nearby, he has to be, because those silver doves are some kind of extension of his shadow magic. Shadow magic that can also somehow be used to worm its way into my mind while I'm sleeping, which explains this lucid dream.

"Seriously, Casimir, this is not what I had planned for tonight. I'm exhausted and need restful sleep."

"Evangeline Blackwood." He addresses me by my full

name, and I whip around to face him. "You can rest later. We need to talk."

He's garbed in a long midnight black cloak, and his inky hair falls around his startling silver eyes. He's watching me like he expects me to try to run. He's terrifying, maybe he's used to women running from him, though, I doubt that's the case. Because he's also beautiful.

"How are you doing?" His cruel mouth grimaces, and I'm pretty sure he couldn't care less how I'm doing.

I raise an eyebrow and scoff. "Really? That's what you're going to ask? This isn't a social visit. What do you want, Casimir?"

"You're right," he steps forward, his suede boots crunching against the gravel, "But I've been instructed to check on your well-being . . ."

I shrug. Might as well tell him the truth. "Well, if you must know, everything is shit, but your plan worked."

"What plan?" he tries, and I laugh.

"The one where you threw me into the vampire's sacred circle and bonded me to their council? Yeah, that one. We confirmed it tonight. I hope you're happy."

His grin is vicious. "Excellent."

The dream begins to fade, the scenery curling into wisps of inky smoke and liquid silver. But as much as I want this to be over, I didn't get anything out of this, and I'm not leaving empty-handed.

"Wait," I yell. "Don't leave yet."

The landscape seems to pause--not disintegrating anymore but not returning to how it was either. The fae stares at me expectantly, shadows pooling at his feet.

"Why did you bond me to the vampires?" His silence causes me to continue. "The fae are incredibly secretive and protective. They keep to themselves. Why meddle in nephilim and vampire affairs?"

"Why would I tell you that?" he asks coldly.

"Because maybe I can help you," I prod. "We might agree, you never know until you give me a chance."

Again, he's quiet, and a dark thought pops into my mind. I blurt it out instantly. "Unless you're planning to sacrifice me for something."

His eyes flicker, as if I just caught him, and my heart skips.

Oh shit.

I keep my mouth shut. As stupid as he thinks I am, I'm definitely not stupid enough to let him know what I'm thinking right now--that I have to figure out a way to best them or at least gain their mercy.

"You want to help us?" he finally asks, his eyebrow practically crooking into a skeptical question mark.

I shrug, feigning nonchalance, but inside I'm reeling. If the fae have marked me for dead, I'm a goner. Surviving vampires and nephilim is one thing, but surviving the fae is something else entirely. They have elemental magic, the kind that's drawn from the earth and the moon, they know just how to use it to their benefit.

Not to mention they use blood magic.

And didn't Isadora once say something about some fae trading their hearts for endless power?

Out. Of. My. League.

I squeeze my hands, knowing that my angelic gift can't hurt the fae. They have no aversion to light. If I'm going to survive them, I'm going to have to prove my worth, which isn't going to be easy if they value me more dead than they do alive.

"I want to help you stop the nephilim from hurting your kind," I say with conviction.

He studies me for a long minute. "Okay," he says at last. "Then get me your cousin."

Surprised, I frown. "Which one?"

"The record keeper."

"Chloe?"

He smiles cruelly, as if I just accidentally let him in on a nephilim secret. "Yes, Chloe. Get her for me, and I'll make sure you live."

"You really have that kind of power?"

He nods. There's something nefarious going on here, but I can't quite put my finger on it. "I won't let my people kill you. I'll make sure you live."

Right . . . so why does this feel like I'm walking into a trap?

"What do you want with Chloe?" I step closer, meeting his pearly gaze. "She's not a bad person. She's the kindest and most gentle one of the entire family. I'm sorry, but I won't hand her over to you if you're going to slaughter her."

"I doubt she's as kind and gentle as she's led you to believe, but don't worry, we have no intention of slaughtering Chloe. We won't hurt her at all. We simply need access to her gift."

What could they possibly need her records for? Off the top of my head, I can't think of anything, but I'm also sure the Unseelie Prince isn't going to tell me either. "And what happens after you're done with her?"

"Her life goes on," he says.

"Where? Does it go on in Faerie or does she get to return to her life in the mortal world?"

He pauses, clearly growing agitated. "She will return to her regularly scheduled life."

I nod, really hoping I'm not about to make a huge mistake. "You've got a deal."

"Excellent."

"How do I let you know when I've got her? Is there somewhere we're supposed to meet?"

His eyes travel me up and down, taking in my bare feet and dress with the pinch of his lips. "Invite her into a dream, and I'll take it from there."

"How does that work?"

"She already knows."

And that's the last thing he says before he steps back into the shadows, the silver swallowing him up, and the dream disappearing entirely. And then I'm falling.

Falling through black nothingness, with nowhere to land.

Two arms catch me as I wake up with a startled scream. I'm gasping for breath, clutching at my chest. Adrian holds me tight.

"It was a dream," he whispers against my ear. "Only a dream."

No, Adrian. It was so much more than a dream.

Immediately, I want to tell him everything that just happened, but I find myself holding back. He might not agree that I should do this. In fact, I'm pretty sure he'll tell me not to trust the fae at all.

But the fae can't lie.

That doesn't mean I can completely trust Casimir, but it does solidify my decision. I need to do this. I just hope Chloe doesn't kill me for it.

I turn over in Adrian's arms, curling up against his cold chest.

I'm hot all over, and his cool body is a comfort to me. It's refreshing, pulling me from the creepy feeling Casimir left behind. Adrian lightly runs his fingers over my back, up and down my spine until my breathing steadies.

"When I asked you how you overcame your nightmares, do you remember what you answered?"

He kisses the top of my head and then inches back to peer down at me. Even in the darkness, I can make out his features. His genuine concern. "Yes, I said that I became the nightmare."

I nod once. "You're not a nightmare, Adrian. Not to me."

He squeezes me tighter. Kisses me again.

"But I think--I think I might be one."

"Why would you say that?" he asks sharply.

"Because I'm willing to be the villain in someone else's story if it means I get to be the hero in my own."

CHAPTER 14

ADRIAN

*A*fter Eva falls back asleep, I slip out of bed and head downstairs, double checking that the doors are locked and the security cameras are working. It makes me nervous to leave her here alone, but I have business to attend to, and she needs her rest. If anyone goes into that penthouse hallway, the advanced motion detectors will alert my phone. But even with security measures in place, I can't trust that someone won't try to get to her, so I also enable the elevator security feature. It makes it so that only my thumb print can enter the penthouse floor. I'd had it disabled when Eva stayed with me the first time, but this time she's just going to have to be okay with waiting for me to move about the property.

I can already picture how that conversation is going to go . . .

From the moment I met her, she's been under my

protection. At first I lied to myself about why, but I've accepted the truth now. It's because not only is she mine, but I'm hers.

The casino is no longer bustling with evening activity. It's five in the morning, and the place is dead. By now, my vampires have retired to their private rooms and communal spaces. We've outfitted an entire floor for the coven to be able to hang out without humans around. Still, a lot like to gamble during the day and paint the town red at night. That's when they're not working. Everyone has a job, too. We all contribute.

Almost all the humans have gone home, save for a few stragglers hanging out at the twenty-four hour bar or the ones here betting on European sporting events. A few more are slumped at the slot machines, mindlessly pushing the max bet button and watching as their credits dwindle down to nothing.

The feelings of pride I had when I walked through the casino aren't what they used to be. When we first came out into society, I made this place my baby. But now, I'm not so sure I love it like I used to. Since returning from Europe, the casino just doesn't look the same. It used to be the thing I felt had brought me back to life, especially once we added on the luxury hotel and made the historic building what it is today. But now I keep seeing it through Eva's eyes, keep feeling what she feels here, and I'm starting to question everything.

I round a corner and find Mangus there. The guy is looking worse for wear. His hair is a mess and he reeks of alcohol. Drinking doesn't do much to our vampire bodies, our metabolism is too fast, but Mangus likes to indulge anyway. Especially since Katerina died.

"We need to talk," he says, waving me into a quiet corner.

"Now isn't the best time." I have a few things to attend to and then I need to get back upstairs to check on Eva.

He ignores that. "Listen, I want to walk in the sun as much as the next vampire, but I'm not willing to risk Eva like that. Not to mention, you know guys like Seb will use it to try to lord over the humans. We have to protect our food source."

"I'm glad we agree," I say carefully. It's hard to know who to trust. Mangus could be saying these things to get closer to Eva, but my gut says he's not.

His eyes search the near-empty casino. "There's something I need to show you."

I sigh, because I really hate leaving Eva alone. I need to get my errand done so I can go back to her. "Can you be quick?"

"Can you pull your head out of your ass? This is important." His eyebrows draw together. "Do you know about the fae witch coven living in the French Quarter?"

My body stiffens. I know all about them, this is my city.

"They're harmless," I say. "They're half-fae outcasts. They sell voodoo trinkets to tourists and keep to themselves. As long as they don't mess with us, we don't mess with them."

Mangus grimaces. "You're sure they're harmless?"

"Well, they're not full-blooded fae. Their magic is diluted. And besides that, I have a good relationship with their coven leader. We have an agreement. They stay away from us and we stay away from them. As far as I know, they hate all supernaturals. And they hate the full-blooded fae who want nothing to do with them."

He retrieves his phone, swiping open the photos app. I glare down at the picture of Sebastian and Antara entering a French Quarter voodoo shop. Even with the night time shadows and dim streetlights, I know exactly which shop I'm looking at. The very same one belonging to the half-fae witches.

"When was this taken?" I ask.

"A few hours ago. I've been tailing Sebastian."

"Shit," I grumble. I don't know what this means, but it can't be good.

"Shit is right." He deletes the photo and slips his phone back into his pocket. "My guess? They're after Eva's gift and hoping to use that witch coven's magic to get it."

I nod. "Either that or they're hoping to mess with the council blood bond."

"Maybe both."

I groan and thank him, then we part ways. He's going back to his suite, and I continue on to attend to my business. This new information makes what I'm about to do even more important. It's critical that I don't let my feelings get in the way.

Feelings.

Since when did I have so many damn feelings?

I find Kenton standing in the middle of his prison cell, staring up into nothing. Using leather gloves, I let myself inside, locking us in together. He can try to fight me to get out of here, but he won't succeed. I could rip his head off his body or his heart out of his chest in two seconds and it would all be over. I didn't bring a stake because I don't need one to kill him. But killing him is exactly what he might want. And I can sympathize with that feeling. How many times have I wanted my immortality to be over? I lost count ages ago.

"What do you want?" Kenton turns on me with a broken expression.

"Where is Brisa?" I come right out with it.

He shrugs. "Why should I tell you?"

"This isn't a request."

"What's in it for me?"

"Nor is it a negotiation." I push him to the floor, coming down on him hard and digging my knee into his chest. Gloves still on, I retrieve the silver knife from my back pocket. "Do you know what silver does to vampires?"

His eyes flash to the knife. "Do it. Kill me. You'd be doing me a favor."

"I'm not going to kill you," I say, releasing a sinister laugh. "But I am going to make you hurt so badly you'll wish you were dead." And then I drive the blade deep into his abdomen.

He screams, and the stench of burnt flesh chars the air.

"Where is Brisa?" I demand again.

"I don't know." His cries are laced with pain and regret, but I can't stop. I won't stop.

In fact, I twist the knife.

He vomits blood. It splatters all over me in a sickening arc, but I don't let up. I keep twisting the damn knife like Eva's life depends on it.

"Where is Brisa?" I demand again.

"Why are you doing this to me?" he sobs. "You know I can't tell you."

But that's not exactly true.

Because what I know is that although she'll have commanded him to do certain things and to keep her whereabouts and plans protected, he is also a young vampire. He can fight back far more than he realizes. Young vampires are notoriously unreliable like that. And I'm counting on this one to break.

Twist. Twist. Twist.

I don't relent.

Finally, something within him begins to crumble. "She was––she was––" He's trying to say it. He's trying, but he just can't get it out.

He will.

I dig the knife in deeper, the silver sizzling his innards, and his sobs come out in gut-wrenching jerks.

Eva thinks she's a monster because she's willing to become the villain when necessary, but she's got nothing on me. If she saw me right now, doing this to her friend, she'd hate me. But I'd do anything to protect her, same as I'd do anything to kill Brisa. In this case, I can do both, and if Kenton is the collateral damage, I'm fine with that.

"Where is your maker?" I demand again.

His eyes roll up into his head, and his body goes limp as he passes out. I know it won't last for long. I pull the knife back out and wipe it clean while watching the wounds in his abdomen stitch themselves back together. Internally, his organs are quickly healing themselves as well. He'll wake up in a few minutes, and then we'll have to start the process all over again.

It could take hours of torture, but eventually, I'll break him.

It's the only way.

I hope that even Kenton can see that this has to happen, but even if he can't, I'm not going to stop. And maybe when all is said and done, he'll want to continue this afterlife. Maybe not. That might depend on how many people he's already killed. I doubt poor old Raymond was the first.

As the boy sleeps, I let my guard drop just enough to be able to see myself in him. I remember all the things I had to go through at Brisa's cruel hands. All the murders. The many betrayals. She even sexually abused me, turned me into a lifelong lover who was never allowed to say no. I was forced to allow it all to happen because my life depended on it. And my revenge did too.

I wanted revenge way more than I ever wanted to live as a vampire.

And now that revenge is at my fingertips, I can practically taste it. And in this moment, it's everything I want.

Just as planned, Kenton wakes up a few minutes later, eyes blinking open and horror dawning. He begins to cry. "I can't tell you where she is." He sounds so young and desperate.

"I feel bad for you, I do, but this is the way it has to go."

"No. Please. You know I can't. Please. Just kill me."

I shake my head slowly, sitting back on my heels and brandishing the silver knife again. There are no surprises this time, he knows exactly what's coming for him. "This is the only way to get the information I need out of you. Did you feel how close we were that time? You almost said it. You almost broke the bond and told me her secrets." He goes silent, just looking at me for a long minute. His eyes slowly widening. "Ah, do you see now? Sometimes it takes pain to get the response needed. Trust me, I know. I taught myself to resist portions of my blood bond with her by doing the same thing."

"Just portions of it?

"Yes, but now I'm free of her, and it's the best feeling."

"How long did it take?" I don't know if he's stalling or genuinely curious.

"It took me years."

"Years?" His voice cracks.

I nod slowly. "But it's not going to take you years. You're young, and that makes you stronger than you realize. That's something she doesn't want you to know, that I didn't know during my youth. It's also why she didn't turn any new children for so long after she made her princes."

"If I let you do this, what will you do to her?"

"I'm doing it whether you let me or not," I growl. "But I thought the answer to your question was rather obvious. I'm going to kill her."

I watch him carefully, looking for signs of loyalty to his maker. But I see none. I only see a boy who reminds me of who I once was, turned against my will, forced into a murderer. He smiles widely, and the blood on his lips is so painfully familiar to me that just for a second I wish I didn't have to do this at all.

"Did you want her to turn you into a vampire?" I ask. "When you were dying in that garden, did you ask for this?"

Because if he did, we might not be as alike as I think we are.

"Never," he says. "I don't even remember when she did it. I think I had passed out by then. All I remember is waking up starving and clawing my way out of a grave to find her waiting for me. I never wanted this. I'd rather

I have died that night." He's no longer crying. The tears have dried up. Maybe he'll never cry again. Something has changed within him, has hardened and calcified.

I know it because it happened to me.

"I've killed six people already."

"Six is a lot, but it could've been much worse."

"Oh really? And how many more will die at my hands? She's told me I can feed on anyone I want, that I can kill as I wish, just so long as I help her."

"Help her do what?"

"I cannot say," he sighs. "Do you know how hard it is to resist killing someone when you're feeding on them?"

I do know, but I'm not focused on that right now. I'm focused on this new development. Brisa never made such commands before. Sure, when I was new we fed and killed all the time, but this is a different century. Vampires can't just go around killing people anymore without serious repercussions.

"Let me ask you this. Are you part of her plan, or were you sent here as a distraction?"

"I don't know," he answers honestly.

"Hmm . . ." I sit back on my heels. "And let me guess, she's commanded that you don't seek true death?"

That's always one of the first things most makers require of their progeny. There's no point in going to the trouble of making a child if they're going to kill themselves within a week of turning.

"Among other things." His dark eyes grow even

darker, even more haunted, and I don't ask him to elaborate.

"You and I are brothers now that we have the same maker." I place my hand on his shoulder and squeeze, leveling his gaze so he can see how much I mean this.

"But you're free of her," he whispers. "We're not the same."

"I am free. And I want to help you be free of her too, which is why I need to know where she is and what her plans are."

He grits his teeth, nodding at the knife. "Do it again."

CHAPTER 15

J wake up with a start. I'm covered in a cold sweat. My body is slow and heavy, but my mind is racing. Everything feels wrong.

Adrian's not here to see me freak out this time, which I'm kind of grateful for. Don't get me wrong, I love his support, but being this vulnerable with someone who has my heart is difficult. I've never had someone I could lean on besides Ayla, and we hurt each other. I find I'm still holding back from Adrian. I'm not lacking self-confidence, but he's just so untouchable; he's seen so much of this world, experienced just about everything there is to experience . . . and I'm a messy human.

No, I'm not even human.

I'm a nephilim who glows every time we make out.

Sighing, I fall back into the bed and start a mental checklist.

I have to find Chloe and take her to Casimir so the fae don't sacrifice me. I have to save my mom from not only the mafia, but from a crippling gambling addiction. I have to stop the nephilim from committing genocide, which seems impossible. I need to save Kenton from true death and somehow help him become a better vampire, the very creature he hated most. Brisa needs to die, and Adrian is intent on being the one to do it, putting him in grave danger. The vampires need to stay in line through all of this, but meanwhile half of the council wants to use my light to make themselves ungodly powerful and dangerous. And others probably want me dead or to turn me, who even knows at this point.

Plus, the nephilim know way too much . . . Tate picked me up from the catacombs for heaven's sakes. We can't forget about that. We still need to figure out who in the vampire organization is a mole for the nephilim.

And I still need to check on Ayla.

Just a typical Monday.

I climb from bed and pad over to the shower. The water feels amazing, and I let it stream down my body for so long that my fingers turn to prunes. The emotions spill out, and I end up crying into the water. I seriously hate crying, but I can't hold it in anymore. It's all too overwhelming. But nobody is here in this shower to judge me, and I don't judge me either. I just let everything go free, and when I'm done, a sense of numb acceptance washes me clean. I can't claim it to be peaceful, but it's still so much better than what it was. At least I can breathe again.

As I get ready for the evening, I wonder when my life will get back to normal or if it ever will. I'm starting to accept that maybe things will never be what they were, or what I thought they would be. And maybe that's okay.

But there is one thing I can do to help get things back on track . . .

I stride into Adrian's walk-in closet, to the massive safe in the back that I'm pretty sure has my phone in it as well as the necklace Gram gave me. I press my hand to the lock and the accompanying keypad, willing it to open, but of course it doesn't.

I could try using the white light. Could I melt it?

"What are you looking for?"

I jump.

I whip around to find Adrian standing in the door-way, his sleeves rolled up and his arms folded over his chest. I don't know what I expected to see on his face, maybe frustration, maybe distrust, but I find none of that. He only appears to be curious.

"The necklace my gram gave me and my phone. You locked them up before we left for France. I'll have to borrow your charger, but I'd like to have my things back."

He brushes past me. "Remember when I told you I made sure that your life was still here for you when you got back?" He dials the lock first and then enters in a code. "Well, I meant it. Your bills are all caught up, including your phone bill. Your apartment is waiting for you, although I'd like you to stay with me instead, at least until we're sure it's safe. Even your job at Pops is ready when you are."

The safe swings open, and he points to the shelf where my phone and necklace are waiting. There are other things in here, documents, a few pieces of fine jewelry, stacks of foreign currencies, and even a silver stake, but nothing too surprising.

I retrieve the necklace, almost expecting something to happen when I touch it, but nothing does. The feather talisman stamped on the back of the crucifix kept the nephilim from finding me, as well as my angelic gift from surfacing. Gram bought it from a voodoo witch in exchange for years off her life. And what do I have to show for her great and noble sacrifice? Nothing. I still received my angelic gift, and I was still found by the De Luca's. And now I'm sleeping with a vampire.

What would she think?

Part of me believes she'd be horrified, that she's turning over in her grave, but in my heart of hearts, I know that's not true. Gram loved people, she always saw the best in them, giving everyone the benefit of the doubt. It's because she cared so much for me that she did what she did. She would've liked Adrian, and she'd understand why things have played out as they have. But would she still be proud of me?

I still don't know the answer to that.

"Are you okay in there, Angel?" Adrian runs a hand down my arm but stops short of where I'm clasping the silver chain.

I shake my troubling thoughts free and retrieve my phone. "Yes, I'm okay. Just a lot on my mind."

He closes the safe and leads me back to the bedroom. "I think I can help you with that."

I laugh. "Oh, what did you have in mind?"

"How about a real date?"

I don't know what I was expecting him to say, but asking me out on a date wasn't it. I eye him playfully. "No offense, but you never struck me as the 'romantic date' kind of guy."

"That's fair, but you never struck me as the 'dating a vampire' kind of girl, and look at us now."

"Okay, fine, let's do it. When and where?"

"We're leaving in an hour, after sunset, and where we're going is a surprise." He sweeps a loose strand of hair from his eyes, gazing down on me with careful consideration. "I've had the closet in the other bedroom outfitted for you. I even brought over some of the things from your apartment. I hope that's okay."

"You did what?" I gape at him then sprint across the penthouse to check it out. Sure enough, the guest bedroom closet is filled with new clothing, the tags still attached, but many of my old items are here as well. I stick my face into my favorite fluffy hoodie and sigh. A wave of nostalgia rolls over me. Ayla gave this to me for my sixteenth birthday. It's hard to believe it's over three years old, that so much has happened. That we don't even talk anymore.

"I can have it all moved back if you want," he offers, sensing my sudden change. "But I really do need you to stay here with me until we know it's safe for you to move back into your apartment. Or you could stay here . . ."

"I'd love to stay here with you," I confess.

He smiles. "You're under my protection, and I won't fail you again."

Something about those words makes me feel what the long shower didn't--a sense of peace. I don't know what all is going to happen, and I can't solve everyone's problems, but at least I have someone looking out for me.

I turn, standing on my tiptoes to press a kiss to his cheek. "I'd better get ready then."

WE HAVE SO MUCH ELSE to worry about right now other than a date, but I find myself excited for the first time in months. My very dead phone is charging, and I'll look through it when we get back, but right now, I've got my hair curled and my eyes lined in a reverse cat eye. I've never tried the style before, but I love it. And best of all, I've got Gram's necklace back where it belongs, sitting at the base of my neck.

I don't feel any magic coming off the necklace. I'm

sure it's all been voided considering everything that's happened, but I still want to wear it. It's my homage to the girl I once was, the girl who will always love her mother and grandmother most in the world.

It's a little chilly out tonight, so I slip into a red sweater dress and black booties and pick out what is probably the most expensive designer coat I'll ever wear. It's sleek and bright red and not my normal black style, but I'm tired of my normal, and I feel good. Accepting lavish gifts is a foreign concept to me. Adrian had to play games to get me to drive his Porsche, and even then I only agreed to borrow it. I don't expect to get it back, not even now that we're dating. I can take the bus again when I need to get somewhere, especially if I'm living here in the center of everything.

"You look gorgeous, but what's that look on your face for?" He peeks into the bathroom at the hour mark. "You look like you're calculating a math problem."

I take in the crease between my eyebrows, just the tip of a very concerned expression on my face, and laugh. "Sorry, I was just wondering if we're dating." My cheeks instantly heat, but I turn and lock my eyes on him.

"I told my coven you're my girlfriend and asked you to live with me." He steps closer, his scent filling the room, eyes roaming my face. "Is this what you want?"

I swallow hard. "Yes, it's what I want."

"Good, because you're mine."

"Good," I repeat.

With a smug smile, he takes my hand and leads me from the penthouse.

THE DATE IS PERFECT. We took a motorcycle to the nicest cajun restaurant in the French Quarter, which was unexpected. I'd thought he was going to bring me to an upscale place with tiny proportioned food I couldn't pronounce. Instead, he booked a private room at the kind of restaurant that makes my favorite foods. He doesn't eat, but he enjoys watching me, and I thoroughly enjoy every morsel.

"It feels like home," I say, swallowing the last bite of buttery pecan pie with a happy groan.

"That's what I was hoping for," he says.

I just stare at him. There's such a big part of me that is waiting for the other shoe to drop. It's only been six months since we met, but we've already been through so many ups and downs. I never thought we'd be sitting here, that we could have come this far, let alone that we'd be dating in the first place.

Or that we'd fall in love.

He pays the bill and takes my hand, leading me outside onto the bustling street. Pulling me back into a darkened alleyway, I expect to start kissing, but instead he holds me in his arms as we levitate, up and up, until we're flying above the city, the dazzling lights far below. I hold on tightly, my nerves flying just as high. I can levitate too, but I'm not well practiced, and this is higher than I've ever gone before.

We finally come to a stop, and I take in the stunning view. The moon isn't full, but it's still large and lighting the night like a silver beacon. That, combined with the venom, allows me to see everything in perfect clarity.

"It's so beautiful," I breathe, emotion catching in my chest.

"You're so beautiful."

I snort. "Is that a line?"

"It's a line, but it's also true. Did it work?"

I grin and press my lips to his. His hands grip me tighter, coming around to lift me up so that I can wrap my legs around his torso and press myself into him further. It feels like we're our own personal sun, and when I begin to glow my familiar warm light, those feelings become a visible thing.

When we're finally done kissing, I'm more than ready to go back to his penthouse and continue sans clothing, but he levels me with an assessing gaze.

"I have another surprise for you."

"Another one?" What else could there possibly be?

"Yes, and I really think you're going to like this one."

"But I don't love surprises," I warn. We're slowly floating back down to earth as we talk, and I suddenly can't wait to get my feet back on the ground. All this lovey-dovey stuff is making me lose my edge. It's so out of my element, and I'm scared that I'm going to lose myself in it.

"You want me to tell you where we're going?" he asks.

I trust him, but I'm also a nosey bitch. "Yes, please."

"Alright," he smiles ruefully, "We're going to get your mother back."

CHAPTER 16

"Armondo lives in the most stereotypical mafia house imaginable," I say, looking down on the place that could, without question, be used to film a mafia flick. It's a white brick mansion with columns all along the front, a huge sweeping yard surrounds it, and a tall wrought-iron fence secures the perimeter. The place demands attention, and even at night, they've got it all lit up for the entire community to see.

"Armondo wants everyone to know just how much power and money is at his fingertips," Adrian explains. "His house is an important extension of his identity."

I wonder if Adrian feels the same way about The Alabaster Heart, but I don't ask.

We're hovering well above Armondo's mansion, waiting for the opportunity to go inside. My golden glow has settled back into my chest, and I've left the red coat behind so that we're camouflaged up here in the darkness. The cold winter air pebbles at my exposed arms and legs, but I don't care, getting Mom back will be worth it. I watch the three guards walking the perimeter of the home, each with automatic rifles strapped to their backs. Each looking for a weak link, just as I'm watching them to see who in their party is the weak link I can break.

"I can't believe my mother is in there, mixed up with these goons."

Adrian is holding me to his chest, my back to his front, and he hugs me tighter. My stomach twists as I remember how Armondo had laid claim to my mother, as if her body belonged to him now. I still feel guilty that I wished vampires away from my friends and family––I still blame myself for what's happened to her. Knowing now that I have control over that aspect of Isadora's spell, I'm going to have to be incredibly intentional about the things I say and do in regards to the vampires.

But I also keep wondering if there's some way I can use that part of the spell to my advantage. I won't know until I talk to Isadora again, and who knows if that will ever happen. Right now, I need to stay focused.

"So what's the plan?" I ask.

Adrian just kisses my jaw in response.

He seems so calm and collected. Meanwhile, I'm a ball of nervous energy. I don't know a lot about the mob, only that they deal in organized crime and they're not to be crossed. They derive their power from using and intimidating and sometimes killing people, and I hate that Mom is with them right now.

"Alright, alright." I shake him off. "We can kiss later. Right now we're getting my mom. What do you need me to do?"

He turns me around, giving me a serious look. "You're staying here and keeping watch. I'm going in to get her."

I scoff. "That's it? That's your master plan?" He really thinks he's just going to walk in and get her, no big deal. "Do you have a backup?"

"I don't need a backup. I've dealt with far worse than these rats."

Good hell. "Okay, but this is a private residence, so how are you getting in there?"

"I've already been invited in before," he says. "On more than one occasion, actually."

"And you think you can just walk in there again?"

"Pretty much," he replies. "Armondo has never verbally rescinded the invitation to me, so until he does, I'm free to do as I please."

I shake my head in disbelief. "Okay, and what if they capture you?"

"They won't." He laughs––he really is that confident.

"The De Lucas did," I point out. "They caught you and tortured you."

"I was being sloppy. I won't let that happen again."

He was being sloppy because I was involved and he

had feelings for me. But guess what? He still has feelings for me, and I'm definitely involved with this.

"Those sound like famous last words to me." I fight to roll my eyes. "I'm going in with you."

"Absolutely not." He tightens his hold.

"Absolutely yes," I counter. "She's my mother, and I'm not weak. I've had months of combat training, an angelic gift that can momentarily blind humans, and I'm pumped full of vampire venom." I nod to the guys with guns far below us. "I'm stronger than all those goons put together."

"But can you dodge bullets?" he asks. "No, you can't. If I get shot, I'll heal. If you get shot, you're gone."

I shrug. "I could get shot out here, same as I could get shot in there."

"I knew I shouldn't have brought you with me," he sighs, but his tone is lightened, and I know I've got him.

"And yet, you did." I squeeze his hand and lay another kiss on him. "So what do you know about this place?"

He points to the light in one of the top floor rooms. "That's her bedroom. We're getting her and we're taking her back to The Alabaster Heart."

"You're sure that's where she is?"

He nods. "I'm positive."

"Okay, so we get her out. Then what? Do you really think a casino is the best place for her right now?"

"All problems we can deal with later." He sounds

exasperated. "Angel, are we going to save your mother tonight or not?"

"Hell yeah, we are."

He kisses me once. Twice.

And then in a flash, he's gone, and I'm still here, levitating in the darkness, and feeling very exposed.

I told him I was going with him.

But damn, he's fast.

I hover for a while, remembering exactly why I never liked the dark. Bad things happen in darkness. And even being able to see in the dark now doesn't make me feel better. In fact, it makes everything worse, because I'll be able to see if Adrian fails. What if one of the guards shoots him down? Or worse? What if they catch him and stake him?

Nerves fire throughout my body, and I hold my breath as he slowly opens the window, inch by torturous inch. The curtains flutter the second he slips inside-- and then he's gone, and everything goes still.

I wait. And wait.

Any minute now he's going to be coming back out with my mother. All I have to do is be patient, but I've never been a wait and watch kind of girl. Adrian knows that, so he shouldn't be surprised when I find myself zooming to the bedroom window and climbing inside.

The stench hits me first.

Cooper and salt. Pungent and strong.

I take in the scene, and my heart catches in my throat. Mom is sitting on the bed in a pink silk nightgown, her red hair smoothed down her back, her face a mask of horror. Next to her is a very dead Armondo. His neck is ripped clear open.

And on Armondo's other side stands Adrian, covered in blood, fangs extended, and eyes bloodshot. In a matter of minutes, he executed the boss of the local Italian mafia, draining him completely.

"What did you do?" I whisper.

He grins at me. "What I should've done the first time he crossed me."

The bedroom door swings open, and a man with a gun sweeps into the room, pointing the barrel straight at us.

CHAPTER 17

I scream, but Adrian moves quickly, grabbing my mother first and then me, and fleeing through the window before the first bullets fly. Shouting and gunfire follow us into the night, but we're moving faster than ever, returning to the casino within minutes.

Adrian's set Mom up in the penthouse across from his own. I figured Mangus or someone else would be living there, but it turns out that's where he had put her when she came to him for help the first time. She was in hiding, and he had everything delivered that she could possibly need. So we're back to that again, but at least this time she has me across the hall. I'm going to make sure she's safe.

Before long, I'm sitting on the end of her bed while she lies back, staring at the ceiling, glassy-eyed. She hasn't said much since we got her away from Armondo and got her cleaned up.

"Mom, say something," I try. "Just tell me what you're thinking."

She sighs, and a tear slips from her eye. "I'm thinking that I've failed as a mother."

My heart breaks at those words. It's never what I wanted her to feel, not in all our time together, not even when it was true. "Because I'm dating a vampire now?"

It's no secret. When we came back here and I told her I was staying with Adrian, I also told her that we're a couple. She didn't even seem surprised. She just told me to be careful.

"Adrian isn't one of the bad guys," she replies. "I never looked down on vampires like you did."

Yeah, because they fed her addiction.

"Adrian isn't all good or all bad. He's complicated." Is Adrian a good guy? Hell no. Is he evil? Not at all. He kills when he needs to kill, but he doesn't do it for sport. He does it when it's necessary and he did it when Brisa commanded him. The memory of him covered in Armondo's blood is still shocking, but I find I don't mind it as much as I thought I would. Because Armondo? He truly was one of the bad guys, and I'm not sorry he's dead. "Mom, you're not a failure, you've just been through a lot. You haven't had as many chances to win as some people."

She shakes her head, her auburn hair tangling against the stark white of the pillowcase. "I couldn't provide for you the way I wanted to, not when you were little and not even when you grew up. I didn't have a lot of family to offer you, only your gram." She pauses for a long minute, the air between us growing thick with the unsaid words. Is she finally going to admit her problem? "And I have an addiction. An addiction that I choose over you too many times."

She hiccups and rolls to her side, then sits up, her feet hanging off the edge of the bed. Our eyes meet, and I fight back the tears. This conversation feels too late, but at least it's happening. Better late than never. "Are you really going to sit there and tell me I haven't failed?"

Okay, that does it. I've already filled my crying quota for the foreseeable future.

I crawl across the bed and wrap her in a hug, then we lie down, and she holds me like she used to do when I was little. We're not the cuddling type, but she needs this right now. And honestly? I think I might need it even more.

"It's okay. What matters is that you're safe now." I take the time to explain everything that's happened to me since I've been gone, going into detail when it's time to explain why she was magically forced from the casino.

"It was terrifying," she recounts, "I had nowhere to go, and I knew that you were in danger too, but I couldn't get to you. I panicked."

"I'm so sorry."

"No, I'm sorry. I should've told you about your dad much sooner. You shouldn't have had to find out about everything the way you did."

We sit in silence for a long time after that, but eventually she speaks again. "I'm going to talk to Adrian tomorrow about moving me out of here."

"Are you sure that's safe?"

"I can't have access to a casino with my mind the way it is, Evangeline." She swallows hard, brushing hair from my face tenderly. "I want to change. It was so wonderful when your boyfriend compelled me not to seek out gambling or any other addictions. I've never felt so free in my life. But it wasn't real. It couldn't possibly last forever if it didn't come from me. Do you see that now, honey?"

I nod reluctantly, trying to ignore the damn frog in my throat.

"I am going to ask him to send me to a rehabilitation center, somewhere that specializes in gambling. It's not going to be an easy addiction to recover from, but I want to do it myself this time." She takes my hand, and hers is shaking. "I want it to be real. Maybe then it will last."

My mother was going to lose everything because of this addiction. It might have killed her. When she was free of it, it was the best thing that had ever happened to me, but it was so short lived. I barely even got to see her like that. I want to hope, to believe that it can happen again.

I understand why the vampires have set things up the way that they have, but it still doesn't make it okay. At the end of it all, people like my mom and their families are getting hurt. I know now that vampires aren't responsible for human vices, humans are going to have those all on their own, but I still firmly believe that manipulating those vices for their blood donation is wrong.

There's got to be a better way.

"I'm proud of you, Mom," I say, pulling her into a hug. "And I'm proud to be your daughter. You're not a failure because you're not giving up."

"You really think so?" She sounds so young, and I can picture her as she was when she met my dad. She was innocent and not that much older than I am now. She had ambitions and was trying to make her way in the world. Vampires had recently come out publicly, and things were uncertain in the world, but she was still so hopeful for her future.

That hope died when he did.

She broke. And I don't know if she ever really healed or if she just pretended for my sake. So it wasn't surprising that Gram dying sent her into a downward spiral. But there's one thing I know about broken people, and it's that even they can be good parents. I know that because she's mine.

"I know so," I repeat my thought out loud, meaning every word.

The next day, we move her out of the casino. She's given an alias and flown to a rehabilitation center in California. One of those fancy places by the ocean we could never have afforded without Adrian's help. I'm not good at accepting gifts, but this one I take without question or an ounce of guilt.

"For the next eight weeks, I can focus on my mental health," she says through the other end of the phone after checking in. "I'll call you twice a week during my visiting hours."

"Sounds perfect." And it really does, I just hope it's not too good to be true. That she gets better for real this time, that it actually lasts.

We hang up, and I scroll over to social media, looking for an update on Ayla.

I've only had my phone back for a day, and I don't know what I was expecting, but it wasn't nothing. She hasn't called. Texted. Messaged me. Tagged me in anything. There are zero notifications from her at all.

The heartbreak is worse than a breakup with some guy because we promised that we'd always be there for each other. Men might come and go throughout our lives, but our friendship was supposed to be forever. I scroll through her posts as a numbness washes over me. From the outside looking in, she's gotten healthy, is out in the world again, and has moved on with her life. She's going out, having fun with new and old friends. She's working at her parent's business. She's even dating a hot new guy I'll never get to meet.

It's like I don't even exist.

But in my gut, I know something is wrong. There's

something I'm missing. It's eluding me. It's big. And it's imperative that I figure it out.

Whatever it is.

CHAPTER 18

The Neon House is exactly as I remember as I weave through the people crowding the dance floor. Adrian wraps his hands around my waist and pulls me against him. We move to the beat, and the man definitely knows what he's doing on the dance floor, but I can't let myself get too distracted.

I also can't let him figure out why I requested to come here tonight, because he'll take me right back to the penthouse.

Now that the human auras are visible to me without the added neon lights, I watch the other dancers carefully. The humans aren't why I'm here tonight. They're just the bait.

The nephilim are my mark.

If Cameron was right, then the energy demons, also known as the nephilim, frequent this nightclub. And if that's true, I'm hoping to find someone who can get me in contact with Chloe. All I need is one conversation with someone in her world who has her phone number. I don't need to see Chloe in person to ask her to visit me in a dream, and I actually would prefer not to.

Adrian and I dance for an hour before I finally catch sight of a nephilim. The woman appears to be in her early twenties, is dressed in a silver halter top and tight jeans, and is dancing between two eager-looking men. She's also siphoning off energy from their auras. It swirls around her in a haze of blues and oranges.

I force myself not to stare, but the confirmation of my time in Faerie hits me upside the head for what feels like the tenth time since I've returned.

They did something.

Because those two weeks went missing from my mind, and I came back here with access to my angelic gift without needing to feed on human emotion. Every time I've been around humans, I haven't felt a desire to steal from their auras, and I think it's because my gift is already well-fed. If I can figure out what the fae did, then maybe I can help the other nephilim do the same.

But what if they already know?

Because Chloe said there was a way to feed without hurting humans. She was going to tell me, but then Camilla sent her away. And then when we were at the Christmas party, Uncle Dario said nephilim have broken into factions, that the most powerful families fight amongst themselves. Could it be because some nephilim know there's a way to feed without hurting humans but they still choose to do it anyway?

My mark breaks away from the two men and heads to the bathroom, giving me my opportunity.

"I have to pee," I yell to Adrian.

He's not necessarily possessive, but he's protective as hell, so I'm not surprised when he walks me off the dance floor and all the way to the bathroom door. Before I go in, he's already casing the hallway, his eyes roaming every corner like he's searching for any possible threats.

"I swear, if you try to follow me into the women's bathroom, I'll scream."

He squeezes my hand. "I'm going to clear it first."

I pin him with a glare. "You asked me what I wanted to do tonight, didn't you? Well, my request includes taking care of myself. I can handle this." I press back on his chest and he lets me walk him to the far wall.

Folding his sexy forearms across his chest, he pins me with a smirk. "Whatever you say, Angel."

I love this man, but he doesn't make it easy to keep secrets. He's got eyes everywhere, and now that we're officially together, he's become my constant shadow. I should hate that, but I kind of love it. Only because I've never had someone care so much. Maybe that makes me pathetic, but I don't let myself think too hard about it. I just want to enjoy where we are in our relationship-- outside of the ladies' room.

I head in and find the nephilim girl reapplying her

lipstick in the mirror. She's radiant, and I wonder how much of that is from her recent feeding.

"Hi," I say brightly. "Do I know you? You look so familiar."

She turns on me, eyes widening with recognition. "You're Evangeline De Luca," she breathes. "I can't believe it's really you."

The fact that she knows my name and face is unsettling, but I don't have time to worry about it. "Actually, it's Eva Blackwood." I inch closer, getting right to the point. "Do you happen to know my cousin Chloe De Luca?"

She nods, confusion creasing between her perfectly sculpted eyebrows. "Sure. She's younger than I am, so we're more acquaintances than anything else."

"Do you know how to contact her?" I ask, trying not to sound too eager.

She shrugs a shoulder. "Yeah, I have her number from the last time she was in town and we went out together. Why? Do you need it?"

I whip out my phone. "Yes, please."

She eyes my phone while releasing a careful breath, whispering to me so the others in the bathroom can't overhear. "You do realize that half the nephilim world is out looking for you, right?"

"Yeah, tell them I'm in New Orleans, I don't care," I say it as if I really don't care, even though I definitely do. But I also definitely think they've figured it out by now anyway. "Either way, I need to talk to

Chloe. We parted ways before I could get her number."

The girl fluffs out her hair and tilts her head at me consideringly. "And why should I help you?"

There are a lot of things I could say here about doing what's right, or I could threaten her with my very scary boyfriend waiting in the hallway, but I don't do any of those things. Instead, I lower my voice, like I'm trying to let her in on a secret. "Because I think she's in trouble."

I'm such a liar. I'll probably burn in nephilim-hell for this.

"Fine." The girl snatches my phone and quickly adds Chloe's number to my contacts. "But you might be in trouble too, your family is a little crazy."

"Tell me about it," I grumble.

"Well, they're offering a reward for information about your whereabouts."

My heart sinks. "And I take it you're going to collect that reward."

"How much?" Adrian's growl echoes through the bathroom, and I would jump if I hadn't expected him to barge in here at some point. The girl takes him in with a mix of agitation and unease, but she doesn't seem afraid. She should be. I've seen what Adrian is capable of.

"We weren't talking to you, bloodsucker." She sticks her nose in the air and turns away from him.

"I asked how much," Adrian snaps. "I'm either going to pay you off or I'm going to kill you and feast on your carcass. Which would you like?"

I roll my eyes, but the poor girl goes ashen, and everyone else left in the bathroom scatters out the door. "I have this under control, Adrian," I chastise him.

He steps closer. "How much? I'm not going to ask again."

"Fifty thousand dollars," she replies quickly, and Adrian practically growls.

She lifts her hands in surrender. "That's how much the De Lucas are offering for information about Eva, and they're willing to triple that if someone can bring her to them." She steps back until she's pressed up against the countertop. "But combat isn't my thing, and neither is kidnapping."

"I'm guessing money is," I say under my breath.

"Everyone has a price," Adrian's reply is silky smooth, but there's a sharp undercurrent there. He's pissed. "Fifty thousand is nothing to me." He retrieves his phone and it's only a matter of minutes before he's transferred the money to her bank account. When it's done, he mocks her with a dark glare. "Eva's worth more than a measly fifty thousand, you should've asked for at least a million."

The girl opens and closes her mouth, her cheeks going pink. "I didn't want to be selfish."

"The audacity to take my money and consider yourself anything but selfish is astounding," he sneers. "If you dare break your word, I will hunt you down and kill you. That's a promise."

She nods, and then she's retreating from the bathroom before I get a chance to ask her about feeding angelic gifts. She'll probably be gone within the minute.

Adrian grabs my hand and drags me from the club and outside into the dark alleyway, pressing me against the brick wall. My breath hitches, and my eyes linger on his full lips. I'm expecting two things. A chastisement and a kiss, both to be filled with the kind of passion that leads to dark and lusty places.

"What aren't you telling me? Why do you need Chloe's number?" he questions.

I try to kiss him, but he pulls back.

"I don't think so. Tell me the truth."

"Do you mean to eavesdrop on my private conversations or does it just come naturally?" I counter.

He laughs, but his mood is still dripping in frustration. "I'm a vampire. My impeccable hearing comes with the territory." Leaning in, he places soft kisses all along my jaw. "Don't you trust me?"

My body melts under his sinful lips, and I sigh. "You've got enough to worry about. I didn't want you to worry about me wanting to keep in touch with my cousin Chloe."

Why am I holding back?

I've told this man so much, but I can't risk him going on a rampage if he believes I'm in danger, and I can't have him getting mixed up with the Unseelie Court either. They're too powerful––even for him.

Besides, all I've got to do is tell Chloe to visit my dreams, and Casimir will take it from there. He's already promised he's not going to hurt her, and if I don't do this, I could end up dead. I just pray that Chloe can find it in herself to forgive me when this is all said and done. As much as I can't stand that side of my family, she's only ever treated me with kindness, and I don't want her to hate me.

I land a quick kiss to his lips, then peer up into his eyes. The storm brewing behind the blue is electrified with worry, and I just want to take it away. I wish I could.

He steps back, and the space between us feels endless. "You can't just call her up. She's your enemy. Or did I just pay off that nephilim tonight for nothing? Promise me you won't call Chloe."

He doesn't understand, and he probably never will. I hate that I'm hurting him, but I can't make promises I have no intention of keeping. "You might have bought me time tonight, Adrian, but I have no doubt that the word is out about my whereabouts. That girl is fifty thousand dollars richer and for what? The De Lucas probably already know where I am by now."

"You don't know that for sure."

"Don't I? There's a mole somewhere in your organization, it's the only explanation for how the nephilim have had so much information on you guys lately." He doesn't try to deny it. "So whoever that mole is will have learned about my whereabouts by now. They probably saw me on your livestream, maybe even talked to me in person. They would've told the De Luca's about me. It's already too late."

He lets out a curse. "Don't you think I know this? Why do you think I can't let you out of my sight? This is why I want to keep you locked up in my bedroom."

I snort. "It's not the only reason why you want to keep me locked up in your bedroom, Adrian."

I'm trying to distract him, it's an obvious move, but it works.

The electricity in his eyes turns molten, and he pushes me up against the wall, breathing me in like I'm his only lifeline. "You smell so good tonight."

Goosebumps erupt over my flesh because I know what he's thinking.

He wants to feed on me.

We only did it that one time on the helicopter, and that was because he needed blood. But now that he's a council member, he's sworn to uphold the vampiric laws. He can't take my blood unless he plans to turn me, kill me, or if he's in grave danger. He may be able to resist the council bond enough to feed on me, but I don't want to cause any trouble. Well, my brain doesn't, but the rest of my body very much does. It felt amazing, the venom unleashing endorphins throughout my entire system, and I can't stop thinking about what it would be like to do it again.

"Are you hungry?" I whisper.

"Let's go." Adrian pulls back, grabbing my hand and marching me from the alleyway to the parking lot where his motorcycle is parked. I climb on behind him, my arms holding tightly to his waist and my body pressed to his muscled back. We zoom back to the casino, pulling into the parking garage, and coming to a stop next to his line of luxury vehicles.

I'm swinging my leg over the back of the bike when his number two, William, approaches.

"What do you need?" Adrian asks. "You're supposed to be on the casino floor."

William tilts his head at us, his eyes narrowing. "Yes, I'm going there now," he says, but his voice sounds off somehow. Something is wrong.

Adrian stiffens. "Go on then."

William nods, turning on his heels and heading toward the elevator. Adrian and I follow, and when William holds the elevator door so his boss can step inside, Adrian only hesitates for a second.

But I can't get into that elevator.

I don't know why--just something in my gut telling me not to.

"What's wrong?" Adrian asks.

My eyes dart to William, and that's the tipping point.

William moves fast, pulling something from his pocket and swinging it at Adrian. At the last second, Adrian moves, and the stake lands in his stomach instead of his heart. Adrian slumps down with a stran-gled growl, and William steps from the elevator. I jump into action, swinging at him with my bare fists as the elevator doors close behind him.

"Are you going to fight me or are you going to join me?" he questions, and again his voice sounds all wrong.

I answer with a kick to his stomach, just as a blunt object slams into the back of my head. The world goes dark. And I fall.

CHAPTER 19

$\mathcal{I}$'m being hitched painfully up under my armpits, and my body is limp, my feet dragging. I blink my eyes open, confusion washing over me. Fear hits me, and I remember.

I remember.

William was acting strange. Adrian stepped into the elevator, but I didn't. William staked Adrian, narrowingly missing his heart. Then something slammed into the back of my head. Why would William do that? Is he working with the nephilim? Is he the mole? But even as I ask myself those questions, something nags at the back of my mind, something to do with William's voice. It wasn't right.

"She's awake," a man says, and whoever is dragging me stops, setting me upright. My legs feel like jello, but I manage to stand. I turn and find Enzo and Nicco on either side of me.

"I should've known it would be you two brutes." I step back, but Nicco is quick to grab hold. "Don't touch me!"

But they stay silent, glowering down as if I were nothing but a petulant child in the middle of a tantrum and not a woman they bludgeoned over the head and kidnapped.

Footsteps echo through some kind of maintenance hallway. It reminds me of the basement in the casino, the very same one Adrian dragged me down to, where we made the fake blood vow all those months ago.

They don't belong down here. And neither does the man that rounds the nearest corner. Leslie Tate. "I'm glad to see you're awake," he says. "I was worried you'd be out for too long when they hit you that hard, but I should've known you have a thick skull."

I can't even be bothered by the insult. "You probably ordered them to do it."

"That's true, I did." He smiles ruefully. By now he's completely dropped the caring mentor act. He's not even pretending to be a decent uncle. He's just a bad man, through and through.

"I can't believe I used to find you charming and fatherly. You're nothing of the sort."

He waves his hand nonchalantly. "My own children might beg to differ."

"Oh, is that why Greyson and Bella are assholes? Or am I supposed to blame their attitudes on your bitchy wife?"

"Enough with that filth!" He strikes me with the back of his hand, the pain sharp against my cheekbone. He's wearing a family ring, and the damn thing cut my cheek. It hurts like hell, but I refuse to react. Blood fills my mouth, and I nearly choke on the acidic taste. But I don't cry. I don't curse. I don't do anything but glare. "We have questions, and we can get those answers from you now, or we can get the answers after we kill off this coven. You decide, but say one more thing against my family and I will make the decision for you."

He's delusional if he thinks he can kill off an entire coven, not to mention all the council members that are still staying here and the entourages they brought along.

"I don't have to answer your questions." But I have one of my own. "Where's Adrian?" The last time I saw him, he had been bleeding and slumped over in that elevator. But he wasn't dead.

He wasn't dead.

And I cling to that thought like my lungs cling to oxygen.

"Your bloodsucker got away," he glares, "And he also left you to us."

That doesn't make sense. Adrian would never leave me with the enemy, not on purpose.

"I know you two are dating," Tate goes on, saying the words as if dating a vampire is truly disgusting. "But how? The vampires aren't able to come near your friends and family."

"As if I'd tell you anything--"

"I think you forgot to include yourself in that bargain with the fae. Not the smartest thinking, but then again, you never were the brightest in the family." He twists the ring on his finger, smiling at the family emblem for a moment before returning his hateful gaze to me. "It seems that your pathetic mother diluted the bloodline."

I grin through the blood between my teeth. "Is that why I'm the first light-bearer in more than a century?"

He goes stone-faced, and I know I've hit a nerve. "Take her to Camilla."

Enzo and Nicco grab me, dragging me between them. My heart bangs against my ribcage for a way out of this. I'm incredibly strong because of the venom, but the twins' angelic gift of strength is too much for me. They've found me, and I can't fight them off.

We approach an unmarked door, and they shove it open, pushing me inside a mechanical room. I'm closely surrounded by a crew of at least forty people, all tucked in like sardines. They're dressed in black tactical gear and are covered head to toe with wooden stakes and guns wielding silver bullets.

They're also staring at me like I'm the embodiment of evil.

There are a few recognizable human vampire hunters, a few people I don't recognize who could be humans or nephilim and I wouldn't know the difference, but the rest of them are the people I spent the last few months with—the nephilim from Italy. Some blood relations and some not. Either way, I won't claim any of them as family. Not after what they've done to me and my real family. Camilla is at their center, pinning me down with her haughty glare.

"Aren't you a little old for all this?" I ask the woman, but the insult rolls right off her back.

"You can answer my questions, or I can get the answers myself."

I push back on the two pairs of vice-like grips holding me in place, but I'm still unable to budge. Frustration floods my system. Resentment too because I don't want her in my mind. She doesn't need to see everything that's happened since Ireland. So much of it is private. And what she would find, she'd most definitely use against me. Against my mom. Against Adrian. Against everybody I love.

"Don't you dare touch me," I warn.

The brightest light ignites from my palms, and even though I'm unable to move my arms, I can still adjust my hands so the light is pointed at her. She covers her face and hisses, and I hope it hurts. I know I can't kill her, if anything it's like the temporary blindness that comes after someone shines a flashlight in your eyes. It's too bad because the old bitch deserves to burn.

"I see you've finally started feeding." Aunt Bianca laughs. "It's about time you accepted your fate."

"My fate? I've been able to access my gift without feeding, so you're dead wrong."

Bianca shakes her head. "Oh, you're still feeding, you just don't know it."

"I'm not," I snap, even as a prickle of doubt surfaces. I ignore it and flash my blinding light directly into her eyes too. She quickly turns away. "But I hope that hurts."

"Come now, Evangeline," Tate says as if he's suddenly the voice of reason when only a few minutes ago he was backhanding me with his gaudy ring. "There's no point in fighting us anymore. We need to know what went wrong at The Gateway, and you're going to show it to us. The more you fight, the harder you're going to make this on yourself."

"You want to know what happened at The Gateway? I didn't want to kill fae, that's what happened."

But those words, as telling as they are, seem to go over their heads . . .

"Bring her to me," Camilla instructs the twins, and just like the good little boys these grown-ass men are, Enzo and Nicco haul me over to their grandmother.

Not mine. Mine was Gram, and she was a saint compared to this snake.

Camilla grabs me, forcing her gift on me like she has every other time, immediately rifling through my memories. She has no real order, no rhyme or reason to where she's looking first. She's reckless, taking zero care with my mind and having no respect for my intimate memories. It's just another day for her.

I cry out when I feel her taking note of my mother's

location in California, especially when her own need for revenge poisons the memories of hope I have for Virginia. She still blames my mother for taking her son away from her all those years ago. Even after everything, after she ordered his death, she still refuses to see her part in it.

Then she leaps into the events that happened when I went to Faerie--she tries to, anyway. But she can't see much, because most of it is still blocked to me. Except for my first day and night there, all the other memories are hazy at best or nonexistent at worst. I'm still not sure if it was the food and drink that did that to me or the king's magic, but I suspect a bit of both. Whatever they did to block the memories, I realize now why they did it. It wasn't to keep me from knowing their plans, it was to keep *her* from knowing them.

Growing agitated, her gift razors in deeper, and the pain of it burns through my brain. It's like the world's worst migraine, and I scream, falling to my knees, begging her to stop.

She doesn't stop.

CHAPTER 20

She fast-forwards to the moment my memories return, to the night I was thrown into the vampiric council. She takes special interest in the sacred circle, replaying those moments over and over again, going through each detail until they begin to bleed and fade together. From there she prys into my most intimate moments with Adrian.

My anger is hot, but her disgust is hotter.

"Those are not for you," I manage between strangled breaths. I want to scream my vitriol, but my voice just sounds like a faraway whisper.

Why can't I push her out this time? I've become impossibly weak. I'm losing the battle and I don't know how much longer I can do this.

But she doesn't care. She continues, ecstatic when she learns that I'm linked into the vampiric council. I can already feel her plotting ways in which she can use that against them. She's trying to figure out how I've been interacting with vampires despite the fae magic, which somehow pops her over to the recent dream with Casimir, and that's my breaking point. Something snaps, and I finally eject her from my mind. She immediately tries to get back in, but she can't. The locks are in place.

I cry in relief.

"You've been a vile girl," she sneers. "And to think, I opened my home to you. You could have had it all, a loyal family, power over your angelic gift, and most of all, you could've lived your purpose and been in God's favor. But you threw it all away, and for one of them."

"What do you know of purpose?" My mind feels shredded, and I press the heels of my palms to my temples. My head hurts so badly. Wetness stains my cheeks, and I realize I've been crying. And I'm so, so tired. It's like she scraped all the energy from my cells.

"God made nephilim so we could rid the earth of unnatural creatures." She reaches out her hand and tugs Chloe to stand above me. I've sunken to my knees at this point. I can't bear to move. "Our sweet Chloe showed you the angel that came down to command it. And yet, despite seeing the truth for yourself, you still choose to partake in such sinful actions. Do you know what that makes you?"

I don't have the energy to respond. And honestly, I'm too exhausted to care anymore. It'll probably have something to do with burning in hell for all eternity.

"It makes you a lost cause." She nods to the others.

"Greyson, Chloe, and Enzo, you three stay here and guard her. The rest of you, please follow me upstairs. It's time to do our duty."

"What about me?" The vampire William steps forward, and my stomach sours.

"How could you?" I hiss. I might be tired, but I have enough energy for this bastard. "Adrian trusted you. These are your own covenmates. You're going to slaughter your own people for nephilim? The nephilim will just turn around and kill you too!"

William laughs, and then something strange passes over his face. It's like the cracking of a shell, and for just a moment, I see him for who he really is: Dario De Luca.

My uncle, Camilla's middle son, the shapeshifter.

My mouth falls open.

William never betrayed us because that man wasn't William at all.

They're quick to leave, stakes at the ready, and I'm left with my guards. Chloe sits in the corner of the little basement room, her eyes shut tightly as if in meditation. There's got to be more to her gift than just record keeping or else Casimir wouldn't have said she could join me in my dream. I just need to talk to her. So much for getting her number. That girl from the club is fifty thousand dollars richer for no reason.

My headache finally begins to fade enough that I can think again. I stand, and Enzo stands with me, holding onto my bicep. I give him a seething glare, but he doesn't care. He doesn't even blink twice.

"Chloe, how are you?" I ask.

Her eyes pop open, and she gazes up at me like I'm a ghost.

"Don't talk to her," Greyson sneers.

"You and I should talk privately," I continue, ignoring everyone else. Her pretty brown eyes are as wide as a deer in headlights. Am I really that frightening?

"I said don't talk to her," Greyson tries again. And again, I ignore him.

"You know how to find me privately, don't you, Chloe?" My gaze bores into hers, and she gives me a small nod. It's all I can hope for—I have no idea if it'll be enough. Will she join my dreams before it's too late? Because it seems that the fae need access to her records, and soon. I just wish I knew why.

"You don't listen to instructions, do you?" Greyson steps in close, looking down on me with a nasty glare. "But maybe you'll listen to them?"

His sinister smile grows as he summons his dark other-worldly creatures. He still believes he can hurt me with them, that he can torture me, terrify me, but not all nephilim can use their gifts on each other. Last time he used his gift on me, I faked my terror to make him believe it was working. But this time? This time, I'm not faking shit. Instead, I gather my strength into my center, lean back on my haunches, and kick him dead-center between his legs.

He goes down like a sack of potatoes.

Enzo startles and loosens his grip, and that's all I

need. I race to the door before anyone can stop me. Greyson's on the floor holding himself, and Chloe isn't one to fight. Enzo is the one I need to worry about, but I have surprise as my advantage. Swinging open the door, I sprint into the hallway. We're somewhere under the hotel or casino, so the vamps aren't far.

I still don't know what happened to Adrian, but he's probably tearing this place down looking for me. Same as I'm about to do for him.

"You can run, but you can't hide," Enzo yells out. It's just about the most predictable comment the meathead could make, and I would laugh if I wasn't hyped up on adrenaline and scared out of my mind.

Lucky for me, Enzo doesn't know all my tricks, and I levitate through the corridors to not make any noise. An exit sign blinks up ahead, and I want to cry with relief. That's my target.

Just as I near the door, Enzo is on me, tackling me in the center and bringing me down hard. His grip is concrete-tight, but I'm able to wiggle my hands free and shoot my white light into his eyes. It blinds him long enough that I'm able to escape his grip, jump back to my feet, and run for my life. I fling open the door to a stairwell. There typically aren't deep basements in this part of the world, but the vampires have enough resources to defy just about anything, including groundwater. They've built several stories underground, and I don't know how deep I am right now. I levitate through the middle of the stairwell, my mind focused on one thing and one thing only.

Save Adrian.

"There's no point in resisting the inevitable," Enzo calls after me, his footsteps close behind on the metal stairs. "We're going to kill this coven tonight, and then we're going through The Gateway with or without you. We'll find a way, and we have a weapon that will kill the fae when we do."

I whip around at that. I shouldn't--I should keep running--but I have to know what he's talking about. "What's the weapon?" I snarl.

He slows, coming up the stairs one at a time, his black eyebrows drawn together. "Join us, and you'll find out," he offers. "Or don't, and you'll still find out, because it's going to happen."

"How quickly will it kill them?"

"If we infect their entire world with iron and seal them inside the realm, I wouldn't expect it to take longer than a few days."

My stomach hardens, and I shake my head. "It's wrong, what you're doing. You think there's some God out there who wants you to kill an entire race of his people? No God would want that."

"They're not God's people," he snaps back. "They're not even people! They have access to dangerous magic that doesn't belong here. They are an abomination. Same with the vampires who are already dead. We're just finishing the job. You, of all people, should understand that. I know my uncle Leslie trained you, that you came to him begging for a spot with his hunters. He helped you."

"Tate lied to me. And you're all lying to yourselves." He's closer, only a few paces from me. It was foolish to stop. I need to distract him. "Aren't there other nephilim who don't believe the things you believe?"

His lips thin as he considers this. "They're mistaken. Chloe has been making the rounds, showing them the truth. It's all right there in the records. Most of them have come around, and, once we complete our mission and God blesses us, the ones who denied their purpose will see how wrong they were."

He's fanatical.

I'd hoped it was just Camilla and Tate and that the others were falling in line because they wanted access to all the family money and power. But I was wrong. Enzo, at least, buys into this completely. The others probably do too.

My mind races back to when Chloe disappeared for a few weeks before Christmas. She later told me she went to New York to visit the nephilim there and help them with something. Showing them the records must have been why she was there, so she could help Camilla bring more people into their way of thinking.

And if that's true, then it's no wonder the fae want to get their hands on Chloe. Am I really foolish enough to believe they're not going to kill her? Fanatical or not, Chloe is a pawn in this, and I don't want her death on my hands. But it's too late, I already relayed the message to her. She's going to come to my dreams, and when she does, Casimir is going to take her away.

I've drifted too close to him and Enzo lunges for me again. Thank God I'm faster this time, using every ounce of strength I have to get away. I bypass the exit to the street and instead head for the casino floor, pushing through the emergency exit doors and flying into the room. Just as I make it there, loud sirens begin to screech, and the entire floor is bathed in bloodred flashing lights.

CHAPTER 21

Most of the patrons are confused, but a few scream and scatter for the exits. It's like dominoes how quickly they all turn frantic, stampeding to get away. I return to my feet, and it's chaos for a good minute as I weave through the crowd, trying to find Adrian. Did the nephilim sound the alarms or did the vampires?

I don't see anyone in tactical gear, but I do catch sight of several vampires looking around with discerning expressions. Ever watchful, there's not a whole lot that can get past them. Maybe for the first time ever, I'm extremely grateful for that party trick. I look back at the exit, but I don't see Enzo. I don't think he followed me here.

"There you are." Mangus appears next to me, clasping my elbow and tugging me back from a group of women teetering in high heels as they try to get out of the building. "Adrian is looking everywhere for you."

I rip my hand away. "Are you really Mangus?"

His eyebrows scrunch. "What are you talking about?"

Dario being here makes it hard to trust anyone, but Mangus's voice--it's the same voice I'm used to. The one that's as deep and salty as the ocean.

It's him.

"The nephilim are here, and they have a shapeshifter with them," I explain. "He looked like William and tricked us. I don't know where Adrian is. We got separated when he tried to kill Adrian and I was ambushed."

Mangus's eyes go steely. "He looked like William?"

I nod. "But he didn't sound like him."

Mangus swears under his breath. "Come on. Most of the coven members are downstairs in the ballroom gathering for a meeting. They're in trouble."

We hurry to the elevator, and when it opens, Adrian is inside with another vampire from the council. They're talking in low calculating voices and when they turn to take us in, Adrian's face sags in relief. He pulls me into his arms, crushing me against his bloodied dress shirt. "I'm so sorry," he whispers into my hair. "I thought I'd lost you."

He almost did. "It's not your fault."

"It is, I should've caught on that it was a shapeshifter and not William the second he opened his mouth."

"Where is the real William?" I ask.

Adrian shakes his head. "I don't know, but I'm guessing they may have already killed him."

I don't have time to process that. "We have to get down to the ballroom. The nephilim are here to attack your coven."

"They already know. I was the one who set off those alarms. The red lights mean we're under attack. Trust me, we're prepared to handle something like this."

I can't help but wonder why he isn't already down there with his coven, though, and I ask him as much.

He inches back, staring at me like I'm missing the obvious. "Because I was looking for you. They failed to kill me, but they left me in that elevator before I could get out. When those doors closed, I thought I'd never see you again. I've been in a panic trying to find you. They took out our cameras. They're all down."

"Probably because they got into your basement somehow and are coming at the coven that way." I imagine the trap Adrian could've walked into while he was out blindly looking for me like he was. "Oh my God," I whisper.

"God has nothing to do with those people," Mangus growls. "I don't care if they have angelic blood in them or not. They've always been like this." I wonder how much blood and gore Mangus has seen over the years because of my kind.

"My family might still think the vampires can't hurt them," I confess. "Because of Isadora's spell and what happened in Ireland, they believe they're untouchable, that they can just come in here and slaughter your entire coven." My voice hardens. "But they're not untouchable."

And Camilla may have realized that when she was in my mind, but if she did, she ordered the attack anyway.

Put her family at risk anyway––because that's how much she wants this.

The elevator doors open into the foyer of the coven ballroom. The battle has already started, pouring out in all directions.

Mangus laughs. "No, they're certainly not untouchable."

The first nephilim to catch my eye is my beautifully evil cousin Bella. She's working side by side with her brother Greyson, and both of them are covered in ash. Apparently Greyson didn't waste any time after I took off. It's a sickening visual representation of what they're here for.

We rush from the elevator, and Greyson's dark gaze locks on mine. He's probably mad as hell that I kicked him in the balls, probably even still in pain, and he grins menacingly. The soot smeared on his face makes his teeth whiter and the brights of his eyes stand out. It's a taunt, but I can't think about it for long because there's no time for his shit. I never thought I'd be the one fighting for the vampires instead of against them, but that's exactly what I do. Jumping high, I levitate across the room and catch sight of Dario. He's back to his regular self, dressed in the same combat gear as the other nephilim, probably so he doesn't accidentally get staked by his own people. Regardless, I don't trust him to stay that way for long.

I land on him with a guttural scream, kicking him in the head. He drops, and I yank the silver tipped stake from his hand, breaking it in half and throwing the pieces across the room.

He blinks up at me, dazed and confused, but I don't wait for him to realize what just happened. I kick him in the head again, and he passes out for good. For just a moment I consider killing him, but I decide against it. I won't be killing anyone here unless it's out of self-defense. It might not feel like there's a choice, but there's always a choice. I'm not going to do to them what they did to my father, and what I know they will do to me eventually if they need to and get the chance.

As if to test my thought, Camilla's voice screeches, "Stop!" I whip around to find her in Adrian's clutches. Her eyes are wide with fear and denial, like she can't believe he's able to touch her. It confirms that she didn't see enough of my memories or she never would've put herself in this position––it's the only explanation as to why she even came here. She usually sends everyone else to do her dirty work, but this time she's the one with blood on her hands, the one who's going to pay the price. She's getting old, she's not a fighter, and she stands zero chance against someone like Adrian.

Someone who doesn't stop, who doesn't even hesitate.

He breaks her neck like it's a twig, and she slumps to the floor.

For a moment, time seems to stand still. She was my grandmother, and maybe in another life she could have actually filled that role. But in this life, she murdered my father, hunted my mother, and imprisoned me. In this life, she was my enemy. And honestly? I'm glad she's dead, but I'm still hit with an immense sense of loss for what could've been.

All at once, the moment breaks, and one of the nephilim calls for their retreat. They stream toward the stairwells, but it's too late. The vampires are out for blood. The attack is merciless, and I'm sure I'm about to witness my entire family line on that side murdered when a black smoke covers the room.

Greyson.

It clouds everyone's visions, but it doesn't do a damn thing to mine. I watch as the vampires keep attacking without their vision, but the nephilim are able to fight them off much better now. They help each other to the exits, even grabbing Dario's unconscious body in the process.

And I'm almost okay with that, with letting them all go free, except for Tate.

Tate's the one I want. He was the one who treated me like a daughter and then manipulated and lied to me. He was the one who recruited humans, took control of their minds, and made them hunt his enemies. Camilla had to die. Tate should have to go too.

But I'm not the only one with a grudge against Tate.

Adrian appears at my side, seemingly unaffected by the black smoke. I know he can't see through it, but he has excellent control over his other senses. He's not going to let a little smoke stop him. Adrian stays true, his eyes fixed on where Leslie is shuffling on a hurt ankle.

"Do you want to take him out or can I?" His voice is that of a predator.

"Can you see him?" I ask.

"I know the man's heartbeat." He nods toward the door where Tate is making his exit. "I don't need to see him."

I'm not going to kill Tate. But I won't judge Adrian for doing it considering Tate was behind Kelli's death and the death of the child Adrian had before her.

"Do what you need to."

Adrian is quick, catching up to Tate in all of two seconds, but Tate is quicker. He swings around, a stake at the ready, and slams it into Adrian's heart.

CHAPTER 22

"**N**o!" I scream and stumble in their direction.

Through the fading smoke, Tate catches my gaze for a long second before disappearing into the stairwell. I want to go after him, but I drop to my knees in front of Adrian instead, carefully pulling the stake from his chest. There was already so much blood on his dress shirt that it's hard to tell how much more is being added. His eyes are bloodshot, and the corners of his mouth have turned crimson. In seconds he will become nothing but ash, and my heart might as well turn to ash with him.

"Don't die on me," I plead. "I can't do this life without you."

He smiles, coughing up blood. "Don't be so dramatic. You nephilim really need to work on your aim." He winces, sitting up slowly, and I break out into a relieved sob.

Tate missed.

We stand and assess the damage, looking over the carnage of the battle. It's not as bad as I first thought it would be because vampires can heal so fast. But that's not to say it isn't bad.

"We only have two prisoners," the real William announces, dragging a man and a woman over to Adrian. I'm glad to see William isn't dead, even if I don't like the guy. "A human hunter and a nephilim without an angelic gift as far as I can tell."

Through a mop of blonde hair, Remi stares up at me with her warm hazel eyes. "Please, Eva," she begs me. "Don't let them kill me."

Everyone turns on me. "This is Remi. She can manipulate emotions. But she helped me on more than one occasion, and she doesn't deserve to die."

"She's a hunter and a nephilim," William spits at her feet. "I'll kill her myself if I have to."

Adrian stops him. "Put them in the prison cells."

"What about him?" I point to the human man. "He's just a kid. He doesn't look a day over seventeen. I bet you Leslie Tate was messing with his mind."

Adrian sighs then kneels down in front of the boy, asking him a few questions. It turns out the boy is only fifteen and was picked up on the way in here, convinced to fight because they had gear for one more. Adrian gives the kid a long-suffering sigh. "You will leave here, get cleaned up, and go on with your life as if this day never even happened. You got it?"

The kid nods, looking absolutely terrified, and scampers off. I can practically feel the annoyance of several wounded vampires who are hurting and needing to feed. They can go suck down a blood bag or two, they'll be fine.

"Tate picked that boy off the street. I knew he would stoop low, but I didn't realize he'd go that low."

"I did," Adrian says, his mind far away for a minute. He turns to look down at Camilla's dead body. It's joined by three others, none of which I recognize. I don't know if they're nephilim or human, if they wanted to be here or if they were manipulated to be here. And I'll never know. "Burn them," Adrian instructs.

"Let's go." Adrian is guiding me to the elevator when Antara approaches us, blood splattered all over her face and her normally perfectly styled curls a tangled mess. I didn't even know she was here for the fight.

She steps over a pile of dust and glares at Adrian. "I lost one of my grandchildren, Adrian. I expect you to answer for what happened tonight." He turns on her with a frown, and she continues. "Seeing as this happened under the protection of your coven, you're to blame, are you not?"

He nods once, and I stare at him. "It's not his fault. The nephilim came here under the misguided belief that the vampires wouldn't be able to touch them. They attacked unprovoked."

She raises a perfectly manicured eyebrow, looking upon me as if I were complete scum. "And why would they think vampires wouldn't be able to touch them?"

There's no hiding this anymore. "It was part of the original council spell."

"Eva--" Adrian warns, and Mangus slides up behind me, planting a hand on my shoulder. It seems neither of them want me to speak, but I go on.

"I made a deal with Isadora when the spell was cast. I gave her blood, and in return, the vampires have to leave me and my friends and family alone should I choose it. It seems to be tied to my intention, so I can make it come and go as I want."

"She's telling the truth." Sebastian walks up to us, his voice dripping in resentment. "It's the only explanation to adequately answer so many of the questions I have when it comes to this girl."

I widen my eyes at both of them. "Right, so if I wished you to get away from me right now, the magic would make you leave. And apparently you'd forget me, too."

Her mask slips, uncovering a mountain of rage.

Sebastian inches forward. "Are you threatening us?"

"Of course not." But my answer must be a little bit too sarcastic from the way Adrian tenses and Mangus chuckles. "I'm part of the vampire council now. I want to be your best friend, Seb."

"Don't be so trite."

"We could get mani-pedi's together," I go on. "My treat."

Mangus snorts. "I'll take you up on that, but I'm not letting anyone paint my nails."

"You're childish," Antara hisses at both me and Mangus. "You have no right to a place on our council, it's an affront to vampires everywhere that you're even breathing the air we stand in."

"And yet, she is," Adrian growls. "If you even attempt to break her from the council, or to kill her, you threaten your own power. Is that really what you want?"

Frustration flickers behind her eyes, frustration and something unreadable, but both are gone before I can get clarity on what she's thinking. I already know what she wants: me dead or serving her with my light. There is no alternative in her mind.

The room is divided as more and more people come to join our conversation. The people behind Sebastian and Antara are all those who support them, those who would use my light to give them enough advantages that they could enslave the humans. But there are just as many vampires on my side, backing me up. And best of all, I have Adrian. As long as I have him, I feel like I've got a fighting chance.

"You're lucky the council members sympathetic to your little angel are all still alive," Sebastian says to Adrian and Mangus, as if making easy conversation with his brothers and not threatening death on council members.

He turns on me, looking so much like Hugo that I'm momentarily brought back to what it felt like when I almost died that September night. The fear that burned through my veins as a cold endless forever loomed. "You might not always be so lucky, Evangeline. You should watch your back." He winks, and then he turns away, walking out with Antara.

I'm left with an uneasy feeling whirling through my stomach. The target on my back is starting to feel like a very real thing.

CHAPTER 23

The next few weeks pass without anything big happening. I feel like a coiled spring waiting for something to set me loose, but nothing ever does. Life is just a string of little moments, mostly good and a few bad--my favorites all wrapped up in Adrian.

There's no word about the nephilim. They've gone into hiding, even abandoning some of their strongholds, including the Italian properties.

Most of the council members have returned to their homelands except for Antara, Sebastian, and Mangus, who've stayed in their temporary residences here, even more of their coven members coming out to join them. Mangus doesn't have a coven or a home or plans to leave. But I'm worried that Antara and Sebastian will find a way to entrap me and kill off Adrian. Sometimes it feels like I'm two steps ahead of them. Other times it feels like I just think I'm ahead and they're actually chasing me into a corner.

And despite everything that happened, even the fae have stayed silent.

Chloe hasn't met me in my dreams. She's probably busy mourning her grandmother and planning revenge. I still have her number and consider calling or texting, but I chicken out every time. She probably hates me. And I don't hate her, but I definitely don't trust her.

I'm on a nocturnal sleeping schedule, and without a job or school I have way too much free time to stew and feel useless. Adrian fears for my safety and doesn't want me leaving the casino without him. I have so many questions, but I can't find the answers stuck in his penthouse scrolling social media and reading fanfics on my phone. That's about the only thing I've been doing between our dates. That and visiting with Kenton and Remi.

Remi won't talk to me, but I talk to her anyway. I sit outside her cell door and assure her that I'm doing everything in my power to make sure that things change for the nephilim so she can have a normal life. I explain that my family isn't normal and that she doesn't need to be wrapped up in what they're doing. She ignores me completely, but I keep trying, hoping that one day I'll get through to her. And I promise to keep her alive, even though I'm worried the vampire council will override me on that. If they realize she had been a servant and spy in Brisa's court, they'll definitely want her dead.

On the other hand, Kenton will talk to me. The only

problem is that everytime he does, I leave our conversations feeling immensely guilty. He hates himself now, talks nonstop about the people he's killed and how he wants a true death. And all along, I keep thinking about how it's my fault. He wouldn't be a vampire if it wasn't for me because he never would've even come to the Palace of Versailles in the first place.

"What's going on with Kenton?" I corner Adrian one evening over dessert. He already finished drinking his wine glass of blood for dinner, and has been watching me eat my slice of chocolate cake with interest.

"What do you mean?" He begins to clean up the dishes, and I follow him into the kitchen.

"Don't play dumb. I know something's going on. You're keeping him locked up, which I guess I understand since he's dangerous and bonded to Brisa, but there's more to the story that you're not telling me."

Because something is wrong with him. Everytime I visit, he's more depressed. More desperate. More exhausted.

"I'm keeping your friend alive." He turns to me, his eyes going all soft and sweet. I'm not going to fall for it. "He broke the rules, and I should've killed him for it."

"And yet you haven't, even though he keeps asking for it. Why not?"

"I might. He doesn't want to be a vampire. Same as you don't want to be turned into a vampire. Should I keep him alive forever? Make him rot for eternity when he doesn't want it?"

"You're avoiding the question."

"And you're avoiding the very real fact that your friend isn't who he once was."

"I know that."

"Do you? He's not the Kenton you knew. He's a killer now; he's like me."

I want to argue, but I stop myself and really take a moment to think about what Adrian is saying. But is Kenton *really* all that different of a person? At first he was, but all new vampires are blood-thirsty. Once that has worn off, he could be similar to the friend I knew. And what about me? If I were to turn into a vampire, would I really change all that much?

Not once has Adrian pressured me to become one, though I wonder if he thinks about it. I'm going to grow old and die a very human death, and he's going to continue on without me, forever locked in the body of a twenty-five-year-old man. I'm not scared of aging and I'm not scared of death, but maybe those are the words of a nineteen-year-old with life stretched out before her. Will I feel different in ten years? Twenty years?

"If I were a vampire," I choose my words carefully, "I wouldn't want to die like Kenton wants to die. I used to think I would, but I don't know that I feel that way anymore. I think maybe I could be like you and do something with myself."

He steps closer, fangs extending and gaze darkening. "You'd be happy to drink blood and live without the sun? You might lose your angelic gift or it might transform into something else. There's no saying what would happen because your vampire self could snuff out your nephilim the way it snuffs out a human."

I nod slowly, but I don't actually mean it, not in the way other humans do. I'm no fledging, and I'm not asking to be turned, I'm just saying that I wouldn't want to die because of it. Kenton has made me rethink everything. Because I want Kenton to live. I really do. And wouldn't I want the same for myself?

But no sunshine would feel like no oxygen. I can't even fathom not having the sun in my life. It fills me up in ways that nothing else can. I take note to spend more time outside in daylight, even if it's just going up to the rooftop. I've missed it too much lately. I've missed it, and I need it.

"You couldn't live without the sun," Adrian whispers.

"Yes I could." We both know I'm lying, and he's happy to call me out.

He leans into my neck, sliding his fangs across my sensitive flesh. Goosebumps prickle over my entire body. He's testing me. Maybe I'm testing him right back.

"Shall I bite you right now? Exchange our blood? I could take you to the graveyard tonight."

I say nothing.

"The angel can join her devil," he prods, voice growing agitated.

I shake my head, and he steps back.

"Because you don't want to be a vampire, but I need you to hear this, Eva." He takes my chin in his hand and tilts my head up to lock with his gaze. "I love you just the way you are. I love you for who you were yesterday, who you are today, and who you will be tomorrow. And in none of those scenarios are you a vampire. The truth is, I love you far too much to ever wish my morbid existence on you." He kisses my lips once, then pulls back. "But if something were to happen and you were to become a vampire, I would love you still, but it wouldn't make me love you more than I do now."

My lips part on a soft whimper, my vulnerability on full display. I wasn't expecting it, but he's just soothed so many of the insecurities I've been harboring deep down about our relationship. "I love you too," I say. The words are still the strangest confession to hear from my own mouth, but they're also the most honest.

He retracts his fangs and presses his cool lips to mine, but I've still got that curiosity burning hot in my chest. I liked the way his fangs felt pressing against my neck. The temptation of it courses through my veins like a devilish question mark. He's only fed from me once, and that was when he needed to in order to survive.

"If I asked you to feed from me, would you?" I breathe.

His pupils dilate. "It's against the rules I'm bound to follow." But his body is saying another thing entirely, pressing to mine and flooding us both with lust. "We can only bite if we need it to survive, if we are killing, or if we are turning someone."

This time, I'm the one to groan. I'm not ready to give

up so easily. "What if you did it in self-defense? What would happen then?"

He pauses for a long second. "I suppose that might fall under survival."

That's the answer I was looking for--whipping around, I grab a knife from the rack and press it against his throat. A small trickle of blood slips down his pale skin, but the wound is shallow and will heal quickly. "If you don't feed from me, I will kill you," I growl.

He grins, hunger mixing with lust plain on his face. "Are you threatening my life?"

I nod, my own expression mirroring his. "I am."

His fangs extend again, and before I can blink, he's deflected the knife and is picking me up and setting me on the countertop. He sinks his fangs into the warm flesh of my neck and I let out a cry of pain, but it's quickly overshadowed by whimpers of pleasure. The venom burns hot as it mixes into my bloodstream, and my entire body buzzes with activity. Suddenly, every-thing in the entire universe is centered on this moment and this man.

He laps at my neck, drinking his fill, and I moan with pleasure. All too soon, he retreats before I grow light-headed. I know it will only be seconds before the wounds heal, thanks to the venom, and I wish we could do it again.

But I'm mortal. I'm breakable. And we have to be careful.

He stares at me for just a moment, just long enough

for me to see the amazement in his eyes, before he presses his mouth to mine and we're kissing again. Our hands, our tongues, our bodies explore each other with abandon--backlit by the warm golden light that emits from within me. That glow is like a love letter from the angel to the devil. I'm not going to join him, but I am going to love him.

I FINALLY CONVINCED Adrian to let me take the Porsche out by myself today. It's sunny and beautiful and I have somewhere I need to be that's most definitely not The Alabaster Heart. He didn't want to agree, but ultimately he walked me to the parking garage and sent me off. I can't stay cooped up in the penthouse forever, and the nephilim have been quiet ever since the attack. There's just one thing I need to do, and I must go alone.

I step from the car and onto the sidewalk, taking a moment to bask in the glorious sunshine. It fills me up in the most delicious way. I could stand here forever, just letting myself soak in its bright warmth.

But I don't have forever.

Taking a deep breath, I stroll up to the familiar blue front door and knock. I haven't been to the Moreno's home in months, and I can't stand to stay away for another day. If Ayla really is done with me, if she's still sure that she wants nothing to do with me, then I'll respect her boundaries and go. But it's been months since she broke off our friendship, and I can't help but hope that there's still a chance for us to put it back together again.

I expect Mrs. Moreno to open the door, or maybe Mr. Moreno, but when it's Ayla who swings it open wide, my thoughts disappear and emotion takes over.

"Ayla," I whisper, tears burning my vision. "It's so good to see you."

For a long second, she just stands there, staring at me like she's seeing a ghost.

She's going to slam the door in my face. She's going to end this once and for all. She's going to shatter my heart. Years of childhood friendship are going to become nothing but bittersweet memories.

She does none of that.

Instead, she jumps forward and wraps me in a tight hug. "Eva," her voice cracks. "Oh my God, where have you been?"

That's when the tears finally break loose and I hug her back, careful not to hurt her with my newfound strength.

Eventually, we peel apart and she's crying too. "Normally I'm the one who cries. You must have really missed me."

"Of course I've missed you," I hiccup. "I've been lost without you."

She takes my hand and leads me out into the bright midday light to go sit on our favorite porch swing. "We have so much to catch up on, but first, you've got to tell me the truth. Do you know where my brother is?"

I blink rapidly, vision narrowing, breaths stuttering. All as the world comes crashing down. All as the memories return at once. I remember exactly what happened in Faerie, and more importantly, I remember exactly who I was with.

And who I left behind.

CHAPTER 24

The fae used Seth and Felix to teach me how to feed on humans without hurting them. There's a way to cycle the energy, to take and give in the same moment. It doesn't drain the auras. But it's not as strengthening as taking the energy outright, which is why a lot of nephilim choose to feed by taking only. Not to give.

And I've been doing this new way of giving without even realizing it, every single time I walk through that casino. Every single time I'm near a human.

Because it's natural.

Because during those two weeks I was in Faerie, the king of the Unseelie Court forced my gift to surface and then made me practice feeding until it became second nature. That's what he does--he taps into others' gifts. He makes them better. Stronger. Or more dangerous. It's why he's so powerful.

And then when it was time for me to leave, he called in a witch who forced me to forget what happened in Faerie, including all about Felix and Seth being there with me. I didn't forget who they were, but they became a barely-there afterthought. Something I couldn't pull to the forefront of my mind. Casimir took me to New Orleans, but Felix and Seth stayed behind as entertainment for the fae courtesans. Apparently it had been a long time since humans had been to Faerie, and the court treated the boys as a novelty.

The king decided to keep them like pets.

It wasn't until this moment, sitting here with Ayla, that everything became clear. I'm horrified that my friends are still in Faerie, still at the mercy of a dark fae king and his court, and I left them behind.

"What is it?" Ayla demands. "You know something?"

I swallow hard, my throat turning dry as sandpaper. How do I explain this to her?

Her eyes are two round saucers. "He said he was studying abroad in Italy with Seth and Kenton, but none of them have responded to our calls or emails. We haven't heard from Felix since Christmas Day. We've been worried sick. It's been over a month. We talked to the police and filed the reports, but we don't know what else to do." Her eyes narrow, taking in my burning cheeks. "You know something. Please, tell me."

"I'm going to get him back," I whisper hoarsely but with conviction. "I promise."

She stiffens, and the porch swing goes complete still. "What do you mean you're going to get him back?"

I have to explain everything. "First off, he's alive," I reassure her, "but he was never studying abroad." She goes ashen as I attempt to explain the truth. "Kenton is a vampire now."

I start with the bad news, because maybe it will make what I have to say next a little more palatable. "But he's alive. He's with Adrian now. We're helping him adjust."

She says nothing, just stares at me. Unblinking.

I force myself to go on. "Your brother and Seth went to Europe to work as vampire hunters, and they even stayed with me for a time in Italy, but right after Christmas, everything changed."

"No," she whispers. "He told me he was done with all that."

"He lied, but it wasn't his fault. He was being brainwashed."

"How? What happened?"

I have to trust her with the information. Even though I'm so scared she won't be able to take it, that she'll hate me for it, or that it will revert her into old ways of staying locked in her bedroom fearing for her life, I can't keep secrets. Secrets are what broke us in the first place. And I have to trust that she's strong enough to handle this.

"What do you know about the fae?" I try.

"I know they're real," she says immediately.

I'm shocked. "How do you know that?"

She looks away with a shrug. I know that shrug, it's her "I've got a secret" shrug, but it's always followed with her telling me that secret. Not this time. "It doesn't matter right now. What matters is that I did my research and now I know about all the supernaturals. How could I not with everything that's happened?" I guess that makes sense, but I'd still like to know what she means by research. This isn't the kind of thing someone can just Google. "Are you suggesting that the fae have my brother?"

"They have him and Seth." Before I think better of it, I continue, "but I have a plan to get them back."

It's the least thought out plan of all time considering it's coming to me on the fly as we're talking, but I want something to offer her. As I explain what I'm going to do, she goes from hopeful, to skeptical, to hopeful again.

She's twisting her blue strands of hair in her nervous way, and something about that is a comfort to me. It's so Ayla. That and the fact that she's kept the vibrant blue that is her signature style gives me a semblance of hope. Maybe she's the same girl she always was. Maybe we can be best friends again. She pins me with a pleading look. "I need to help."

"I don't think that's even possible." I go on to explain that the only way I know to get into Faerie is through The Gateway in Ireland, except the fae prince Casimir must have another way with his magic because he's taken me through the realms using his shadows. He can travel in ways that the rest of us can't, and he can take people with him. People he chooses. It's through Casimir that I intend to get Felix and Seth back.

She takes my hand and squeezes, and it feels like the first time in ages that I can relax again, even if it's short lived as she demands I still teach her how to get to Faerie through The Gateway. So I explain how the magical wards work, giving as many details as I can remember. She dutifully types it into her phone, and it makes me nervous because what if she somehow finds The Gateway and ends up trapped in Faerie with her brother? If both the Moreno children go missing because of me, I don't know how I could live with myself.

"Your parents can't lose you both," I plead. "Please, don't attempt to go there. It's not like here in the mortal world. It's so much more dangerous."

"I'm not scared of the fae," she snaps, sounding like she really means it.

I study her, admittedly a little bit confused. Last time I saw her, she was hiding in her bedroom and wouldn't even go outside because she was terrified of vampires. And now she's done research on supernatural beings and she's not scared?

"I've been going to lots of therapy," she says, placating my skepticism. A warm smile brightens her cheeks. "And also, I met someone."

She says that last part with an air of wistfulness that I've never heard from her before, not even when she fancied herself in love every other week back in middle school. My heart warms for my friend because she deserves to feel what I feel with Adrian. She always dated around but never had anyone serious. No relationship lasted longer than a month, that's if you could even call them relationships. They were more like passing flirtations. She would get bored quickly and move on to a new crush the same way other people scroll social media. Always something better to look at.

"Tell me about him."

She grins and opens up the photos on her phone. "His name is Dominic, but he goes by Dom." She pulls up a pic of a tall guy with closely cropped brown hair, soft green eyes, and a sexy smirk. He doesn't look too much older than us, but he's much, much bigger. His muscular tattooed arms are wrapped around her waist in the photo. She's smiling up at him like he's her own personal sun, and he's smirking at the camera.

"Where did you meet Dom?"

She closes her phone. "We met at college, actually. I know, I was only there for a month, but he was one of the people I met before I came home."

"Oh, wow, so is he still there?" She went to school up north but dropped out pretty quickly, deciding it wasn't for her, so I'm surprised she met a guy. She certainly never told me about him. I thought she was pretty much hiding out in her dorm room the whole time.

She shakes her head. "He just graduated, actually. He moved back home and only lives a few miles from here. He went to our rival high school if you can believe it. He was the star of the football team and everything," she snorts at that. "But he graduated three years ahead of us so it's not like we would've known him anyway."

This is a lot to take in. An older guy, already graduated college, big and tattooed and smirky. "Is he good to you?"

"He's amazing," she gushes, "he makes me so happy."

That makes me smile. She deserves happiness. We all do. But what will she say when I tell her about Adrian? Will she understand or will she judge me for it? I want to keep the information to myself, but I'm also really trying not to keep secrets from her since that's what broke us up in the first place.

"I'm dating someone too," I blurt out.

She side-eyes me knowingly. "Let me guess, you're dating Adrianos Teresi?" She bats her eyelashes. "*The vampire prince.*"

"How did you know?"

"Oh, I saw the way he looked at you that night in the alleyway. He wanted to do more than just drink your blood." She wiggles her eyebrows suggestively, and I snort.

Okay, so maybe she's not going to hold it against me.

"Do you love him?" she asks, becoming serious.

I nod. "I do. And he loves me back."

"Of course he loves you, what's not to love?" Her lips pucker. "But did you break my brother's heart?"

My own heart drops. "I don't think so, but I did hurt him. I'm really sorry."

"I was right, you know," she tuts. "You two never should've dated."

I nod because she was right, but what I don't say is she was also wrong in trying to force her opinions on us. We had to figure things out for ourselves, even if it meant doing it the hard way. But that's all water under the bridge now, and I don't want to go back there.

"Be careful with Adrian," she says coolly, and I can tell she doesn't like me dating him anymore than she liked me dating her brother. At least she's not lecturing me about it. She doesn't understand. I don't know if anyone really will. But it's not for them to understand because me and Adrian do.

And I am being careful, but not for the reasons she's thinking. She's still worried about my well-being, but I'm past that. It's my heart that's in the most danger. I've given it to the man––it's completely in his cold, dead hands––and if he decides to break it, I won't be able to stop him.

As lame as it sounds, that's scarier to me than anything else I'm dealing with right now. And I know that's selfish, that there are so many more important things than my love life, but it's the truth.

"I'm going to get your brother back," I promise her.

She hugs me again, and it feels like I'm the one with her heart in my hands now. Felix's life depends on what I do next, and I can't let her down. Not again. Nor can I let Felix and Seth down. Not like I did with Kenton.

The people I love keep getting hurt because of me,

and it's time for that to stop. I just hope Casimir doesn't rip my head off when I betray him. But first, I've got to get Chloe into my dreams. Finally feeling brave enough to use her phone number, I text her before heading back to the casino.

Meet me at midnight.

--Eva

She'll know what that means.

CHAPTER 25

I'm standing dead-center in the hunter's bank vault training facility. I'd recognize this place anywhere with its shiny glass dividers, concrete walls, and sense of righteous purpose permeating the air with the scent of sweaty coeds.

Spinning around, I find myself in the middle of the sparring mat where I first learned how to fight. I spent so much time here, it meant so much to me, but now I hate this place. I know what it truly is, who's behind it, and why. At least today the large room is empty and I don't have to face anyone I'd rather never see again.

"Hello?" My voice seems to be swallowed up by the walls. I turn in a wide circle, searching for her.

"I'm here," Chloe says, her voice ringing out.

She's suddenly standing right in front of me with her arms folded across her chest and a murderous expression on her heart-shaped face. She's wearing a black silk nightgown that hugs her curvy body in a way that makes me envious. My simple cotton shorts and tank top could never hold a candle to her outfit. "Well, you got me here, now what do you want?" she demands.

Oh...

The realization that this is a dream sets me off my axis and I nearly lose my balance. She rolls her eyes but grabs onto my arm, steadying me. When I was visited by Casimir in my old school playground I knew I was dreaming from the first second. This time, I didn't know until she pointed it out. I feel so out of sorts here.

And I feel guilty.

"Aren't you going to say something? My grandma is dead because of you," she sneers.

That accusation snaps me out of it. "She's dead because of her. And my father is dead because of her. Do you really believe everything you were taught by that monster?" I shift back from her, glaring. "I thought you were different, that you wouldn't really support genocide."

Her face goes red. "There's more to the story than you know."

I shrug. "I've got all night for you to explain it to me."

But really, I'm stalling for time because Casimir said if I got her into my dream, he would know and he would come for her.

So where is that prince?

My promise to Ayla depends on him showing up.

"Dreams don't really work like that," Chloe explains, annoyed. "You don't get unlimited time in here. Sometimes it will feel like we're here for minutes but it will be hours out there, and sometimes it can feel like hours in here but be seconds out there. I never know which one I'm getting until it's over."

"That actually makes a lot of sense. It explains why sometimes I can wake up from a full eight hours of sleep and feel exhausted. Or the other way around, sometimes I'll sleep and it will only feel like a couple minutes but really--"

"--I know you're stalling. Cut it out. If there's something you need to tell me, you'd better do it now before one of us wakes up because I'm not meeting you here again. I'd rather never see your face again."

I don't know what to say. I don't know how to keep her here. Or how to make Casimir show up. But I don't have to wait long because one of his strange silver doves with the ruby eyes pierces its way into our dreamscape, landing on her shoulder. She squeaks and swats it away.

"Dreams are so weird, aren't they?" I laugh. Black shadows descend on us, and I breathe out a sigh of relief.

Relief that is short lived the second Prince Casimir steps from the shadows. The man is a terrifying sight to behold, and when Chloe takes him in, her mouth thins to a line.

"Eva, what did you do?" she whispers.

"I'm sorry. I had to."

Casimir laughs. "She's not sorry. Neither am I."

He lunges for Chloe, and at the same moment, I lunge for him, grabbing onto his arm and holding tight. And all at once, the three of us are swept into his shadows, tumbling through the darkness. It feels like falling and being catapulted at the same time, my insides practically rearranging themselves.

We reappear moments later, the three of us sprawled out on a plush bed.

It's not Adrian's bed in New Orleans where I fell asleep.

No, it's a huge bed with tall posts and drapes of black and purple silk. And it has an elf lying between me and Chloe, laughing his head off.

Not what I expected.

At least we're no longer in a dream.

"You're a sneaky little devil," Casimir says, his eyes sparkling as he looks at me. "I think I like you after all."

I groan. I'm not here to be liked by him. I'm here to get my friends back.

"Did you come to join in the fun?" he questions. "I've shared my bed with multiple women before, so I assure you I know what I'm doing."

I scrunch up my nose. "You wish," I snap, but he just laughs again. And then he rolls over, pinning Chloe's body under his own. He looks down at her with a savage grin, like he's about to bite her.

"Get off me," she growls.

He doesn't move, though, he just stares at her for a long moment, his black hair hanging around the two of them as he studies her. Slowly, that grin falls into a frown of pure disgust, as if he hates her.

She spits at him, actually spits, and he curls his lip and rolls away, wiping his face clean. "You're a nasty creature," he growls. "I should whip you for that."

"It takes one to know one," she retorts, sitting up and folding her arms over her chest.

They kind of remind me of how we were when Adrian and I first met, and I hold back a smirk. There's a fine line between attraction and hate, and these two are obviously harboring attraction even though they want to kill each other. Despite everything, Adrian and I found a way to turn our hate into love. That was our miracle. These two? These two won't get a miracle. She's a nephilim, trained her whole life to hunt down his kind and kill them all. And he's an immortal fae prince, ruthless and cunning and just as prejudiced as she is.

"Remember our deal?" I say to Casimir. "You can't sacrifice me now, and you promised not to hurt Chloe either."

He levels me with an annoyed grimace while Chloe scrutinizes me like she wants to rip my head off. I can't say I blame her.

"I remember our deal," he says coolly, "and lucky for you that was never the plan for either of you, though,

I'm sure my father won't hesitate to execute you should you prove yourselves to be villains."

I raise my hands. "Hey, I don't claim my nephilim family or their ways."

He nods once, turning his vitriol on Chloe. "But she does. She's all in on the nephilim ways."

"What do you want from me, fae?" she snaps.

"You'll see." He grabs her arm and tugs her out of the bedroom, and I scramble after them. He stops and turns on me. "You tricked your way into coming here, you can figure out how to get yourself back home."

"Don't you think I came for a reason? You people still have my human friends. I'm taking them home with me."

His face is glacial and unreadable. "They're not my property. I cannot return them to you."

"Who said anything about property?" I growl. "They're nobody's property, they're humans."

"Tell that to my father."

Then he turns back on his heels, still clutching onto Chloe, and drags her away. I have no choice but to follow. I got myself into this mess, and it seems the king is the only one who can get me out of it. The first time I met him, he terrified me and he knew it. This time, I'm sure he's still going to terrify me, but I'm not going to let him know it. There are too many people depending on me to be strong.

"Whatever you do, don't drink or eat anything here," I advise Chloe as I catch up to the pair.

"Obviously." Her natural sweet nature has all but turned sour toward me, but given the circumstances, I can't say I really blame her. "I never thought I'd have to actually worry about all those lessons about Faerie, so thanks a lot for this."

"If it's any consolation, you probably know a lot more than I do."

"It's not," she snaps.

"That's enough," Casimir orders, and when Chloe tries to argue, his creepy shadows sweep up to wrap around her mouth, silencing her.

"You're going to suffocate her!" That proves to be a stupid thing to say because he extends that shadow gag to me as well. It muffles the air around my mouth and silences my vocal cords. Panicked, I attempt to say something, but I can't. I swipe at him, but he easily out-maneuvers me.

"Just breathe. I didn't cut off your lungs or your nose."

Oh . . .

I relax as my lungs swell with oxygen. I shoot Chloe a conspiratorial look, but she just turns away from me. Okay, I deserved that.

We hurry through the castle corridors, ignoring the onlookers as we pass by. Glimpses of recognition hit me at many of the fae in all shapes and sizes. They come in all colors too, and most of them are beautiful, but some look like they crawled out of the depths of hell. None of them look all that human except for the elves with their pointed ears. I remember some of these people from my time here, but I was so drunk on wine and food half the time that I blush seeing them now. They witnessed me at my worst, but in my defense, it wasn't like I could starve myself for two weeks.

We enter the throne room, and King Orlyc gazes down at us from his creepy bone throne with equal parts amused pleasure and cunning strategy. He was expecting us.

"You both look so much like your namesakes," Orlyc says. "That's not a compliment, by the way. Your family should be ashamed of themselves. Anything you'd like to say?"

Our voices become freed from the shadows, and Chloe uses the opportunity to put her foot in her mouth. "I'm proud of my family name," she declares, standing tall. I want to kick her.

"Well, I don't claim them. My last name is Black-wood," I add because it's true, and also because I don't have a death wish.

"Ah, would you like me to change your DNA?" Orlyc cackles at me. "That could be arranged, though it's not something I would do lightly, and I would have to magick you to secrecy. . ."

I gape at him. "I have no idea what you're even talking about."

He grins. "Do you like being a nephilim?"

I frown. "I don't know. . ."

Chloe glares. "Touch my DNA and die."

Does my meek little cousin have no sense of self preservation? Her angelic gift can't save her from the fae, and it's not as if her family can follow her here. They obviously still haven't figured out how to cross The Gateway because if they had, the fae would either be sick and dying right now or already dead.

Casimir is quick to return those ghastly shadows to our mouths, silencing both of us for her stupid comments.

It's a damn good thing I love Felix and Seth.

The king turns to his son. "Why are there two of them? I thought we got rid of Eva." He nods at me, and my insides become like ice.

"I did as I was told and placed her in the vampire council," Casimir responds, shooting me a pointed look. "But I needed her to get to Chloe, and Eva was sneaky, grabbing onto me when I brought her cousin back."

A crease forms between Orlyc's eyebrows. "And why would she do that?"

"We still have her two human friends. She wants them back."

The king appears thoughtful before turning on me. "I'd forgotten all about those humans. Where are they now?" He motions to one of his attendants hovering near his throne, an elfin man with a dog-like swamp creature at his side. From what I remember of my studies, I think it's a kelpie. The little guy would be cute if its teeth weren't as long and sharp as knives.

"They've been entertaining the courtesans," the man

replies simply. I have no idea what that means for Felix and Seth, but I just hope they're unharmed.

The king returns to me. "Ah, very well, I have no real use for your friends now that the novelty of humans has worn off on me. You can have them back, but I'd rather like some entertainment for myself first. I think you'll do just fine."

What does he want? Because I swear, if this is some kind of sexual advance, it's not happening.

As if reading my mind, his dark blue features contort in disgust. "I would never sink as low as to have sex with a nephilim. None of us would."

Good--because I'm not having sex with a fae.

But if not that, then what does he want from me? He's already surfaced my angelic gift and taught me how to feed, then threw me into the vampiric council's sacred circle in the eleventh hour. He's already taken weeks off my life that I'll never get back. What kind of entertainment can I possibly offer?

"How's her gift coming along?" he asks Casimir. "Still sharp?"

Flashes of his hands gripping my head, forcing my gift to burn from within my body out onto the surface, return to my mind. My stomach goes hard. Chloe shoots me a questioning look, but I ignore her.

"It's coming along well." Casimir's reply lacks emotion, and I wonder if this is how the prince always interacts with his father. "The light is under control, and her feeding is still happening naturally. Don't forget, she's still carrying vampire venom. Can't you smell it on her?"

Standing from his throne, Orlyc strides to me. I keep my posture straight, imagining a rod through my spine. I refuse to flinch when the imposing man leans down and sniffs me.

"Indeed," he says, stepping back. "I don't think I've smelled this much vampire venom on a nephilim in at least a century."

I don't think I'll ever get used to the immortals' sense of time, of how many lifetimes they can live, on and on and on until someone eventually kills them or they decide they've had enough.

Orlyc grins, and those creepy silvery-white eyes peer into mine as if he's looking down into my very soul. "Don't worry, I don't want you dead. I need your soul to stay bound to that council."

My soul?

"Your soul is stronger than I expected. That's good. You're very promising."

Uhh--what the heck? First he was talking about my DNA and now he's talking about my soul. They're two different things, neither of which I understand much about. Maybe I should start asking questions. Or maybe I'd better not...

"How about we play a little game? Complete a task for me, and you and your humans can go home. Fail, and you will still go home, but they will belong to me indefinitely."

He means every word he's saying. He doesn't care about humans. This is the Unseelie Court, and humans are of little consequence here. But how can he threaten such a thing? Do my friends truly mean nothing?

Casimir releases my vocal cords from his shadows, and I snap at the king. "My friends aren't your slaves. You need me in that vampiric council, it's all part of your secret plan. So I'm bargaining with you to get my friends back. Let them come home with me and I won't do anything to mess up my standing with the vampires."

I expect him to be angry, to demand I heed to his will. But he just laughs, and then he snaps his fingers. Seconds later, Felix and Seth are dragged into the throne room by a pair of warrior fae. My friends look very mortal standing between the elves in golden armor.

Without thinking, I run to them. "Are you okay?"

But they look at me with wide weary eyes. Confused. Lost.

It's like they're not even *seeing* me.

"What have you done to them?" I whip around on the king.

"You already know what our food and drink does to outsiders. They've been in Faerie for weeks now. I'm not sure how much longer their minds will be able to survive this realm."

He laughs again, more maniacal this time, and his people follow suit. They don't care. None of them do. This is all a game.

"How are you planning to keep them indefinitely if you're killing them?" I raise an eyebrow.

"Believe me, there are ways . . . now, are you prepared to win your friends back or do you want to keep arguing with me?"

"Fine. What do you want me to do?"

CHAPTER 26

ADRIAN

She's gone, but at least this time I haven't forgotten her. She's burned onto my soul, a part of me, and I can't imagine forgetting her again. But it happened before, there's no denying that. It could happen again. I would continue on living with a gaping wound inside of me, never able to heal it, and driving myself mad trying to figure out why I was hurting in the first place. The fae need to be checked. What else are they capable of?

I've been scouring the hotel and casino security footage for over an hour, searching for signs of Eva but coming up with nothing. I left her in my bedroom earlier tonight, double checking that the locks and security cameras were working when I went. Hell, I even tested the motion detectors in the hallway outside the penthouse myself. All were intact. So where is she?

"Who would want her?" Mangus asks.

I give him a rageful glare, and he shrugs like this is the obvious place to start. Doesn't he realize I know that? "Everyone wants her. The nephilim, the fae, the council, Brisa . . . take your pick."

Mangus folds his arms over his chest. "Calm down, brother. This isn't like you."

"I need to get her back." I know I'm frantic, that I'm acting much younger than my age, that my normal demeanor is completely gone, but I can't help it. I'll do anything to get her back. I promised her my protection. I always keep my promises.

"You're in love." He tilts his head, assessing me with amusement. "I didn't realize it had come to that already."

Maybe I should be embarrassed, but I'm not in the slightest. "Yes, it has come to that. Now can you help me find her or not?"

"We need a tracker. I would say you should call Hugo but . . ."

I grumble and drop my face into my hands. A tracker isn't a bad idea, but I'd need more than just someone who can sniff out her blood scent and follow the trail. She straight up disappeared from our penthouse. Whatever happened to her had to have involved magic. Unless there's someone who has better tech than I do and has managed to override my cameras without my knowledge.

Both are possible.

Both are infuriating.

I need to follow all the leads until I find her, and the

closest one I have to me right now is Kenton. Trying to break his blood bond to Brisa has been relentless. Everyday, while Eva sleeps, I go to him, and we try. And everyday the bond is too strong. But he's young and determined--we're so close. I just don't know how much more torture he can take.

"Go see if you can find out why Sebastian and Antara were talking to the fae coven in the French Quarter and report back to me," I command Mangus.

He rolls his eyes. "You know, I don't answer to you, Adrian. We're supposed to be equals." I open my mouth to argue, but he stops me. "I will take pity on you because I like you and Eva together. I never thought I'd see you fall in love. I'll admit it's a cruel form of torture for a man who recently lost his wife, but all the same, I want this for you."

With that, he leaves the security room. I follow shortly after, heading down to meet Kenton. It's time to find Brisa. I know for a fact she's been trying to get to Eva, so Brisa is the best place to start. And if she doesn't have her, then I guess I'm flying to Ireland because the fae are the next best lead.

Kenton is waiting for me. He's always waiting for me.

He wants this to be over, to be free of her. He also wants to be free of this afterlife, but I'm not sure I agree. He doesn't know what's possible for his future. If we can tame his bloodlust, he can live a good life without killing anymore. It doesn't have to be over for him, and

I'm willing to take on the VEC on his behalf if he'll let me.

"Is today the day?" he practically begs.

"It has to be. Eva is missing. Brisa might have her."

Kenton's normally resigned eyes turn dark and determined. "Don't stop. Kill me if that's what it takes to get the information you need."

He doesn't deserve that. Getting to know him the last few weeks, I believe him to be a good guy. A lot of good people turn bad when they get a taste of the kind of power vampires have. Kenton partook in that power, but even still, he's still good deep down. I don't blame him for what he's done, not in the way he blames himself. I blame Brisa. And after she's dead, I plan to offer him a place in my coven. If he lets me, I'll help him, give him a new family and a job, something to live for.

But I don't think he will accept it.

He's still so stuck on the life he lost. Now that the initial bloodlust of being a newly turned vampire has worn off, he's ready to be done. I can't even blame him.

Sliding my hands into my leather gloves, I retrieve the silver knife and get to work.

It's different this time, maybe it's the sense of urgency, maybe it's that we both care about Eva, or maybe it's that we're both tired of Brisa getting away with things, but something starts to crack at a much faster pace than ever before. He sobs through the pain while simultaneously begging me to keep going. And I do. Even when I want to stop, I don't relent.

Finally, the cracks break wide open, revealing the truth. "Brisa's in the nearby countryside," he mumbles. Blood drips from his mouth. His eyes.

"Where exactly?"

Through the pain, he manages to explain the area. There's a certain look and layout of the house, there's a nearby forest and swamp. He remembers the numbers on the house and the name of the closest road. I'm sure with a little online searching I'll have an address within the hour.

"She's gathering an army," he warns me. "She kidnaps the strays, finds people that nobody will miss. She brings them in, has her new vampires feed on them until they're close to death, and then she turns the victims herself."

"And what's her plan with this army?" Now that he's able to speak, the confessions pour out of him. I still keep the knife lodged in his abdomen just in case, ignoring the scent of burning flesh.

"She wants to attack the council, but it's all a distraction to get to Eva."

"What does she want with Eva?"

"I don't know," he replies honestly. "I thought she still wanted to turn her, but sometimes she talked as if she wanted to kill her. Other times she would talk about her light. I can't say what her plan is, I honestly don't know, now please," he begs. "Let it be over. Please just kill me."

I release him just as he passes out. He's not dead, and he won't be getting a true death anytime soon, but he's going to be in a world of pain for the next hour as his body heals from the massacre of my knife. I'll come back for him later, will thank him, and will convince him to let me help him. He doesn't deserve to die, but if he truly decides that's what he needs, I won't stand in his way. I can't force this life on anyone, and I wouldn't begin to try.

But right now, I've got a vampire to kill.

CHAPTER 27

I seriously hate Faerie.

That's all I can think as I stare at the nasty humanoid troll standing with me in the middle of the small dirt-floored arena. He's at least seven feet tall, with large yellowing teeth, pointy gray scales covering his bare back, long coiled hair on his bare chest, and hands the size of boulders. He's also hungry, and apparently he has a thirst for flesh––my flesh, if he gets his way.

"Don't worry," King Orlyc calls out from the overhead gallery, watching down on me while everyone laughs. "We won't let you die. Maybe just lose an arm or two, but we can heal those before we send you back to the mortal world. This is just for pure entertainment."

"And when I'm done *entertaining* you, you'll let me and my friends go home?" I call back up.

"That's our agreement." But the way he says it makes

me think he probably has much more than this rolled up his sleeve.

Several of the spectators snicker at his response, and I grit my teeth. I need to stay focused. How in the hell am I supposed to kill this thing? Because that's the favor the king has asked for. Kill the troll. If I don't kill the troll, he'll still let me and my friends go home, but that's after I've healed. Because the troll is absolutely going to beat the shit out of me. And try to eat me, apparently.

This troll is an inmate on their fae-equivalent to a death row. It's here because it literally *ate* a fae child. Yup, it's disgusting, so either way, this creature is going to die. But why me? Why do I have to be the one to do it? Again, it's all about games and entertainment. Just another day in the Unseelie Court.

"Sorry, buddy," I say to the troll. "You're dead either way, but I think you already knew that."

He grunts, and I jump into action, summoning my light and blinding the creature. It's a temporary advantage, but at least it's a start.

It's also a big mistake.

Because the troll snarls with intense rage and dives for my hands. Maybe I really will lose my arms in this fight. I crouch down and roll out of his way, and he slams into the stone wall that surrounds us, cracking it. But the wall instantly repairs itself with earthen elemental magic, and the people sitting on the benches above applaud gleefully. It's enough of a distraction that the troll gains ground, knocking me to the floor. I can't let him get me down–– if I do, it's all over.

I scramble up, using my levitation to fly above him. Several of the fae cheer at that while others shout disapproval. I catch sight of Chloe in the crowd sitting with Casimir. They both look downright miserable to be here. I catch Chloe's gaze, and she just looks away. Casimir does the same. *Well, I'm sorry, but are you two the ones fighting a troll right now? I don't think so.*

Refocusing, I come down on the troll's head, kicking it as hard as I can. I've got loads of vampire venom, so it should do something. Nope. Nada. He's like a steel mountain.

My legs buckle.

I cry out as I fall to the ground, pain rocketing through my lower half, and the back of my head hits the dirt floor with a thud. Stars shoot through my vision, and pain zaps at all my nerve endings. I scream, wanting nothing more than to end this, to call a truce and be done, but this isn't some sparring match.

And I can't stay down.

The troll is too quick, climbing on top of me and nearly crushing me with his weight. His smile is grotesque as his putrid breath surrounds me, reeking of coppery blood and rotting garbage. I gag, trying to squirm away. It's useless. I can't move, and we both know it. The crowd goes downright feral––they know it too.

He leans in, smelling my neck.

Sure, King Orlyc said he wasn't going to let me die, but at this moment I have zero faith in him. They say before you die that your life flashes before your eyes, but that's not what happens to me. It's not slow or surreal. It's frantic and terrifying, the emotions slamming me like a head-on collision with a semi truck, my life's memories coming at me all at once.

I don't want to die.

Using every ounce of strength and willpower I can muster, I free my hands from underneath him and thrust my palms into his face. I shine the light again, harder than ever before, brighter than I knew was possible. Blinding and hot. So hot that it burns.

The troll wails and rears back as heat blisters erupt across his body. I don't stop, letting it pummel him as I stand. My ribs are aching and my heart is pounding and the screams of the spectators are deafening, but I'm only focused on the troll.

I have to kill him before he kills me.

Guess I'm a killer afterall. Maybe none of us are all good or all bad. Maybe we're just doing the best we can with the shitty circumstances we have, and sometimes that means fighting a troll to the death. But I would rather be the predator than the prey. I'm done being anyone's prey. And I'm done holding back.

"You're going to die now," I announce. "I will make it as quick and painless as I can, not that you deserve that."

I don't have a weapon. I only have this angelic gift and the heightened senses and strength from the venom, but deep down, I know it will be enough to finish him. And King Orlyc must know it too. Maybe this is all part of his plan to show me what my gift is really capable of. It's more than just angelic light that streams from my hands, *it's angelic fire.*

The crowd is loving this: they're laughing, cheering, making bets, and most of all, they're feeding off the sickening energy of this fight. It's disgusting, but I can't worry about it right now. I just have to get it done.

But it's not working.

I'm burning him, he's in pain, he's down, but he's not dying. Maybe his skin is too thick? Am I not strong enough? Cruel enough?

Well, I know I'm not cruel enough to just stand here and let this continue.

Without pausing to overthink, I jump up and fly at the gallery, grabbing hold of the closest soldier. The elf cries out when I grab onto him, but I've surprised him enough to topple us both over the railing. We land on our backs on the arena's dusty and blood-soaked floor.

To do this, I've had to abandon the light, and the troll is back on his feet and furious. He's half burned, and he comes for me, but I push the soldier in his way. Just as I expected, the elf is quick, retrieving his long sword and pointing it at the troll. The troll slows to a stop and grunts with fury.

"End him," I instruct the soldier.

The man growls but quickly retrieves another

weapon and hands me the sword. "I'll kill you for this," he sneers.

"Only if your king allows it." Which won't happen because the king wants me alive.

I wield my powerful new weapon, aiming it at the troll. The monster is circling us now, his beady eyes focused only on me. I'm the one he wants.

"So I take it you're not going to kill him for me?" I ask the elf.

"No, but I should let him eat you," he growls.

And that sets my resolve because I will not feel sorry for this damn troll.

He charges forward, and I jump and spin, the long silver sword cutting through the air in a circular arc and slamming into his neck. Using every ounce of strength I have left, I press down and slice through sinew and bone and muscle. Hot blood flies as his body crumples to the dirt, head rolling several feet away. Grimacing, I pick up the decapitated head by the oily hair and hoist it in the air like a trophy.

Half the crowd cheers wildly and the other half boos, but I don't care. I'm just glad it's done and I can go home.

"Are you happy now?" I call out to the king.

"Very." He nods, and the firelight of the many overhead torches reflects off his crown. "That was fun."

I suppose they get bored living as long as they do, but I'd rather not be the entertainment anymore. "Great, now send me and my friends back home."

When the king stands, the room grows silent. I drop the troll's head and step away, beyond grossed out that its blood is all over the combat clothing and boots the fae provided for this very event. I turn and hand the sword back to the soldier, who shoots me a glare before returning it to his sheath.

"Casimir will take you home after you dine with us," Orlyc says.

I snort. "I'm not eating your fae food. Good try, though."

"Then join us while we eat," he insists. He still sounds jovial, but his eyes are like ice. I don't trust him for a second. "I won't take no for an answer."

I agree, feigning resignation, but I'm actually more on guard than before. A troll was one thing. Dinner with the dark king? That's something else entirely.

CHAPTER 28

ADRIAN

There aren't a lot of basements in New Orleans because of the high water table. We built a several-levels deep basement into the hotel, but it took a substantial amount of money to engineer and complete. Most of the developers who bid for us discouraged the basement levels altogether, but I insisted on having an underground sanctuary for my coven. And a lavish one at that.

For as long as I've known her, Brisa never settled for anything less than total extravagance. I figured that she wouldn't hole up and plan my demise just anywhere. She would want to be in a luxury hotel or apartment somewhere close by, and probably somewhere that also had access to comfortable underground accommodations in case of an emergency. She'd definitely stay within the city limits, probably in the French Quarter. That way she could strike at a moment's notice.

But I was wrong--because she's not in the city at all. She's in the swamp.

And so, I am in the swamp now too, hunting her down. It's filled with life, even in January, the croaking toads being the loudest of all. It's not even their mating season and they're obnoxious. There's no peace and quiet out here.

I wonder what Brisa thinks of that--she's not actually *in* the swamp, but she's taken over a property that backs up to it. The large antebellum house is old and gothic, but decently maintained. I wonder who owned it, and I also wonder if she killed them or turned them. I'm going to assume they're her children now after everything Kenton confessed.

Hovering over the dark swamp bordering the home, I catch a glimpse of the old graveyard on the other side of the property. That graveyard alone explains why she chose this estate for her plans. Graveyards can be hard to find in family estates like this. They're illegal in most places, but this one would've been grandfathered into the property. There shouldn't be any new souls resting here, but from the looks of several freshly dug graves, it's obvious she's been siring new vampires.

Kenton's still back at the casino, locked away, but he was right. She's building an army. I won't release him from his cell until after she's dead. And once she's gone, I'll have more new vampires without a master to deal with. That will create unintended consequences--I may be hunting new vampires for weeks. They won't be under the council bond like all others, so it will be best to kill them. It's going to be hard enough to get the council to agree to let Kenton live.

I've trusted five vampires to come with me tonight. After we left the car at the closest highway exit, I levitated and the rest came on foot. Mangus is leading William and three of Will's oldest and fiercest children. I hope the six of us will be enough because seeing the large house now makes me a little nervous. She's in there with God knows how many new children. They might even be waiting for us.

The others catch up, and I levitate down to meet them. "We'll go in and lure the new children out. Don't hesitate to kill them, they'll be instructed to do the same to you."

"You're sure we can go in?" William asks.

"Whoever owns this place is long dead by now. There's a family graveyard on the other side of the estate. I'm certain that's why she chose this location."

"She could've turned a thousand vampires by now."

Mangus shakes his head. "We would've known. There would've been reports of people going missing. You can pick off loners here and there, but you can't pick off a thousand humans in a matter of weeks without notice."

"And it's a small graveyard," I add, "So no, not a thousand, but possibly a hundred. They're young, dangerous, and operating outside of the council's blood bonds. They all need to be eliminated."

A line forms between the eyebrows of one of William's men. He doesn't like the sound of that; he probably thinks I'm being cruel and ruthless. Well, I am. I have to be. There is no room for mercy in tonight's mission. I level him with a hard glare. "Do not hesitate," I repeat. "They won't hesitate to kill you, and it's either us or it's them." He nods, and I continue.

"We get in, we kill, and we find Eva if she's there. But leave Brisa to me. Got it?" They nod, their killer instincts come out to play. "Alright, let's go." The six of us take off in a group, Mangus at the forefront and me just steps behind. We gather on the porch and he throws open the front door, the first to go in.

"It's clear," he whispers low, and we follow him inside.

I don't normally get nervous, but I'm a wreck right now. I can admit that. Because Eva could be in here. She could be hurt. Or worse. And the sickest thing about it is that I hope she's here, because if she's not, I won't be able to save her tonight. And I'm not going to stop searching until I do. I don't care if I have to comb through every corner on this planet, starting with the fae realm.

But right now, she needs me alive, and I need to stay focused. So I force her from my mind and think of Brisa instead. She's the one I want to question, that I need to kill.

But the house is eerily silent.

Did Kenton lead me to the wrong place, or did Brisa

already move on to a new location? Or maybe they're off doing something else right now. For a second, I imagine her army has moved into the casino in my absence, that I've just walked into the perfect trap. That Kenton planned this all along.

We round the corner into the large kitchen, and Mangus points to the refrigerator. "Can you smell that?"

I inhale the scent of cold blood. It's being stored for later, and it smells fresh, like it was taken within the last twenty-four hours. She can't be too far.

"Split up," I instruct. "When you find her, call for the others." We're fast––it'll only take seconds for us to catch up to whoever finds her first.

We peel apart in different directions, and I head toward the back of the house, hovering inches above the floor to keep completely silent. I really hope I'm the first to find her. But the back of my neck prickles in an old familiar way, and that's when I know the truth.

She's found me first.

CHAPTER 29

$\mathcal{A}$ pair of pixies bathe and dress me for the evening. They're barely a foot tall with large gossamer moth-like wings. They weave pink flowers into my hair and make me dress in a matching pastel pink tulle dress. "I hate this color," I mutter to myself, but the pixies take that as an insult and hiss, one of them pinching my cheeks.

"Ouch!" I try to brush her away, but she flashes sharp teeth at me, and I stop.

"This feels like some kind of cosmic joke." Chloe glowers down at her own pastel green dress. The dress looks way better on her than it does on me. "Thanks to you," she adds, shooting me an arched eyebrow.

"What would you do for Greyson and Bella? Or for your twin brothers? What about all the friends you made when you trained?" I smooth out the dress and release a breath. "Because I'm pretty sure you'd have done the same thing I did."

"You're asking a manipulative question, and I won't fall for it."

I sigh, overcome with exhaustion, and rub my eyes. A pixie hisses and swats my hand away, whining over the messed up makeup she just applied. "Geez, you're stronger than you look," I say to the pixie.

She giggles, snapping her sharp teeth again. "I'm a lot of things you'll never know, nephilim. Now let me do my job, or I really will bite."

Okay, note to self, they definitely bite and they understand English, so don't say anything that can't be repeated outside of this room.

But I really am beyond exhausted right now––I couldn't care less.

When Casimir brought us to Faerie, I was in another time zone sleeping. I didn't get much sleep at all before being pulled here, and now the sun is rising here in Faerie. I assume we're somewhere near Ireland still, which makes me think it's setting or has already set back home. I really wouldn't know anymore, the time zones make no sense to me, especially adding in the fact that I'm no longer in the mortal world. All I do know is that I'm dying to get some decent sleep.

"I'm not trying to manipulate you." I return to my conversation with Chloe, stifling a yawn that earns me another hissing pixie. "I just want you to understand why I did what I did. They're not going to kill you, I made sure that was promised, and fae can't tell lies, but my friends would've been stuck here forever. They didn't deserve that."

She hums to herself, not yet convinced, but I can tell I'm cracking her shell. I still believe she's a good person deep down.

"And besides, they were kind to you. Don't you remember them? Seth and Felix lived at the Casa with us for a while." She stiffens, and I think I've almost cracked her. "And Felix is such a great guy. I've known him since I was a kid and believe me, he doesn't deserve to be stuck in this place. And Seth? Well, Seth is kind of a crotchety old man even though he's the young and broody type, but he's got a soft heart. "

"Fine," her voice drops an octave. "Whatever. I get it. You did what you had to do. Now can you stop talking? I'm still mad at you even though I understand."

Success--I've got her!

"I'll take it." I offer her a wink, and she rolls her eyes.

The pixies finish with us, fashioning us into what looks to me like a pair of sugar-plum fairies from *The Nutcracker*. Casimir appears from the shadows of the dressing room, stepping out of them as if striding through a doorway. His creepy dove sits on his shoulder.

"What is that thing?" I ask him, not caring that he hates when I ask him questions about his magic.

He ignores my question completely, inspecting us,

and taking way more interest in Chloe's appearance than my own. "This will do. Let's go."

We have no choice but to follow him outside.

The dinner has been set up in the castle's courtyard, and even though it's a cold winter's night, the air has been magicked to feel like a warm summer's evening. Little fairy lights flitter above the crowd, lighting the entire space. I squint up at the lights when I realize that they're actual fairies dancing around up there. They look to be enjoying a party all their own.

Long rectangular dining tables are set off to one side and covered in decadent food and drink. The dance floor is on the other side, already filled with dancers. Huge white roses overflow from centerpieces and archways. They're five times the size of any rose I've seen before, and the thorns tucked in their stems look sharp as knives. I take note to stay away from them.

The fae are dressed in some of the most beautiful gowns and suits I've ever seen. And also some of the strangest. They wear silks of every color, many covered in beaded embroidery or gems. And several with slits in the backs for wings. The wings are just as varied as the gowns are.

"Welcome to the Unseelie Court," Casimir says, sounding bored, probably because he's been to these parties a thousand times before. "You do know what Unseelie means, don't you?" He directs this question to Chloe.

"Evil and malevolent," she quips.

"That's one way to put it," he replies evenly. "There are light fae and there are dark fae. We are the dark fae. This is our side of Faerie."

The fae are comprised of many mythical creatures besides the elves, and I'm pretty sure all of them are immortals. They can still be killed, but they don't age once they reach maturity. For most that means they look to be in their twenties, and for others it's their thirties. But nobody here appears to be a day over forty. There's no way to tell who has the power, who has the secrets, and who belongs where. Aging and generations are such a human thing, but they just make sense to me. This? This is unsettling, to say the least.

I wonder what that makes of fae lives––do they still live it to the fullest? Or do they grow bored, coming up with malevolent games to occupy their time? I think I already know the answer to that question . . .

As far as I know, the elves are at the top of the fae food chain, ruling the Seelie and the Unseelie Courts. They're also the most like humans, but that's all I really know of them. There might be others in Faerie that challenge them, mages and such. It's not my place to know, nor do I really care so long as I can get out of here tonight.

"And does your father have a queen?" Chloe asks, gazing at the crowd. I think she's looking for King Orlyc, but he's nowhere to be found. "I'd like to talk to a woman about all this."

"There is no Unseelie Queen," is all Casimir replies,

then he takes both of our arms and drags us to the head table. "Sit and enjoy yourselves." He sounds sarcastic, pushing us into chairs, but I wonder if he's actually being sarcastic or if he's filling a role. This could all be another game.

And then he's strolling away to go dance with an elf who has the prettiest hair I've ever seen. It streams down her back in a glossy red wave, sparkling like rubies in the dim light.

The king is the last to arrive, and when he does, everyone else takes their seats and begins to devour the food. It looks and smells delicious, but Chloe and I don't move a muscle. In fact, I sit on my hands, just in case. I'm not tempted this time because I know where it will get me. It also helps that I'm barely hungry.

We stay like that all through the dinner, and although we're sitting next to the king, he never speaks to us or even acknowledges our presence. It's as if he wants us here to be seen, but not to participate.

Fine by me.

After the dinner and dessert are finished, and after the people have started to grow tired of the dancing, King Orlyc motions to one of his servants. It's the very same elf that always has that kelpie dog at his side. Together, they scamper into the castle.

"I have your friends," Orlyc says, and my heart jumps. Then he turns to Chloe, "and I have someone I think you'd be very interested to meet."

The crowd parts, and Seth and Felix come strolling

in. They look healthy, like their minds have been returned to them. At least compared to when I saw them a few hours ago, it's a night and day difference. I jump up and run to them, wrapping them both in a double bear-hug. Chloe follows close behind, though she refrains from hugging anyone.

"Eva, we've been so worried about you." Felix is the first to speak. "They sent you away and wouldn't tell us anything."

"I've been worried about you," I counter. "What have you been doing here?"

They exchange guarded looks. "Not now," Seth supplies. "But just know, we're okay. We're not traumatized. At least, I don't think we are."

Seeing their eyes so clear right now makes me wonder what the fae have done to make them return to their normal selves. There must be a safe way to survive this place if my human friends can go from being drunk on food and wine to being completely alert and sober like this. And it's only been a few hours. But it doesn't matter right now because we're leaving Faerie and never coming back.

"Let's go home." I turn back to the king to ask for just that when the crowd falls to complete silence, parting for a newcomer.

CHAPTER 30

The tall elfin man saunters into the courtyard followed by several of his attendants, all of them dressed in gold and white silks. There's no question they belong together. The leader is stunning and impossibly tall, with golden ringlets that fall all around his face like a heavenly halo. A prickle of familiarity runs through me. I feel like I've met this man before, but that's impossible.

Is it impossible?

"Why have you requested an audience tonight, King Orlyc?" the man booms, seeming completely unaware of my little group huddled off to his right.

"Is it so strange for us to want to host our friends?" Orlyc teases.

The man responds with a deep scowl as massive white feathered wings explode from his back. The tips of the feathers seem to be ignited with an unearthly fire.

And that's when I realize how I know him.

"Oh, don't be like that." Orlyc laughs at this obvious display of power. He turns in a wide circle, arms outstretched in introduction. "Welcome King Alberich Mikael, High King of the Seelie Court." The party guests clap, but I don't. I can barely even move. I'm too stunned. "It's so kind of you to take time from your busy schedule to join us." He steps to the side, motioning Chloe forward. But she can't seem to move either. "How I've longed for you two to meet."

Chloe's knees begin to slump, and I grab her, helping her stay upright. Seth and Felix step forward as well. Chloe doesn't seem to notice any of us, though, her eyes are glued to the light fae king. And I get it, because as shocked as I'm feeling right now, she must be feeling complete betrayal. Her mouth hangs open. Eyes glossy. Unmoving.

"It can't be." Her voice cracks in equal parts horror and pain.

"Oh, but I assure you, it can," Casimir says, appearing at her other side. He frowns at her with pity, and that's almost worse than when he looked at her with disdain.

"That's right, your avenging angel is actually a light fae," King Orlyc confirms.

So it's true then. That is how I "know" Alberich. I saw him in Chloe's records.

"And to think, all along you thought our Al here was God's avenging angel, come down to command his precious nephilim seed to rid the world of supernaturals," Orlyc continues. "How wrong you are, Chloe. And how very wrong your ancestors were."

The fire on the light king's wings has only grown at this, as if it's tied to his fury. "This is why you brought me here, Orlyc?" His wings lift, as if he's preparing to take flight. "For these women? I don't have to entertain nephilim."

Orlyc rounds on Alberich. "The nephilim must be stopped. The truth is the only thing that will set us all free."

Alberich shakes his head. "I did what needed to be done in order to protect our realm from theirs. They were a virus, infecting our kind and diluting our bloodlines."

"And so you lied?" Chloe asks, growing bolder.

"It worked didn't it?" He stalks in close, and I hold on tighter to her shoulder, not willing to let her go. We're in this together. "I did what I had to do, and your kind easily believed it. They wanted something to do with themselves. They needed a purpose."

"You pretended you were an angel of God," Chloe hisses. "You spoke in tongues."

"I used elfin magic." His blue eyes bore down on her, and his wings flap once more, sending a gust of wind in our direction. "I did what had to be done to protect my kind. And I would do it again."

Prince Casimir's been watching this exchange with his mouth set in a grim line, not saying much, but at this he growls at the light king. "What you did cost thousands of innocent lives."

"But I saved generations of fae in the process. Do not act as if you understand the ways of kings, Prince."

Shadows dance around Casimir's knuckles, and I'm certain he's fighting the urge to set them loose on Alberich.

King Orlyc simply laughs––more entertainment to fill his evening. "The nephilim have a record keeper born to every generation, someone who can access the memories of what you did and continue to spread your message. The mission you tasked them with has never ceased. They've used it to justify countless deaths, claiming their God decreed it. But the truth is, the nephilim are mortals with watered-down angelic blood and nothing more."

He points to Chloe, and Casimir's shadows shove her forward, wrapping up her arms and legs in a cocoon of darkness.

"This is the current record keeper. Do you know what you've created? What kind of weapon this youth has become for her people?"

"Her *people* don't belong in our world, and we don't belong in theirs. I ensured they would drive the fae back into our world, which they did. The portals wouldn't have been sealed if it wasn't for my ingenuity." His wings are flapping again, that terrible fire growing taller and taller. "Yes, there were sacrifices. Yes, people died. But our kind has stopped mixing with the wrong bloodlines, and as a result, we're stronger than ever. We've returned to the old customs. Our courts have flourished. Our children grow up healthy. Our way of life is that of kings and queens. What does their mortal realm matter to us now that Faerie is thriving?"

Chloe's eyes release a well of unshed tears as she speaks the truth. "It matters because the war continues on in the mortal realm."

"Not my problem," he sneers.

She continues, "and because my people will find a way into Faerie, and when they do, they will unleash a weapon. A weapon the likes of which you've never seen. A weapon that will destroy this realm and everyone born of it."

CHAPTER 31

Choices are made quickly after Chloe's confession, mainly because King Alberich pulls his head out of his ass, and also because Chloe agrees to help the fae. She understands now that she's been as blinded by the records as the rest of her family, and she wants to set things right. Can we go back and save the thousands who've died in this centuries-long war? No. But can we stop it from continuing? We don't know, but we hope so——we believe it's possible.

The meeting winds down, and the exhaustion pulls me under. All I want right now is sleep. *Dreamless* sleep, if I can help it. I'm sure Adrian is losing his mind looking for me, but once I get home and tell him what happened, I'm going to bed.

Chloe doesn't know it yet, but I have a feeling she's going to struggle getting the truth out. She loves her family and believes the best of them, but

I'm not so sure they'll accept her word on this. These prejudices are lifelong, are they really going to be able to give them up? What if they don't believe her or they find a way to twist her words into something ugly?

"Are you ready then?" Casimir says to the group of us ready to go back to the mortal world. He sounds bored by all of this, like there are more interesting things he could be doing with his time right now. His eyes flick to Chloe, and his nose wrinkles. "You're crying again. Please stop that."

She wipes at the tears. "Leave me alone, Casimir."

He stiffens at the mention of his name, like hearing it on her lips is an insult.

I'm quick to defend her. "She's just realized that her friends and family have been killing people for generations for no good reason and everything she was raised to believe is based on a lie. I would cry too."

"You would?" Her lip trembles. She sounds skeptical. That's what I get for having resting-bitch-face.

"I mean, probably. But if I didn't, it's only because I'm a bitter old hag."

"How old are you?" Casimir frowns in confusion. "You don't look old for a mortal."

"It's just an expression." I bug my eyes out at him. "Now can you take us home please?"

One of the party fairies has come down to buzz around Chloe, trying to collect her tears into a crystal vial. Chloe brushes her away, and the fairy throws sparkly dust in her face. Chloe sneezes. "I think I'm allergic to that stuff."

"It's pixie dust," Casimir says. "It's a gift."

"Does it make you fly?"

He frowns. "No. Wherever did you get that idea?"

"Never . . . mind," she mumbles but he seems genuinely curious.

"Let's get going." I shoot Casimir a pleading look, not really wanting to get into the tale of Peter Pan and Neverland. "Please take me to Adrian."

"I just want to go home." Chloe wipes up the last of her tears.

"Which home?" I snort. "Don't you people have houses all over?" Her eyes water again, and I backpedal. "Damn, I'm sorry. I didn't mean to make you upset."

Casimir bristles, giving me a death-glare. "What did I say about crying?"

Geeze, it's not my fault she's so sensitive.

"Take me to my brothers, Enzo and Nicco," Chloe interrupts. "Can you do that?"

I almost think he's going to say no, but he simply nods.

"Just take us to my house," Felix says.

I don't know how Casimir's magic works, that he can know where to take everyone, but he must because he stretches out his arms like what we're about to do is no big deal. He needed me to get to Chloe, so he must have some limitations, but I'm not about to slow us down by asking him questions he won't want to answer anyway.

We all grab on at once and he pulls our group into his shadows.

We tumble through the darkness with no end.

Flashes of the twin's faces appear, and then Chloe is gone. We hover nearby for just a second, watching her reunite with her brothers in the living room of a home I don't recognize. It reminds me of when I was a kid and my mom would drop one of my friends off at their house. She'd always wait to make sure they got inside safely before driving away. Casimir is doing the same thing to Chloe right now. I try to speak, to ask him if he's developed a soft spot for her, but the shadows are cutting off my voice.

Chloe looks up, catching sight of us with her large caramel eyes, and then we're gone, falling back into the ether again. The inertia slams through my body at a sickening pace. We're moving much faster this time. It's like being on a horrible roller coaster, and all I can think is that Chloe got lucky to be dropped off first.

And then we're in the Moreno's kitchen where Felix and Seth are stumbling out of the shadows. But we don't stick around to make sure they're home safe, we're gone again.

Now it's just me and Casimir, and he turns his grip on me. It's so impossibly tight that I would cry out if I could speak, but the shadows keep me in silence. All I can do is hold on for the ride, everything spinning faster and faster, my mind nearly floating away.

I'm dropped in an unfamiliar place.

Catching my breath, I sit up and look around. I'm in a random backyard and it's night out.

Great job, Cas . . .

The grass is mossy and wet, the trees are tall and probably old, and up ahead looms a creepy antebellum mansion. There are no lights on, and it looks very much like it could be the set for a horror film. Except, this isn't a movie, this is my real life. I shiver and look around for Casimir, wanting to tell him that he dropped me in the wrong place, but he's gone. He didn't bother to stick around to make sure I made it home safe either.

Cursing the fae, I stand and brush myself off. At least the sunrise looks like it's coming soon. The sky is that shade of blue it turns when the sun is about to crest the eastern horizon. The one relief in all this is I won't have to try to find my way back to the casino in the dark. I take in the many gnarled trees and the huge weeping willows, the nearby croaking of toads and cicadas, and determine that a swamp is nearby. At least I'm probably in Louisiana, but how far to New Orleans?

I might be able to levitate back to the city, but I need to know where I am before I can know which direction to go, so reluctantly, I trudge up to the house. Let's just pray that whoever lives here isn't a "shoot first and ask questions later" type of southerner, but more of a "hospitality is our birthright" type. I almost channel light into my hands as a makeshift flashlight but decide better of it. That's a surefire way to scare someone. I'm already dressed in an ugly tulle pastel pink gown with loads of flowers braided into my hair. I look like a homecoming queen reject.

Just as I step onto the front porch, a guttural moan catches my attention. I pause to listen, a sense of foreboding creeping over me. The moaning continues, and I realize it's not actually moaning that I'm hearing. It's the sound of muffled speech.

This is the part in the horror film where I would be screaming at the television, telling the dumb girl to run the other direction. And I'd definitely be throwing popcorn at the screen when she goes to investigate the muffled voice. Rule number one of surviving a horror movie: don't put yourself in the wrong place at the wrong time on purpose. I guess today I'm that girl, because I back off the porch and head toward the noise.

All at once, three things happen: the sound grows urgent, the sun begins to peek over the trees, and my eyesight adjusts completely to the dim light.

And there he is.

Adrian.

Moments from death.

CHAPTER 32

He's tied to a tree with thick silver chains and a gag is shoved into his mouth.

I don't think, I just act.

Racing across the lawn, I reach him and begin frantically removing the chains. He groans hard as his exposed flesh sizzles against the metal. His eyes search mine, then dart back to the house, as if trying to tell me something.

It takes a second, but I pull the gag from his mouth. "How did you get here?"

His voice is ragged and more angry than ever. "Brisa's in there with her new vampires. Don't go inside. Untie me and get away from here."

"And what are you going to do?" I question as I work on the chains. My heart is going a million miles a minute because I know that rising sun is going to kill him soon.

"I'm going to go back in there to kill her," he snarls.

"Good. I'm going with you."

He levels me with a look that says he knows better than to argue with me but he's really not happy about it. "Fine." He breaks free of the chains. His body is weakened from the silver, and he needs time to heal. He also needs to get away from the sun. That house is not safe for either of us, but he's got thirty seconds at most.

He breaks a branch from the tree and fashions it into two makeshift stakes, handing me the sharper one. "Bring some of that chain," he instructs.

I pick the smallest length of it up and wrap it around my left hand, keeping the stake in my right. Then we race back to the house, crossing the threshold seconds before the sunlight hits the earth.

I have to hold my breath to keep from audibly panting. That was so close, and now we're walking into an equally dangerous situation because Brisa wants Adrian dead. Because she was surely watching everything we just did.

Because she knows exactly where we are.

Vampires come at me from all sides, and I don't have time to orient myself. I fight back immediately. I'm still tired and disoriented from the longest day of my life, and my movements are slower than normal. And there are just so many vampires. I can't count them all, but I'd guess at least thirty. Thirty of them, and there's only two of us. I manage to stake one, but seconds later another has me pinned against the floor. Meanwhile, Adrian is covered in them. He's so much faster and stronger, but he's vastly outnumbered. They're going to rip him to shreds.

Slamming my silver-wrapped fist into my current vampire attacker's face, the man rears back with a guttural roar. I jump to my feet, dropping both the stake and the silver, and channel my gift instead. I'm going to aim it at all of them. They're already dead as far as I'm concerned, and luckily Adrian is safe from my light since the council bond magic makes it impossible for me to kill him. The angelic firelight erupts from my hands, and I point at the attackers, spinning in a circle to make sure I hit them all. They scream and hit the floor, but I don't stop. And I won't stop. Not until they burn alive. And they do, one by one, crumbling into ash.

I never saw Brisa among them. She must still be in here, still hiding somewhere in this house. And I'm going to hunt her down and kill her for this.

I let my hands drop, the light disappearing for now. I cough, covered in the ash. I have to wipe it from my eyes.

I expect Adrian to be on the floor where I last saw him.

But he's gone.

My stomach roils with revulsion and adrenaline. I know I couldn't have killed him, so he must have been dragged away.

God, I hope I didn't accidentally kill him.

Ignoring my growing panic, I release a frustrated

scream and race upstairs to search. I don't know why I think he's upstairs, but I just do. He could be anywhere in this huge house, but there's something about the grand staircase that calls to me.

It's *very* Brisa.

I go from room to room. The windows are all boarded up, but little streams of light are beginning to come through the cracks. It's enough sun to injure a vampire if they were directly in it, but I don't think it's enough to kill one. As far as I know, only full sunlight exposure can do that.

Jazz music begins to faintly play from a scratchy record player. I freeze. It's coming from a room farther down the hallway. A door cracks open, and what looks like candlelight flickers from within. It's a production, a show for my benefit, and it's creepy as hell.

Also, very Brisa.

Rushing forward, I slam open the door.

Adrian is lying on the bed, and Brisa is curled up at his side like a lover. But she's no lover because pressed to his heart, ready to kill, is a long wooden stake. And around his neck, coils a black and brown cottonmouth snake. It's one of the most poisonous snakes in the area, and seeing it sends a streak of panic through me.

Because she's controlling that snake . . .

I almost forgot that she can communicate with animals, commanding them to do things for her. And just beyond these walls is a swamp full of all kinds of dangerous creatures at her disposal. I imagine what she could do with all those snakes and gators, and my fear triples.

"Your girlfriend is here," Brisa whispers to Adrian in a breathy tone. "How very fortunate. I wanted her to see you die."

CHAPTER 33

"Just tell me what you want from me. I'll do it, and you can stop this."

She tilts her head in my direction, her eyes narrowing into hateful slits. "I want my crown back. I lost it because of you. Once he dies, you're next. I don't care what you are or what you can do. I've made up my mind. I want you gone."

"Eva, don't," Adrian hisses, and she shifts her weight so she's straddling him, the tip of the stake never leaving its mark. She's not going to miss his heart. All it will take is one simple wrist movement, and he'll be gone forever. I'm not sure my gift would be fast enough to stop her in time. And still, the cottonmouth tightens around his neck, then turns to hiss at me, baring its fangs.

"Don't kill Adrian, and I'll help you," I plead.

She smiles her most calculated smile, the one that doesn't reach her eyes. "Here's what you're going to do," she instructs. "You're going to call a council meeting in three nights' time to meet in City Park at two a.m. sharp. You will ensure that every council member attends, insisting that the full moon requires another forging. Once you are all together, you will join bloodied hands, and I will arrive. That is when you will transfer the blood bond back to me."

"The hell she will," Adrian snarls, and she tuts, pressing the tip of her stake hard enough to pierce through his shirt and into his chest. He swallows a groan, shaking his head at me. He'd rather die than let her win. But I can't let him die. I just can't.

"And if word of my impending arrival leaks to anyone," she adds. "Not only will I kill Adrian, but I will hunt down anyone you've ever associated with, anyone at all, and I will kill them too. Friends, family, old teachers, co-workers––*anyone.*"

I can see it in her eyes and hear it in her voice––she means every word. This is more than a threat, it's an oath.

"Okay," I agree, "I'll do my part, I will get them all there and help you do whatever you want. *But* if transferring the bond fails, you cannot blame me. You're forgetting that the fae are part of this equation too, it's their magic you want to change, and they already forged the bond. They said it couldn't be changed."

She smiles again, and this time it does reach her eyes. And it's terrifying. "I already have everything I need from the fae. You just make sure everyone arrives on time and that they don't suspect my arrival."

"And what about Adrian? You're going to have to let him go so he can show up with the rest of the council."

She mocks me with her tone. "Do you really think I'm foolish enough to do that? No, Adrian will come when I do. You'll have to cover for his absence."

Adrian stares at me with wide eyes, shaking his head over and over again. The snake grows agitated and bites him. He groans and stops moving, and the snake relaxes again. The snake's venom can't hurt him, but my heart still breaks to see him this way. To see him hurt and bound. Once again under Brisa's control.

He doesn't want me to do this. And I get it, because I wouldn't either if I were in his position right now. But I'm not, and if there's a chance to save him, I have to take it. I'll worry about the blood bonds when we actually get to that point.

"Please, just let Adrian go," I try one last time.

"Adrianos is mine. He will always be mine. It is my right to keep him alive or end him."

I shake my head. She's so wrong. "You have no right to anybody but yourself."

"Don't speak," she screams, then she speaks more calmly. "I will let him walk free once I have my royal bond returned to me."

I nod. There's nothing else I can do.

"Now leave."

"But--"

"Leave!"

The cottonmouth slips from Adrian's neck. It slithers off the bed quickly, snapping its fangs at me and hissing. I back away, but it doesn't stop coming at me. I turn and run, and the damn thing chases me from the house entirely. It's only when I'm fully outside that it finally doubles back to its master.

And even from way out here, I can hear the warning sound of Brisa's maniacal laughter.

Spinning around to take in my surroundings, I'm overwhelmed with panic. I don't know where I am. I don't have a phone. And I'm dressed in a pink gown, covered in blood and ash. What the hell am I supposed to do?

I could levitate, and I definitely will if needed, but I'm exhausted and worry I won't be able to hold it for long. Plus, it's daylight out. What if someone sees me? How will I explain myself?

Either way, I really hate snakes. There ain't no way I'm getting bitten by that cottonmouth, so I take off at a dead sprint away from the house and toward the long gravel driveway. It disappears into the trees up ahead, and I'm hoping whatever road it leads to will be an easy enough one for me to follow to civilization.

I run faster than I ever have before, but just as I'm about to hit the treeline, I notice a small cemetery off to my right. I've had enough cemeteries to last me a lifetime, and from the looks of this one, recent graves have been dug here.

Graves for all those new vampires I just killed.

It's probably stupid, but I don't want Brisa having any new children with her when she comes to the council meeting in three days' time. It takes three nights to make a new vampire, so she won't have time to make new ones to replace the ones I killed back in the house. But what if she has more buried here? Stifling a groan, I force myself to be brave and veer off toward the cemetery. I'll dig up any fresh graves and kill the vampires before they're fully turned. It's now or never.

Fighting back a nervous shiver, I swing open the wrought iron gate and edge my way inside. In this part of the world, bodies aren't able to be buried underground because of the water table, so the cemetery is a labyrinth of above-ground tombs and vaults. But vampires still have to be buried underground in order to turn, so I go straight to the areas of disturbed soil. There are several large holes, and I peer down into them to see open coffins at the bottoms.

Open and empty.

I exhale and find that I'm shaking so badly I need to sit down. But I can't. I have to search the place thoroughly, and then I have to go. And quickly, before Brisa realizes what I'm doing and sends her cottonmouth out here.

I shiver at the thought of having to dig up any graves should I find one. At least all I'll have to do is open the coffins. If an actual vamp is in one, the sun can do the work in killing them for me. And if I find a half-dead human, I can help them to safety, lock them up somewhere until the three days are up.

I round a corner of a particularly overgrown area surrounding a tomb, and reluctantly find what I was looking for.

A row of four more disturbed graves.

There are four in all, each haphazardly piled with dark, wet soil. Falling to my knees, I set to work digging up the graves. I'm so much faster than I would've been when I was still human, and there's not that much soil to begin with, so it doesn't take long. And I'm already disgusting with blood and ash, what's some dirt going to do?

By the time I hit the first coffin, I want to puke from the nerves coiled in my belly. It's the last thing I want to do, but I throw open the coffin lid anyway.

A vampire hisses.

CHAPTER 34

I scramble back, holding in my scream. I expected to find a human, someone slowly being turned. Maybe they'd already be undead, maybe not. But the man in the coffin is a fully formed vampire in black tactical gear.

He reacts in a flash, pulling me into the coffin with him and slamming the lid shut overtop us. He's screaming, the sun already starting to sizzle his flesh, but I'm also screaming now. Because I'm trapped in a coffin!

"Let me out," I cry, pushing against the lid. Despite his fresh wounds, the creature holds me so tightly that I'm locked in a vice. I will the light to come to my hands when the man growls into my ear.

I know that voice.

"Calm down," Mangus says. "You're going to get me killed. And whisper, please. Brisa's hearing is excellent. She doesn't know where we are."

My heart rate is still beating a million miles an hour, but I shift my weight slightly to lie next to Mangus instead of on top of him. My eyes adjust to the complete darkness of this godforsaken coffin, and I take in the man pressed next to me. His hair is a tangled mess, his eyes are closed in pain, and he smells like burnt flesh.

"What are you doing out here?" I demand.

"There were five of us that came with Adrian to kill Brisa and look for you," he explains slowly, gritting his teeth as his body starts to heal itself. "Unfortunately, Brisa already killed William. And I hate to be the one to tell you this, but I think she killed Adrian, too. She had him tied up to a tree so he'd burn with the sunrise."

"No, I saved him," I quickly add, and he visibly relaxes. "*But* he's now her prisoner."

We both want the other to explain what they know, but I make him go first.

"After she killed William and tied Adrian up outside, she also tied us up and told us we were going to die after her children had a chance to play with us." He grimaces, but doesn't expand on that part. "Fortunately, her and her children all went to the other side of the house to watch Adrian burn. That's when we were able to get away. But we only had minutes to find somewhere safe to spend the daylight hours. It was by sheer luck that we found these coffins open. We quickly buried ourselves just as the sun was rising."

His story checks out. I was on the other side of the property with Adrian when they came over here, so I wouldn't have seen or heard them. I'm a little peeved that they didn't first go try to help Adrian, but there wasn't a lot of time.

"Now you explain how you got here," he says.

"I will when I have more oxygen." I'm trying to stay calm, but this coffin is really starting to feel like it's going to suffocate me. "I can't stay in here too much longer," I whisper. "I need air."

"Right, okay, I'll let you out in a minute, but at least explain what happened in there to make Adrian her prisoner."

I slow my breathing and nod.

This is still Mangus. I like him, but I don't necessarily trust him. I barely even trust Adrian, and I'm madly in love with the guy. But I do go into detail about Brisa's plan to get the council together and transfer the bond. I know she said I wasn't supposed to tell anyone, but I was never going to stick to that side of our agreement anyway.

"Adrian won't let you do it. We can't give her the royal bond. She'll have control over us again. He'd rather die, and so would I." Mangus is adamant about this, and I can't say I blame him.

"Obviously I don't actually intend to give her the bond, but we have to get her into our territory so we can kill her and save him."

He thinks on it for a long minute. "Or we just storm in there the second the sun sets and get it over with now." He wants revenge, and although I know he cares for Adrian, I think it has very little to do with Adrian, and a lot to do with his dead wife.

"Except when I questioned her on her plan, she told me that she already had what she needed from the fae. Don't you want to know what she meant by that? What if she has something big planned? And more importantly, shouldn't we find out who has been working with her so we can stop them too? As much as I want to storm in there and get Adrian back, we need to be more strategic about this." He doesn't have an answer to those questions, probably because he knows I'm right. "Besides, half the vampire council still wants to access my light. What if they're willing to work with Brisa to get to me? What if they'd even go so far as to give up their blood bond for it? If we just go in there and kill Brisa, we will lose our chance to find out the truth."

Mangus is still quiet. Too quiet. And I'm worried he's going to disagree with me again. I don't know what I'll do if he turns on me. "You're smarter than I gave you credit for," he finally says, much to my relief. "Now let me ask you this, who's the mole for the nephilim? Because we know that someone has been working with them and giving them information that only those deep within our organization could know. So, Eva, if you're so smart, tell me who it is?"

From the tone of his voice, I can tell he's desperate for me to know. All at once, the answer hits me, everything clicking into place at once.

The favor he owed Isadora.

How he seems to be everywhere in all of this, always in everyone's business.

And why he wants me to figure it out––to name the traitor.

Maybe this is a mistake, maybe he's going to kill me for this, but I whisper the truth anyway. "You are, Mangus. You're the mole."

He doesn't react. He doesn't even move. Which is the exact opposite of what I thought he was going to do.

I take a breath of the musty air and continue, "But I don't think you're a bad guy. I don't think you would've done this for just any reason. And I know you hate the nephilim."

"There's only so much I can say here . . ." he replies, practically admitting it.

"And that proves my point. You can't tell me anything because you've been spelled not to, which makes me think back to our interaction with the fae witch. She broke your bond to Brisa, but not without a favor. We were led to believe the favor hadn't been required of you yet, but actually, it was an ongoing one. It was something you had already started."

He's silent as only the undead can be, and that's all the affirmation I need.

"The fae wanted you to spy on the nephilim, but you couldn't do that unless you pretended to be on the nephilim's side. Turning on your own kind was the only way."

"The fae are tricky," he says bitterly. "They can make

you do things you never thought you'd do, and even when you try to stop, if you've made an agreement with them that's been magicked, you will be forced to hold up your end."

"So you're basically a triple agent. You are trying to help the vampires, but you also have to help the nephilim so you can be the spy the fae demanded you to be."

"Well that sounds pathetic." His voice is lost and forlorn. He's still grieving, and he always will be so long as he's immortal.

"And meanwhile, the whole reason you even agreed to do this in the first place is gone," I say softly. "Brisa blamed your wife, used her as a scapegoat for something she was actually doing herself, and Katerina paid the ultimate price."

"And that's why we should go back in there and kill Brisa tonight."

"But we won't, because Adrian's life depends on this plan working. We're going to beat Brisa at her own game, and you're going to help me do it."

"And then we kill her," he growls.

"And then we kill her," I agree.

Three nights later, the moon is hanging like a silver dollar in the black sky, shining down on the vacant city park. Even though it's a beautiful winter's night, the chill that breezes through the trees is bitter. We're in the center of the large park, gathering our group in the middle of a clearing. The nearby trees hide us from the view of anyone who could be wandering through, but nobody's out here at this time of night anyway. Not even the homeless will hang around New Orleans for long these days. Too many things go bump in the night around here.

I stare up at the moon, equally mesmerized by its beauty and intimidated by its mysticism. There's something about full moons and new moons that the fae, especially the witchy kind, love, so it's only fitting that we're back out here during another full moon. That knowledge alone makes me feel like there is so much more to this world than I ever thought possible. Magic is proof enough of that.

It's been six months since I met Adrian, and so much about my life has changed since then. I know things I never wanted to know, but I can't go back, even if I wanted to. And I don't want to. I've accepted where I am now, accepted that this is the life I'm meant to be living. This is the way in which I'm going to help the world. Not by running around staking vampires, but by making it so that vampires don't need to be staked in the first place. It's no small feat, but I believe there's a way I can make things better for all people. Being on the council is just the beginning.

Working with the fae is also part of that.

And tricking Brisa . . .

There's a lot of loose strings to be pulled tonight. If I'm lucky, I'll be able to do it. And if I'm not, I'm going to create a big tangled web and a lot more dead bodies.

And even more ash . . .

"They're all here," Mangus says, sliding in next to me. He nods toward the shadowy trees where the other council members have appeared. I quickly count to make sure they're all here and release a slow relieved breath.

Antara and Sebastian are already exchanging conspiratory glances, setting off my inner alarm bells. I'm not sure if they are working with Brisa, but I think they are or else they wouldn't be so gleeful. Because I was right--they want power, but they want to be able to walk in the sun more.

They want my angelic gift.

And somehow, Brisa has promised to give it to them.

Which is funny, considering she told me she wanted to kill me. Maybe she thinks she can have both. Steal my gift for herself and then kill what's left of me.

My mind reels at that thought, and my insides go hollow.

We form a circle. Santino is the first to speak, his accent thicker than usual tonight. "Why did you call this meeting, Mangus? I had to travel all the way from Brazil for this. It had better be good."

"You're here because I wanted you here," Brisa's voice rains down like glass as she levitates from the darkened sky. She's dressed in a billowing bloodred gown. And she's alone. I glance to the thick trees, wondering who's eyes are watching us right now. And wondering where Adrian is.

"Where is he?" I demand, unable to wait a second longer.

She settles to the earth softly and presses her index finger to her lips. "Shh, you've done your part. Now be quiet and let the grown-ups talk."

Sebastian nods toward the forest, and several women dressed in long white fur coats amble out. Adrian comes stumbling out with them. Once again, he's wrapped in silver chains. His body heals fast, but the silver slows that process down, and he looks like he's been beaten within an inch of his life recently. Bruises purple up and down his arms and face. His lips are split open. But his eyes––his eyes are completely bloodshot, indicating that he's fed recently.

Good. He'll be stronger if he's fed. But I still want to cry seeing him like this. And I want to claw Brisa's face off.

"What's going on here?" Nadia demands. She's the councilwoman from Russia, a very take-no-prisoners type of personality. She turns on Sebastian. "Have you allied with Brisa? Are you working against us?"

Sebastian replies coolly. "I'm working for the betterment of our entire race, and that includes you."

Antara smiles softly, taking Nadia's hand like they're the best of friends. "Don't you see? Eva was given to us as a gift. We must use her now or else risk losing her forever. Don't forget, she's a mortal girl."

"Excuse me," I growl. "I'm standing right here, and I belong to nobody but myself."

Brisa addresses the group. "Evangeline belongs to the vampires, whether she agrees or not. Why else would she be bonded to the council?"

"What do you want, Brisa?" Mangus asks. "Stop playing pretty with your words and just tell us why you're here so we can get on with it."

She shoots him a nasty look but answers his question. "These fae witches have so graciously agreed to bring me into the council bond."

That's a bold-faced lie. She doesn't want to be

brought into the bond, she wants to have the bond returned to her. She wants to be queen again.

Mangus snorts. "You'll never settle for a share of the power when you are used to having it all to yourself. You're selfish, you always have been."

Her eyes flare. "Quiet! You are not to speak to me that way."

"You've just proved my point. You're always going to think you're better than the rest of us."

"None of you would exist if it weren't for me!"

"Some of us didn't ask to exist," Adrian speaks up, his voice ragged and pained. His hair hangs down in his eyes, and he glowers at Brisa as if she were evil incarnate. My heart shatters for him, taking in his words more deeply than I ever have before. I know he didn't ask for this life, and I wouldn't wish it on anyone, but I'm also so glad that he's here, that I met him, that I love him.

"You were always so ungrateful," Brisa tuts at Adrian, "but I'm willing to overlook it." She points to the moon. "I'm here now. You have ten council members with Eva and need a tiebreaker to join your ranks, and that's what I am going to do. You don't have to like it or even agree, but it's happening." Then she crooks a finger toward the fae women. "Witches, come do it now while the moon is high enough to bless our sacred circle."

The women step forward, removing the furred hoods of their beautiful cloaks. They don't look like fae witches to me, they look like normal human women.

What can they possibly do here? I still don't want to believe this is possible. This is Isadora's spell. They can't change it. It's already been forged. It's already done. But then the last woman removes her hood, settling it back against long tresses of white hair, revealing lovely green skin and pointed ears. My knees go weak.

Isadora . . .

CHAPTER 36

Mangus and Adrian appear stunned, and I'm sure I do too, but I'm not giving up hope. Not yet. Her presence isn't the worst thing that could happen tonight. I expected that something like this might surprise us, which is exactly why we called the people we did, and why Mangus and I made our plan in that dank coffin.

"She doesn't want to join our council," I challenge. "She wants to take the bond for herself. That's why she called us here. This meeting wasn't Mangus's idea, it was hers." I nod toward Adrian. "Why do you think he's in chains? He's her leverage."

"And I can still kill him," she hisses. "If you don't shut your mouth, I will."

"Is this true?" Nadia demands.

"It's true I used them to get you here, that much is obvious. It's not true that I am trying to take the bond back. As much as I'd love to, it's not possible. All I can do now is be added to your circle." Her eyes sparkle, and she gives me a sly grin. "And help you take Eva's light as our own."

I'm horrified as we're pushed into a circle, Brisa included. *Myself included.* Adrian is at her side and still covered in chains. He looks two seconds away from murdering everyone aligning with Brisa. And about one second away from murdering Brisa herself. My hands are itching to unleash the angelic fire, but I hold back.

"Let's get started," Isadora instructs. "But first, we must remove the silver." She sets out to unwind Adrian's binds, and when he's free, I expect him to come to me, but he doesn't move from his spot next to Brisa. And when the blade is passed from person to person, I cut my own palms, forcing myself not to think about it. Adrian shows no emotion as he slices open his palms. Brisa does the same, and then Adrian takes her hand in his own.

My already shattered heart breaks even more, and tears spring to my eyes.

Should I just do it? Just kill her now? Would she have time to retaliate? To fight me? To hurt him? Because this is the last thing Adrian deserves. She won't have the same power as before, but if she joins the council, she'll always have something over him. She's the reason for most of his trauma. She deserves true death, not to be allowed into our sacred circle, and not to be in a position where nobody within this circle can ever attempt to kill her once the spell is done. And that's all assuming she doesn't get the bonds entirely to herself. I still don't trust any of this. She's not one to compromise so easily.

"I cannot remove the blood bonds," Isadora eases our fears. "The spell has already been forged and nothing can undo it, but I can add your maker to the council."

"We have to put it to a vote," Nadia insists.

"I vote no," Adrian snaps.

The vote will tie, at least that's what he expects, but when it gets to me and Mangus, we both vote to add Brisa to the council. Adrian stares at me like I've lost my mind and then at Mangus like he's just staked him in the damn back.

"Just stop fighting her," I tell him, and it nearly kills me to say those words that I don't mean. But it's all part of the plan, and it's going to work. It has to. "I don't believe they'll be able to get to my light anyway. It's not something that can just be passed around."

Brisa exchanges a knowing glance with Sebastian.

Mangus mutters, "It's better to have her as our ally than our enemy." And I'm pretty sure it just about killed him to say that.

"So it's settled." Brisa grins like we're old friends, but her eyes are still cruel, and I know she still plans to use me like she does everybody else. She turns back to Isadora, waving at her like she used to wave at her servants. "Now hurry, witch. We don't have much moonlight left."

The moon isn't going anywhere, though, and Isadora

begins her chanting. It's eerily similar to the chants she used when she first cast the spell weeks ago, but at least this time I'm not being held down by vines. Not that this is much better. I'm currently clasping the hands of the vampires next to me--Mangus and Santino--our bloodied palms pressing together.

There are eleven of us in the circle now as the moon shines down, lighting all our faces in its silvery light. This light is so different to the angelic gift in my hands that seems to mimic the sun. I'm still not sure what the golden glow mimics, considering it doesn't hurt Adrian. For just a moment, I close my eyes and soak up the moonlight. It seems to compliment my gift, creating a calming balance deep down within me. For just a second, I imagine I'm alone out here, that I'm in meditation and not worried.

Crack.

My eyes fly open. Shadows have descended. Several of the vampires step back, widening the circle to its fullest as they try to drop each other's hands. They cannot.

And then none of us can move at all because we're being magicked...

Magicked by King Orlyc himself. The imposing man stands centered in our sacred circle, tall and magnificent and entirely fae. And he's not alone. He's brought seven other fae into the circle with him.

We're still unable to speak, which normally would piss me off, but I don't want to hear what the vampires have to say about this right now. When it's all over? Oh, absolutely, I can't wait to hear them bitch about it. But right now, everyone needs to let Isadora work her magic.

But then I catch sight of Adrian, his eyes narrowed on me in confusion, and I wish I could relay a telepathic message to him. *Hang tight. It's going to be okay.* But I'm not even sure I believe it because this is just the beginning of our plan, and there are still so many things that could go wrong.

Starting with trusting the Unseelie Court.

The fae have us right where they want us, and they could kill us if that was their endgame. It would be so easy. But I'm pretty sure they won't because that wouldn't solve the problem of the nephilim, nor does it create a lasting solution for anyone. And while most of the fae are prejudiced against other supernaturals, that doesn't make them murderers.

And besides, we have a plan.

The magic builds as Isadora continues her ancient chanting. It's obvious what's happening here--the Unseelie King is bringing himself and his most trusted allies into the council bond. The vampires must know it too, even though they can't move or speak. Because their eyes are huge--some angry, some awed, and all but Mangus's are shocked.

The shadows descend, thick and almost dark enough to block out the moon. Then one of Casimir's silver doves flies around the circle. I'm beginning to think his birds are like his own version of the Secret Service, always checking on things before Casimir himself arrives, always guarding him, ever present.

As expected, Casimir appears with the nephilim representation hanging off of him. Chloe, of course, and she's brought along Nicco, Greyson, Tate, her mother Lainey, two nephilim I don't recognize, and Remi.

Remi shoots me a thank you nod, and I'm happy to see they got her out of the casino prison. Casimir had said he wouldn't have a problem, and he was right. I'll admit, I'm happy that Remi is joining the council. She was always a kind person, and I know she'll be willing to fight for what's right. By now, the nephilim have seen Chloe's true memories. They had to agree to change in order to get an invite to come.

But the one person I wasn't expecting is the very same person I'd hoped I wouldn't see here tonight. Leslie Tate.

Everyone's packed tightly into the circle now. There are nine fae including Casimir, nine nephilim including myself, and ten vampires.

But I don't expect Brisa to last for much longer . . .

Without her, we'll have twenty-seven council members in all. Twenty-seven people prepared to govern the supernatural community.

But as I look at Brisa now, her chestnut hair billowing around her face with the rest of us, her eyes molten with rage, her hands clasped tightly onto Adrian and Antara, I'm suddenly worried she's about to be connected to us forever.

I should've just killed her. . .

Isadora's chanting grows louder. Stronger.

The magic continues to build into a crescendo, seeming to rocket from one bloodied palm to the next. I feel it when it splits, shooting into the people inside the inner circle and back out to us. Over and over again.

It's too much.

Chloe nearly falls over, but Casimir steadies her. King Orlyc continues to use his fae magic to hold the outer circle of vampires frozen while the people inside the circle form two inner circles facing outwards toward us. Even though there are three circles, we are all one.

The electric magic stabilizes.

"Now!" King Orlyc yells, and Chloe's eyes roll into the back of her head, going white. And then everything goes dark.

For all of us.

She immediately pulls us into her vision, right to those records stored within her mind. She shows us the past, when the wars first started, then she shows us what happened for her to recently learn the truth--and everything King Alberich of the light fae confessed that night in Faerie.

After seeing these records, I can only hope the rest of the council agrees that this is the right thing to do. The deadly consequences of the supernatural wars need to end. It's time for change, for new growth, and a better world for everyone.

My voice becomes free and I yell out, "Are we all in agreement?"

"Yes!" they all reply back, but I don't trust it.

Words are one thing.

Actions are another.

And intention is everything.

Which is why Isadora says what she says next, "Your hearts have been tested. Not all have proven worthy of this sacred bond."

And with that, two members are thrown from the circle. Physically tossed out. Removed. Hearts failed to be worthy of our common goal.

Brisa and Tate.

All at once, the moonlight brightens on those still in the circle, a blessing of magic. And then it stops, and King Orlyc releases our bodies. We can move again.

Brisa releases a rage-filled scream, charging right for me. One second I'm standing with the others, and the next I'm flat on my back. My vision blurs from my head slamming against the cold hard earth. Her knees pin down my hands, and she rears back, her fangs extending.

Her plan failed. Ours succeeded. And now I'm dead.

CHAPTER 37

Just as her fangs sink into my neck, sharp and punishing and final, she's gone.

Nothing but ash.

I cough and sit up, gaping at everyone. Adrian's standing above me, a bloodied stake in his hand.

"Where did you get that?" Sebastian deadpans.

Mangus raises his hand and winks. "I may have brought one along, just in case."

Everyone stands there, stunned. In the quick seconds that Brisa was preparing to kill me, Mangus was tossing a stake to Adrian.

And Adrian finally got his revenge.

Isadora steps forward. "What was a vampiric council is now a supernatural council. Decisions made here will be for the betterment of all." She smiles, a blissful calm relaxing her sharp fae features. "The magic is three times stronger with the addition of nephilim blood and fae royalty. It would be impossible to break your council bond apart, but you may adjust members as necessary with my help."

"And what about me?" Tate steps forward from where he was tossed from our sacred space. I've never seen him look so much like an old man.

"You didn't make the cut," Chloe explains regretfully. "Your heart was tested by the magic. You're still hardened to better treatment for other supernaturals."

His jaw tenses, and he glares at us before motioning to Greyson. "Come along, son, we're leaving."

Greyson slowly shakes his head. "No, I'm not going anywhere with you." It's surprising, I never thought I'd see the sour-faced boy have a backbone for anything other than torturing people. "I'm tired of fighting demons for you."

I don't know what he means by that, but Tate goes still, then nods as if finally accepting the truth. He begins to walk away, but King Orlyc holds out his hand and Tate is physically moved back to us through Orlyc's power. He stops Tate right at his feet, glaring at the man.

"You have a weapon that can infect my world and kill my people. Where is it? It must be destroyed." Orlyc demands.

"It can't just be destroyed," Tate snaps.

"Do not lie to me. You do not want to know what I am capable of, what I will do to you if you keep this secret."

Tate's eyes are furious. "The weapon is a nephilim

child. You cannot destroy it because it is a person. And didn't you just swear to protect all supernaturals?"

Orlyc's lip turns up. "That is up for debate."

"No, it's not, because this person has done nothing wrong."

I assumed the weapon was some kind of iron they were going to put in the water supply, but this? A person with the power to destroy an entire race? I glance down at my hands, understanding how that feels. The pressure of such an angelic gift is hard to fathom, but it's something I hold within my palms, that I could turn on vampires at any second and burn them alive. People will always want me dead for it. Or they'll always be trying to find a way to get it for themselves.

I look to the other nephilim, expecting one of them to confess more on this person who is the weapon, but all of their mouths stay shut.

"We cannot say any more than that," Chloe finally tells the king. "We've been oathed by one of our comrade's gifts not to confess. But I assure you, there's nothing to worry about. The person with the weapon is kind and gentle. They won't harm you. They never wanted to in the first place."

The king scowls, but there's nothing he can do. They're at a stalemate. "Consider this mutually assured destruction. You do one thing to hurt my realm, and I will rain hellfire down on all nephilim."

Everyone begins to bicker like school children.

"Okay, that's enough!" I yell. The group quiets, many

of them looking at me with new eyes. "Are you forgetting that we're in a council bond together? We can't just go making these threats anymore."

"I'm not in the council," Tate grinds out defensively, but then he releases a long breath. "But I'm tired. I'm too old for this war. I just want to retire, go lie on a beach with Bianca, drink wine everyday, and enjoy the rest of my life."

"You're serious?" I question with a snort.

He shrugs, his bushy salt and pepper eyebrows coming together. "I'm being completely serious. Camilla was the driving factor in this family, and at this point, I'm just happy to pass the mantle down to the next generation. I've been fighting for so long, and what for? It was all a lie. So now I want to take my wife and retire on the coast, maybe I'll try writing or painting. I don't even have a hobby."

Okay, he actually does sound serious.

But it still doesn't make up for everything he did, for all the humans he manipulated and controlled. I still don't trust him as far as I can throw him, but I also have to find compromises here too. As much as I hate him, he's my uncle, and there are several people here who love him.

"Fine, but make one move against supernaturals and you will be executed," Orlyc states.

"Noted." He grimaces, and he really does look tired. But also, a little bit relieved. "If you need me, I'll be in Italy."

And with that, he walks away.

"Why do all this?" Adrian turns on the Unseelie King. "What's your endgame?"

The circles split apart, but King Orlyc stays rooted in the middle. "I wanted the nephilim to know the truth, that they are no better than other supernaturals, especially not better than immortal elemental fae." His words drip with royal snobbery. "I've long wanted to return to this realm, and after the vampires successfully returned to human society, I knew it would be possible for us to as well. The issue, however, were nephilim hellbent on killing us." His eyes land on me. "And then we found Eva."

My cheeks burn. "Mutual assured destruction is the only way we're all ever going to get along." Several of them nod, but others don't seem too happy about all this, especially Antara and Sebastian.

Orlyc continues. "Many of the original pieces of the council spell cannot be altered. Royalty who enter into this council cannot be removed. Everyone else here was voted in by their people, and new elections will still occur every decade."

"We already voted," Chloe explains. "I went to my people and showed them the truth. It's going to take some getting used to."

Everyone goes quiet for a moment, and then Adrian speaks up. "Since everyone traveled so far to be here, I propose our first council meeting to happen in this very spot tomorrow at midnight. Right now, however, the sunrise is fast approaching and the vampires need to get home."

We split up in our different directions, but I don't go with the nephilim. I'm with Adrian.

The trip back to the casino is uneventful. We have cars with drivers waiting for us, so at least we don't have to exert our energy on the way back.

I lie my head on Adrian's shoulder and recount everything that happened to get us to this point. I leave out the part about Mangus being the mole. It's not his fault, and I plan to keep that information to myself for as long as I possibly can. Maybe that's foolish, but I'd rather be a fool than be responsible for whatever will happen to Mangus if the vampires find out he's been magicked into being a traitor.

"You're a genius." Adrian chuckles, kissing me on the forehead.

"I don't know, the fae are pretty cunning. I couldn't have pulled this off without them."

"The fae don't hold a candle to you, Angel."

"You're grossing me out," Mangus complains from the seat next to us. "Can you two please wait until we get back?"

"You're just jealous," Adrian teases.

Mangus sighs. "I am. I miss my wife."

That sobers us up real quick, and I pat his knee. Nobody says another word.

We pull into the casino's parking garage a few minutes before sunrise. For the first time in ages, a sense of peace washes over me. We did it. Brisa is gone. Camilla's gone. Tate is no longer a threat. It turns out the half-fae witches that Brisa brought along with her actually went to Isadora a few weeks ago and brokered a deal for themselves. They'll have partial access to Faerie now that they've helped the fae.

And before leaving the park, I stopped Isadora for a quick chat. She assured me of a few things. First, that Brisa's plan to steal my gift and kill me required fae magic, but the fae double crossed her because they're loyal to me. And second, that my anti-vampire bargain in the original spell has now been voided. It was my one request of Orlyc back when we devised our plans to put this council together. I no longer need to worry about being forgotten or lost by the man I love. All in all, it seems like everything worked out.

I should know better than to let my guard down . . .

We're climbing from the armored cars to head inside when gunshots rain down. There's no confrontation, no time to plan, no time to react.

It just happens.

A bullet slams through my abdomen, and I go down.

CHAPTER 38

*M*y vision blurs, tunneling in on Adrian's face. He's lying beside me, wounded with what must've been silver bullets. Our blood puddles between us, and I have the stark realization that this is the end. He must think so too, because he reaches out, grabs my hand, and squeezes it three times. Each squeeze is weaker than the previous.

I squeeze back four times. *I. Love. You. Too.*

A man is walking up to us, heavy boots echoing on the pavement. He's got his wooden stake ready, pointed right at Adrian. "You really thought you could kill my boss and get away with it, didn't you?" he taunts. "This is for Armondo."

He swings the stake right for Adrian's heart.

But just before he hits the mark, someone is yelling, someone is pushing, someone is grabbing the attacker and getting staked instead.

Mangus.

The weapon slices into Mangus's chest at the exact same moment that Mangus rips open the attacker's neck. Both go down, crumpling on top of each other. But Mangus's body quickly turns to ash. And the man bleeds out.

A horrified sob wracks my stomach, and more blood gushes from the bullet wound. My whole body is cold. The sound of clattering against concrete draws my attention, and I find Adrian on all fours, the bullets naturally being ejected from his body. They fall like long silver raindrops. The same won't happen for me.

I'm going to die.

He could change me, could turn me into a vampire. But that's only assuming he could find a cemetery quickly, and I doubt I'd live long enough to make it through a three-night transition. But in this moment, I would take the very existence I feared most if it meant I would get to continue a life with him. Because I don't want to die.

Adrian scoops me into his arms. He's saying things, things about my life, things about holding on, but the words don't register. Nothing sticks. It's all fading too fast. He carries me out of the parking garage, outside into the fading darkness, and I give up the fight.

Light. Everywhere. Beautiful, wonderful, golden, warm, eternal light.

I'm floating in the sunrise, made new by its rays.

And Adrian is here, kneeling over me. So this must be the afterlife, because vampires can't survive in the sun. But here we are together, the angel and the vampire. The pain in my abdomen is gone. My mind is returning.

"Are we dead?" I whisper, and his eyes go wild with relief.

"No, we're not dead." He laughs the kind of laugh I don't think I've ever heard from him before. It's so incredibly free. It's not the laugh of a vampire. "Well, you're not. I've been dead for a long time now."

Is he trying to make a joke? I blink and look around, but the light cocooning us is just so warm and bright, it's hard to see anything.

"Where are we?" My vision finally focuses, and I can see that we're not in a graveyard, nor are we in some kind of heaven. We're a few blocks from the casino, lying in a grassy area of the downtown riverwalk.

Lying in the hot pink sunrise.

"Adrian, no! You can't be out here."

He smiles, kissing my forehead. "How are you feeling?"

Is he serious right now? He's about to be burned alive, and he wants to know how I'm feeling? His mouth finds mine, and I'm momentarily lost in the sensation of being alive, of still being able to kiss him. But there's no time.

Is this a goodbye kiss?

I pull away, so utterly confused. "You didn't turn me?"

"I'll never turn you, not unless you beg me to. I'll never ever take that choice from you like it was taken from me."

More and more, my senses are coming back to me. I sit up and glance around, realization pounding against my ribcage. We're outside, the sun has risen, and Adrian isn't ash.

He's not ash, because he's *glowing.*

"You're golden," I breathe out, and he nods.

He's so beautiful. His hair sparkles like spun gold, and his skin looks warmed and healthy. This is a man that was always meant to be in the sun but was forced to live in the darkness. And seeing him like this? It's a treasure.

"How?" I mutter. Because somehow, maybe even by the grace of God, he's managed to make it out alive. My gift has saved him--I'm glowing too. And my bullet wound has been healed, which I'm assuming Adrian handled with his venom.

"Why are we out here? Why didn't you just take me back up to the casino?"

"You lost so much blood. I thought you would need the sun to heal."

The sun to heal? I blink at him.

He nods. "Haven't you noticed? When you spend time in the sun, you come back with more energy and your gift is stronger. You can feed your gift with human auras, and I think you've been doing it naturally every time we've been near humans, but I also think you've learned to feed your gift by going outside." He shakes his head. "I'm sorry I kept you cooped up in the casino. I'll never do that again."

Now that he says all that, I suddenly realize how right he is. It makes the most sense. Of course my gift would love the sun. "But what about you?" I counter. "You were just going to die to bring me out here?"

"For your life, I would gladly die. So I came to the place where I knew I could get you the most sun the fastest. We're only a few blocks from The Alabaster Heart."

"You healed me with your venom?"

He shakes his head. "No, you healed yourself with the golden light."

Realization hits me. *Of course.* My light is two sides of the same coin.

"And I stopped you from dying."

He nods, and I just stare at him. I still can't believe it. He was going to die to make sure I would live. And I was willing to become a vampire just so I didn't have to lose him. Laughing, I jump on his lap and wrap him into a hug.

I've never viewed my light as a gift, never wanted it, never asked for it, but it's a part of me. And maybe for the first time in my life, I accept everything that I am. The light and the darkness, the good and the bad. There are unspeakable things I would do for the ones I love.

The killing white light is a part of me, but so is the golden healing light. And both have saved lives. I'm sure the good fight isn't over, but at least for today, we can put down our weapons.

I press my lips to Adrian's, and together we glow.

CHAPTER 39

TWO MONTHS LATER

The sprawling city of Rio De Janeiro, Brazil is a vista of asphalt and greenery stretched between the mountains and the sea. We came early so we could acclimate, and I've spent the last few days playing tourist, especially enjoying the landmarks and the white-sand beaches. I even swam in the South Atlantic Ocean, checking off a bucket-list item.

Rio is one big bucket-list item, actually.

From the cars honking down the streets, to the tropical flowers, the incredible food, and especially the grand mansions built right up next to rainbows of graffiti——there's just something so *alive* about this city.

I'll admit I've imagined myself living here with Adrian, daydreaming scenarios of what it would be like to be able to do everything together, to be able to go out in the sun every single day with him. Because this city needs to be enjoyed with some sweat on your neck and a little bit of a sunburn on your cheeks.

But we can't do that--not yet. We haven't told the vampires about what my gift can do for them. We've been putting everything together first, waiting for the perfect moment to present our case to the council.

That perfect moment is almost here.

Santino's coven has welcomed the entire supernatural council to their headquarters, an opulent building high in the mountains overlooking the city. We've all been given luxury accommodations for ourselves and our entourages. Just as with the New Orleans meetings, council members have flown from all over the globe for this event. The security is tight, but I'm not worried about getting attacked. The dust has settled, and the supernatural council has only grown stronger in popularity with all of our communities. Besides that, Adrian and his coven, the fae, and nephilim have my back. And I think everyone is going to like what I'm going to offer tonight.

We're meeting under the full moon to welcome our newest members onto the council. To even things out after Mangus's death and Tate's forced retirement, we needed one more vampire and one more nephilim in our ranks.

The vampires have elected a coven leader from Canada, and the nephilim have elected Dario. Adding a shapeshifter to the council has me nervous, but I guess what they say about keeping your enemies close is going to be proven true or false with this guy. Especially considering this is the shapeshifter who helped lead an attack on Adrian's coven, who tried to kill him. But we have to move on from all that, things are different now. At least, I really hope they are.

After sunset, the council pours out onto the sprawling lawn. It overlooks the city, which sparkles in the darkness like a million fireflies. Adrian takes my hand and squeezes. "Are you ready for this?"

I nod. "I've been ready for this since that first time I saw my mom giving blood in exchange for poker chips."

His eyes dim, and he threads his fingers through mine.

We all mingle for a bit, waiting for the moon to reach its peak position for our new members to be forged into our bond. Butterflies swirl in my stomach as I wait. And when it's finally time to join hands and bring the two newest members into our ranks, rounding us out at nine council members for each of the vampires, nephilim, and the fae, I still wait.

"I want to join you!" a male voice calls out from the darkness, interrupting our ceremony minutes before it's scheduled to start. A young man strides up to us, determination etched into his handsome face. Something about him is familiar, though I can't place it right away.

"And who are you?" Adrian demands. "This is a private meeting."

Not to mention, how the hell did he get past the security?

"I'm a werewolf," the young man says boldly.

"They are extinct. Do not lie to this council," Orlyc booms.

The supposed werewolf shakes his head, eyes narrowing toward the huddle of nearby nephilim. "They thought they wiped us out, but they didn't."

"If you're a werewolf, then where's your pack? And why are you able to stand here in this human form tonight?" Adrian points to the moon.

The wereboy laughs. "You don't know much about us, do you?"

Adrian stares at him for a long moment. "I'll admit werewolves have eluded most of the supernatural community for centuries. There weren't many to begin with."

"I don't have to disclose our secrets, but I will prove to you that I am what I say I am. It's why I am here, to demand my rightful place on this council." He says all this while simultaneously removing his clothing. He has zero sense of shyness about his nudity as he stands before us. And then his body changes, shifting into a massive dusty brown wolf.

The circle drops hands and stumbles back as he howls into the moon. Blood pools between our fingertips. Does he smell that blood? Does it call to him? I don't know a thing about werewolves or if I'm in danger right now.

But just as quickly as he did the first time, he shifts back into his human form and begins putting on his clothing.

"The nephilim have no objections to you joining our council," Chloe says softly. "Shall we put it to a vote?"

It's unanimous––nobody else has any objections either. He's only one more person on the council, not nine. How much damage could he possibly do?

"What's your name?" King Orlyc questions.

"I'm Dominic," he answers boldly. "That's all you need to know about me."

My insides go cold, and I rethink my vote––I know why he looks so familiar.

This is the boy that Ayla is dating.

I've only seen him in a few pictures, and seeing him out of context like this didn't jog my memory fast enough. As if sensing my distress, he turns and offers a smug wink, and then he cuts his palms with his damn teeth and forces himself into the circle.

I don't know what to do, I have too much else riding on tonight to worry about werewolf drama, but I wonder if Ayla knows this about her boyfriend. She must. Didn't she say she knew all about the supernaturals and the fae? This must be how she knows. *He told her.*

Taking a deep breath, I join the sacred circle and continue on with my waiting. It's harder to stay calm with these new questions swirling around in my head, but somehow, I manage.

And I wait, and I wait, all the way until the three new members are forged into our council bond.

Until Isadora has muttered her final word.

Until the electric magic flowing between us crawls to a stop.

And then I make my move.

"I have a proposal I'd like us to vote on tonight." My voice carries on the midnight breeze, and everyone turns on me.

"This can't wait until tomorrow?" Dario deadpans. "Some of us aren't nocturnal and would like to get decent sleep."

Touché. But in my defense, I am dating a vampire.

That said, I've mostly returned to a normal sleeping schedule. I've even started working at Pops again and am applying for college. I've decided I want to go to medical school and work in the Emergency Intensive Care Unit. It's going to take a lot of work and many years to get there, but I have enough time and self-confidence to know I'm going to do it. I also know I'll never have a normal life, but I'd still like to have one that I feel is my own. Not one that revolves around my boyfriend, even if I do love the guy.

"No, this can't wait," I say louder.

They gather around to hear me out, and Adrian offers an encouraging smile.

"It's no secret that the vampires have set up businesses that help them exchange human addictions for human blood. This has been a brilliant way for them to keep their kind well fed without having to bite anybody." I feel my cheeks burning as most of the vamps send me death-glares. "But I would like to propose a change to that system." I don't let myself stop to take questions. "I have access to light that will make it so vampires can walk in the sun. I know it works because I've successfully used it with Adrian."

Whispers erupt.

"Is this true?" Nadia demands, turning on Adrian.

"It's true," he confirms. "Now let her talk."

I clear my throat as they fall back to silence. "Thank you. I have two kinds of light. White angelic fire that comes from my palms and can kill . . . and warm golden light that can heal. Something about the healing light allows Adrian to survive in the sunlight."

"And how do you know this for sure?" Santino asks.

"The morning Mangus died, I naturally and unknowingly gave my light to Adrian. I believe I had been giving it to him for weeks . . . because I love him." Saying those three words in front of everyone is very uncomfortable for me, but it's an important part of my story. "I have talked with the fae witches, and they have assured me there's a way I can share it with more vampires. And I'm willing to do that, under a few conditions."

"Anything," Antara cries, her eyes going round. She suddenly looks less like an evil vampire and more like a young woman desperate to get her girlhood back.

My heart squeezes––this was the right decision.

"If you agree to *pay* for human blood from now on,

then I can magick my golden light to live within any vampires who are tested to have worthy hearts."

"What the hell does that mean?" Sebastian sneers. "Worthy hearts?"

"It means that you can't ever use the gift of walking in the sunlight to harm humans." I pin him with a knowing look. "No more big plans for world domination."

"You're asking too much."

"I'm not asking enough," I snap. "But I'll do it, and in return, you're getting what you've missed for so long."

He steps forward, his features going rigid. "You're asking us to give up our businesses. How are we supposed to pay for blood without those?"

I shake my head. "You can still operate your bars and casinos and whatever else, but no more exchanging vices for blood. No more of your shitty manipulation and compulsion to get these humans roped into horrible addictions just so they'll give you blood that you could just as easily pay for." My voice turns to ice. "If you want blood, then you use your profits to pay for it."

They're thinking about it . . . I can tell they're close to agreeing.

"You're young now," Sebastian carries on. "But what happens when you're gone in a few decades? We need more than a *mortal girl,* we need to extract your gift like Brisa had planned."

There. He said it. What I knew he wanted all along.

But I had a feeling this might happen. I knew he would still be looking for a way to take my gift away from me forever, probably at the cost of my life. That's why I did what I did. It's exactly why I chose to be brave. Why I recently traveled back to Faerie and made even more agreements with the King Orlyc--the very same king who has the ability to manipulate the magic within people, to change their DNA and turn them into something new.

I shake my head and then I turn to the group of fae. I first assumed they were wicked, but they're not. They're not all good either, they're like the rest of us--a menagerie of dark and light.

King Orlyc's eyes sparkle with mischief. Of course he demanded to be the one to announce the final reveal. This is the epitome of entertainment, and he's nothing if not a grand entertainer.

"She's not mortal anymore," he says boldly. His eyes sparkle with triumph as everyone turns on me. Pulling back the hair covering my pointy ears, I show the council what I've become: a fae.

"She's one of us now."

EPILOGUE

FOUR MONTHS LATER

"*I*'m going to melt if we sit out here much longer," I tease Adrian, though it feels true.

We're lounging on our hotel balcony, soaking up the late afternoon Spanish sun. After the July council meeting in England, the two of us set out on a month-long adventure through Europe. Well, the two of us and my ever-present vampire bodyguards. Now that I hold so much power to help both the vampires and the humans, I'm always protected. As we speak, three of them are standing outside the hotel door and several more are down below casing the lively city streets.

Spain is our last destination before heading back to New Orleans. We'll be home just in time for me to start college next week. I'll admit I wasn't sad to leave New Orleans behind for the hot summer months, but our week in Spain has turned out to be just as hot and humid. That's okay--the country is stunning, and the company isn't so bad either.

"Just five more minutes," Adrian mumbles, his eyes closed and his face raised to the sun. We've done this every day since coming out to the council. That's okay, Adrian needs this sunbathing just as much as I do.

Once we figured out what I could do that morning on the riverbank, I knew I had to use my golden light to help the humans. I also knew that I would never really be a human. And that's when I contacted King Orlyc to see if there was a way that we could use my gift to leverage the vampires. Orlyc was the one who helped me learn to feed. He was the one who helped me create the supernatural council. And with everything that happened to me in Faerie, I suspected he would be able to help me with this too.

Well, he was, but the price was my mortality.

As Unseelie King, Orlyc's throne allows him to not only manipulate magical gifts, but he can manipulate actual DNA. He can change people. And so we agreed to transform me into a fae so that I could become immortal. I don't even remember the ancient ritual--they made sure of that--but I was made fae a week before our trip to Rio.

At least my soul is mine. That will never change.

Even now, months later, I'm still adjusting. But I don't plan to go live in Faerie, and I'm not a natural born fae. Besides the fact that most will never accept me as one of their own, the natural fae have way more abilities than I do. They're also allergic to iron. I'm not. Lying hasn't been easy, though. Technically, I can still lie, but it takes a lot more effort and it's hardly worth it.

Basically, I'm an immortal nephilim with pointed elf ears and an aversion to lying, who is filled with vampire venom. I'll always be a nephilim by birth, and Orlyc says my angelic gift is mine forever because it's tied to my soul, but I'm now so much more than just part angel. Adrian teases me, calling me a triple threat. I guess he's right.

"I have a fantastic idea," I say. "How about we build a pool on the roof of the Alabaster? That way, we can both enjoy the sun and the heat without melting."

He grins, eyes popping open to gaze at me. "I like that idea. I'll get it done by next summer."

If Adrian says it's going to happen, then it's going to happen. His word is as strong as steel. Just like how he said he would keep me protected and hired the body-guards, or how he brought me into his coven even though I'm not a vampire. Crazy enough, most of those people are starting to feel like family.

My actual blood relations are doing much better. I sort of have a relationship with my dad's side of the family, even though I doubt we'll ever be close. And my mom is doing amazing since getting released from rehab. She got a fancy new office job and hasn't stepped foot in a casino since returning from California.

And the Moreno family--my other family--are all doing great, too. We're not as close as we used to be, but my relationship with Ayla is at least doing better. She's still dating the werewolf, but she insists she can't talk about it. Felix is home and back in school full-time, and he's still hanging out with most of his same friends. Although last I heard, Seth isn't around as much now that he's come out and gotten himself an exciting social life with the LGBTQ community.

I'm just grateful they're not out hunting anymore.

"I've been thinking," Adrian interrupts my thoughts. "What if we found our own place and moved out of The Alabaster Heart?"

I freeze, and he sits up, taking my hands in his. "I mean it. I hate what The Alabaster did to you. I don't want you to have to keep living there just to be with me."

I imagine us playing house for a second, how nice it would be to have a life to ourselves, and then I shake my head.

"I'm okay with living there. Besides, I avoid the casino and stick to the hotel anyway. And I like our penthouse." He tries to argue, and I cut him off. "You're the coven leader. I don't want you to give that up for me. Maybe there will be a time when someone else can take over and you and I can have a break, but for now I don't want to change anything."

My mind flashes to Kenton. My friend has fit in with the other vampires far better than he ever imagined he could. Adrian got him into regular therapy with someone who specializes in this kind of thing, and he's been doing really well now that he's forgiven himself for what happened when he was a new vampire. He's moving forward with his new life.

"I think we should stay where we are," I reaffirm.

"Are you sure?"

I lean over and kiss him softly. "Yes. I like our home."

There was a time when I thought meeting Adrian was the worst thing that had ever happened to me. I was so wrong because he's the best thing. He sees all the sides of me. He loves me because of who I am, not despite it. And most of all, he's taught me how to do the same. Me, in love with a vampire? A year ago I wouldn't have taken that bet for all the money in the world.

I guess it's a good thing I don't gamble.

Brisa

A LETTER FROM THE AUTHOR

Would you like to read the first kiss scene from Adrian's point of view? You can get that bonus chapter and other fun goodies by joining my Facebook reader group called "Nina's Reading Party". Thank you for taking a chance on *Vampires & Vices*. I've been working on this series for years, so to finally have it finished is a dream. If you liked it, please leave a quick written review on Amazon and Goodreads, and please tell your reader friends. I would love to keep writing in this world, but I can't without readers like you. Thanks again!

Much Love,
Nina Walker

ALSO BY NINA WALKER

Young Adult Dystopian Fantasy Romance
The Color Alchemist

Dark Paranormal Romance/Urban Fantasy
Vampires & Vices
New World Shifters

New Adult High Fantasy/Paranormal Romance
Bleeding Realms: Dragon Blessed

Young Adult Standalone Dystopian Fantasy
Dark Ocean Princess

Romance Pen Name: Grace Costello
Twinfluence
Ivy League Liars

ACKNOWLEDGMENTS

Thank you to everyone who championed this series. Thank you first and foremost to all the readers, I couldn't do this without you. Thanks to the amazing fans and moderators in my Nina Reading Party FB group, to everyone on social media who shared this series, to my proofers Kate, Sarah, and Cassie, to my incredible editor Ailene Kubricky, to my character illustrator Kalynne Art, and my talented cover designer Clarissa at Joy Design. And of course thanks goes out to my family, and especially to my supportive husband.

You're the best!

ABOUT THE AUTHOR

Nina Walker writes YA paranormal romance, urban fantasy, dystopian fantasy and more. *Truth Death* is her 19th book. She lives in Southern Utah with her sweetheart, 2 kids, and 4 pets. She loves to spend as much time outdoors exploring the real world as she does exploring her own imagination.

www.ingramcontent.com/pod-product-compliance
Lightning Source LLC
Chambersburg PA
CBHW031313210726
48287CB00005B/1533